THE RED HOUSE

THE RED HOUSE

A NOVEL

MARY MORRIS

DOUBLEDAY   NEW YORK

FIRST DOUBLEDAY HARDCOVER EDITION 2025

Copyright © 2025 by Mary Morris

Published by Doubleday, a division of Penguin Random House LLC,
1745 Broadway, New York, NY 10019.

DOUBLEDAY and the portrayal of an anchor with a dolphin are
registered trademarks of Penguin Random House LLC.

LIBRARY OF CONGRESS CATALOGING-IN-PUBLICATION DATA
Names: Morris, Mary, [date] author.
Title: The red house : a novel / Mary Morris.
Description: First edition. | New York : Doubleday, 2025.
Identifiers: LCCN 2024024167 (print) | LCCN 2024024168 (ebook) |
ISBN 9780385544986 (hardcover) | ISBN 9780385544993 (ebook)
Subjects: LCSH: World War, 1939–1945—Italy—Fiction. | Internment
camps—Italy—Fiction. | LCGFT: Historical fiction. | Novels.
Classification: LCC PS3563.O87445 R43 2025 (print) |
LCC PS3563.O87445 (ebook) | DDC 813/.54—dc23/eng/20240607
LC record available at https://lccn.loc.gov/2024024167
LC ebook record available at https://lccn.loc.gov/2024024168

penguinrandomhouse.com | doubleday.com

Printed in the United States of America

1 3 5 7 9 10 8 6 4 2

The authorized representative in the EU for product safety and
compliance is Penguin Random House Ireland, Morrison Chambers,
32 Nassau Street, Dublin D02 YH68, Ireland,
https://eu-contact.penguin.ie.

This book is for Maria and Nino Marangi and their family,

who are family to me.

When a person disappears, the detective must look at what she took with her when she left—not only the material items, but what is gone without her; what she carries with her to the underworld; what words will go unspoken; what no longer exists if she is made to disappear.

—JACQUES SILETTE, FRENCH CRIMINOLOGIST,
FROM HIS BOOK, *DÉTECTION*

The ground is like a beautiful woman. If you treat her gently, she'll tell you all her secrets.

—CLYDE SNOW, FORENSIC SCIENTIST

. . . all of human wisdom is contained in these two words— "Wait and hope."

—ALEXANDRE DUMAS, *THE COUNT OF MONTE CRISTO*

This is a work of fiction. The Red House is an actual place I stumbled on a few years ago. Though I have taken some liberties with its history, I have taken none with the truth.

THE

FIRST STORY

———

1

I WAKE UP IN A MOTEL ROOM and realize I've been dreaming about my mother. I can't say I've thought about her that much in recent years. But since the phone call, she's been slipping back into my mind, and now into my dreams. It's been a couple weeks since I listened to the message. His voice, one I haven't heard in a long time, saying, "Laura, it's Charlie Hendricks." Then he hesitated, as if he thought I wouldn't remember. As if I could forget. "Detective Hendricks. I'd like to talk to you. If you could, please give me a call."

I listened for an inflection. Some hint of why he might be calling, but there was none. What could he want, after all this time? Still, his voice riveted me to the spot, the way it always has. Most people's lives are a river, a flow from womb to tomb. But not mine. My life divides itself right down the middle; it's a fault line, a slice, a scar, a gully between before and after. An egg cracked in two.

The room in which I wake is unfamiliar, and at first I'm not certain where I am. The curtains are drawn, and I hear a shower running. The sheets are still warm, but I'm alone. Is it my husband or my lover in the shower? Am I in some tacky motel off the Palisades, or a room where I haven't slept since I was a child? Or perhaps I'm just in my own bed, in Brooklyn. I try to get up, but it seems as if I'm paralyzed. I can't move my hands or my feet. Sleep paralysis, it's called. A kind of stasis I've been experiencing more and more of late.

And then I remember the dream. I am a schoolgirl, dressed in a uniform that I never wore, with my satchel of books, on my way home. It is a spring day—perhaps an April afternoon, because the crocuses and daffodils are in bloom, and the air has that freshness that it only has at the start of a new growing season. The sun is shining and there's a ball field. A girls' softball team is playing, and from the back I recognize my mother. She's the coach—something she never was when I was growing up—and she's shouting instructions to the girls.

I call out to her. At first, she doesn't hear me. She keeps encouraging the players, telling one girl to steal second. Then she seems to notice me. I am shouting and waving as she turns slowly, a smile on her lips, and looks my way. But she cannot see me because she has no eyes.

I sit up in bed, my heart pounding in my chest, and I recall that I am in Brindisi, Italy, the place where I was born, and where I have not returned since I was a little girl. But after Charlie Hendricks called, I knew it was time. I have come to find my mother. Or if not her, at least what is left of her. I am looking for the shards. Some remnant. Her story, if you will.

I GET UP AND THROW OPEN the thick curtains. A blaze of sun pours in. Before me, the Adriatic glistens. The sound of the shower, I realize, is from another boarder in this pensione where I'm staying. There's no husband or lover with me. I am alone in this dreary room on the other side of the world. My mother used to say that on a clear day she could see Albania, but I never have. If I were staying longer, I'd redecorate this room. I'd eliminate the heavy curtains, the bed frames. I'd let in more light. Strip it down to bare bones. There are too many pictures on the wall. Someone's grandfather from World War I. A painting of a dog and a water-color of the sea. I'd get rid of it all.

It's what I do for a living. I stage things. Though I went to art school for painting, in the end I needed a job and I stumbled onto this one. I don't stage for the theater but for residential real estate. I make rooms look bigger or cozier. I bring in snazzy furnishings, fancy mirrors. I give people ancestors and histories they've never known. I rifle through boxes at flea markets and buy photographs of strangers on yachts or a glowing family in front of the Eiffel Tower. I create elegant, affluent lives. Love for the brokenhearted. A couple kissing, a child's first swim. I invent warm memories for the sad houses of widows and divorcées.

I acquired this skill when my father decided to sell our house. We had to make it look as if happy people lived there. We hung bright curtains, planted bulbs in the yard. If it was winter, my father was always sure to have a fire roaring in the fireplace. But when the new family learned that this was a house from which a woman had disappeared, they soon lost interest. Eventually a couple bought it after our father, once more, lowered the price. Over the years, on drunken nights, he'd remark that it was "a steal."

But I am only in Brindisi for a few days, a week at best, and, despite the heavy tapestries and bad art, I must make do. I've rented this room in a pensione by the sea. I am here in the hopes that some small piece of the past will slip into the present. Brindisi, after all, is where I spent my earliest years. Now, in the T-shirt I slept in, I step onto the balcony. Below, the sea laps at the shore. As far as I can see, there is nothing but water, sky, and sun. Already the breeze is warm and sultry. I breathe it all in, then close the doors to the balcony, get dressed, and go downstairs.

Though it's just past seven, Signora Piazza already has my break-fast laid out. A pastry, a hard-boiled egg, a bowl of strawberries, yogurt, and coffee. I am not hungry, but I don't want to hurt her feelings. "So," she says in her rapid-fire Italian, which I can barely follow, "what will you see today?"

I arrived in the late afternoon yesterday, and after a brief sojourn and early dinner I've spent most of my time sleeping. Now I'll ven-ture out into the city. Signora Piazza thinks I am here to look at architectural restoration—which is what my husband does. She has no idea what my real purpose is, but then I'm not entirely sure I do, either. I eat quickly as she watches me. "Ah, *che caldo,*" she says, fanning herself and rushing around, closing the shutters, trying to keep the cool air of the night in the rooms.

Now, as we sit in almost darkness, she keeps trying to speak with me in Italian. She seems puzzled that I spent the first six years of my life here, yet I speak very little of my native tongue—though I understand her, more or less. Still, at times I play dumb—just to avoid the questions. She is also perplexed that I am studying a map. "But you grew up in this city." I have tried to tell her about my childhood, in the years after the war, but she can't seem to grasp that I lived here a long time ago.

2

I HEAD OUT. IT IS A WARM late-summer morning as I stroll along the esplanade. The sun is already blazing, blinding as it shimmers off the harbor, and I have to squint to see. I fear the heat will be almost too much to bear. There's the pungent smell of brine and fish. On the docks, fishermen are coiling their nets. Their catch fills plastic bins that are being carted up to the market. Blood stains the cobblestones. Gulls squabble over the guts the fishermen have left behind. Other vendors line the walk. They sell sunglasses, sunscreen, or souvenirs. I take a deep breath and gaze out to sea.

I didn't remember much about Brindisi before I arrived. Yet since I got here, a strange feeling has swept over me. It is like muscle memory, I suppose. Like riding a bike. The way a place can come back to you. My mother and I walked this promenade. She'd clutch my hand, as if she were afraid I'd slip away if she let go. Normally she walked quickly, as if she was always late. She raced down the streets. She dashed for every light. "What's the hurry, Viola?" my father called out to her, but, even if we were early, she rushed. Sometimes it seemed as if she was running for her life, and in the end, I suppose she was. But with me she ambled, taking her time.

We lived across the harbor, and most mornings we'd ride the small ferry that charged only a few cents and could carry four or five people. Women sparred on their way to market over who had gotten there first. My mother seemed to relish these spats. She often paid for our ferry ride with the coins she picked up along the way. (Not that we were poor; my father's job paid quite well.) But she'd cross the street for the glint of a shiny coin. My mother was always picking up things she found outside—mostly objects other people discarded, like books, ratty sweaters, old furniture she'd take home and restore. "Junk," my father called it. But my mother loved her "finds." She'd leave little gifts under our pillows or beside our beds, the way crows have been known to do. Beer-colored sea glass, a blue paper clip, a stone in the shape of a heart.

I still have most of the things she left for me. I keep them in a box in the back of my closet. I don't know if Janine, who is five years younger than I, kept hers. Janine and I are polar opposites. We look nothing alike and no one would take us for sisters. I am darker, small, and full-bodied, like our mother. And Janine is taller and fair. She takes after our father. I suppose there is a resemblance around the eyes. We both have our mother's wide brow. But otherwise there is little we share.

People have always said that my hair is my best feature. Perhaps now that it's salt-and-peppery this is less true, but when I was growing up it was lush and dark like hers, unlike Janine's thin, dirty blond. Our father used to tease Janine that if she were a man, she'd be bald by the time she was twenty. Then he'd rub his own bald pate. Janine never found this funny. But I was different. Thick curls fell across my face and my mother would gently push them away. At times my hair got tangled ("a rat's nest," my mother joked—though I've never seen a rat's nest and I doubt she had, either). And then it had to be untangled.

My mother liked to sit beside me on the sofa while we watched a show, and pluck the strands apart. And if that failed, she'd get out her soft-bristle brush. She'd clasp a hank of hair so that she wouldn't pull my scalp, and start to tug. She'd work her way through one clump at a time. Only rarely would she lose patience, when the snarl was especially stubborn or if I'd yelp in pain. She'd lean over and wrap her arms around my neck. "Oh, Pigeon," she'd say. "You know I never want to hurt you." She said she called me that because I fluttered around.

At times, she grew angry. She pursed her lips, and a look came over her face, and then she'd tug as if she were pulling the hair out of my head. If I screamed, she cursed. A few times she threw the brush down. It was as if a monster lived in her, one she was struggling to tame even as she did battle with my thick curls. Once or twice she threatened, "I'm going to cut it all off." But she never did.

AFTER SHE LEFT, I SAT in front of her vanity table in the bathroom. She looked at herself in this mirror every day. I wanted to see what she saw. I picked up one of the brushes she used for her own lush hair. I opened the little drawers that held her lipsticks and brow pencils. I put on her lipstick. I brushed my hair. I dug deeper. Tucked far in the back, I found her old hair clasp—the tortoiseshell one she always wore. I held the clasp, turning it back and forth, then used it to pin up my own hair. I assumed she'd taken it with her, but here it was. Now I knew she was really gone.

I haven't talked to my sister in a while. We didn't officially stop speaking. She just wanted to move on. She's younger, and it seems that we "process" things differently. That was what the family therapist who saw us both for a while said. I tended to act out in anger toward others—blow up at friends at school, talk back to teachers—whereas Janine took her grief out on herself. So, it's not that anything happened between us. We didn't have a falling-out as much as we fell apart. If we run into each other, we say hello. We might even embrace. It's not as if there's bad blood between us. It's more like there is no blood. As if it all drained away. Anyway, Janine lived in Brindisi for only a short time.

My mother loved the markets. She walked among the fishmongers, the fruit and vegetable vendors, the ones who sold nuts and dried fruit. Others where she bought pasta and bread. She haggled and bartered and bantered back and forth with the merchants, arguing over how many grams. They often tried to give us more calamari than she wanted or make a case for a finer cut of meat, the more expensive mushrooms. She was a frugal, practical woman and never bought more than we needed. By one o'clock, we'd be on our way home.

My first memories are here, but they are vague, unformed. Fading in and out. Flashes, more than anything I can hold on to. A seagull soaring overhead, catching bread mid-flight, a stony stairwell, a child crying. In the streets, children playing. My mother's laughter. As if no time has passed at all.

3

AT THE DOCKS I SEARCH for a ferryman, but it's not as easy as I recall. Before, the ferries ran regularly and there was always one waiting, but now you have to hire a small boat to take you across the harbor, and these seem few and far between. A couple of seamen with dinghies refuse, but, after some negotiating, I find one who will shepherd me for a euro. He is a dour, silent man who neither smiles nor helps me aboard, but as soon as I am settled, he turns on his motor and the boat putters, spewing exhaust.

It is a breezy day and little waves slap the boat. Once or twice the boatman, who has a scruffy beard and not many teeth, scowls at me. Perhaps he doesn't like tourists, or perhaps he has just been doing this for too long. Without a word, he takes me to the dock below the monument and drops me off.

The Monument to the Italian Sailor looms above the harbor. It's a tall, imposing statue of a lonely man, lost at sea, perched on a pedestal. My mother and I strolled by it every day on our way to the ferry. It's in a pleasant park, and our apartment was nearby. I don't remember the exact address where we lived, but I'm hoping that I'll know the building when I see it. It was oddly shaped, with four separate wings, like a crucifix. This detail always seemed important to my mother. Though we were technically Catholic, we never went to church, nor did we celebrate any holidays except with a Christmas tree and an egg hunt for Easter. But when she referred to the building, she always said that it was in the shape of a cross.

I stand on the sidewalk, looking up at the old buildings—many with scaffolding holding them up. They are in various states of decay and disrepair. In the porticos, there are restaurants and a trendy wine bar. Again, I follow the sea, weaving in and out of the residential streets. Now they start to feel familiar, unlike the strangeness I felt when I arrived, as if some kind of map memory has taken over. I let my feet lead me through streets lined with small shops, trash piled high in alleyways, laundry hanging overhead, sheets flapping in the breeze.

Then I turn onto a street whose name rings a bell. It has a narrow stretch of buildings in various states of disrepair. Some modern, some old, but all neglected. I look at one storefront, then another. I follow my nose and it is not long before I find myself in front of an edifice with wide balconies that wrap around and look out to the airport and, beyond, to the sea. I count the floors. Six. And the building appears to be in the shape of a cross, with four apartments on each floor. I'm fairly certain of what I'll find inside. A crumbling stairwell, no elevator, and residents dragging themselves, along with their children and groceries, up and down all day.

Shivers run along my arms. The kind you feel when a ghost is near. That's what my mother used to say when I got goose bumps: a ghost is walking by. I am fairly certain that this is the building where we lived, but of course, after all these years, I could be wrong. On one of the high balconies, I see a woman, her hair wrapped in a bandanna, hanging laundry out to dry. How easily this could have been me. Who knows how many families have lived here? How many have come and gone? How many children have grown up and moved on? What made me think that there would be anything left of me, left of us, after all these years? And what made me think that coming back would be a good idea?

I suppose a part of me has always wondered. Did she decide to come here? Perhaps she came home. Yet, as I stand in front of the building, I realize how futile this is. My mother was never one to backtrack. She used to believe it was instinctual. Like wolves, our survival depends upon our moving in a circular track. Or sharks, always moving forward. After all these years, it seems unlikely she would return.

And yet I had to come. I am forty-two years old. My marriage is on the rocks, and I am having a fling with a former client whose apartment I staged. Then Charlie Hendricks called. I probably listened to his message twenty times before deleting it. I tried to decipher some innuendo in his words, some sense of what he was calling about. What does he need to tell me? Couldn't he give me a hint, a clue? But his voice was flat, without any hint or inflection—the way I remembered. I couldn't bring myself to call him back. Instead,

I fled. I came here. But now I realize what should have been obvious all along. I am the same age that my mother was when she disappeared.

4

IT'S AN ORDINARY DAY in March. A Tuesday just before spring break. Thirty years ago. Mud season in New Jersey, 1972. The kind of day you aren't supposed to remember. Uneventful. One day melting into the next, until we have what we call a life. This would be just another day, forgotten. Except it's not.

The ground is mushy and ready to spring back to life. I love the loamy smell, the new growth pushing through. Mom yelling for us to hurry. Our breakfast of cereal and juice, scrambled eggs, bacon, and wheat toast is laid out. Breakfast is an elaborate affair. All our meals are. But especially breakfast. She squeezes the juice and makes muffins from scratch with fresh blueberries and buttery scrambled eggs. "It's the most important meal of the day," she says as she hovers over us.

She's a small woman—though she no longer has that tiny waist our father could wrap his fingers around. She eats and eats. She eats the way a dog does, gulping her food down, as if fearing that someone will take it away. It's as if she's starving, and at times I wonder if she's not. And not only does she eat but she insists that we do, too. We have to have full meals. We must finish everything. "Eat," she says, but not in some affectionate Italian mother way. It's more insistent than that—like a warning, a threat. "You never know," she says cryptically.

"Know what?" Janine or I ask, and then laugh our heads off, as if this were incredibly funny. But we never get much of an answer. Just the glare in her eyes as she waits for us to take the last swallow before we can get on with our day. It's only years later that I understand what she was saying. *You never know what lies ahead. You never know what might happen to you.*

I want Lucky Charms. There isn't enough milk and we have to use cream. My mother curses under her breath. Not really curses. More like "darn it" or "drat." She never uses strong words. She's mad at herself that she's forgotten the milk, but also annoyed with me because, despite her elaborate breakfast, I want something else.

"I think you just do it to be contrary," she says.

She pushes the hair away from my face. Her hair is black and pinned up with the clasp she always used. The tortoiseshell one I coveted until it was mine, then I didn't want it anymore.

Our father comes down, ready for work. He has a little shaving cream behind his ear that she rubs away with her thumb. He kisses her on the neck, and she pats his cheek. They're lovey-dovey in a way that embarrasses us. He's always kissing her on the neck, the arm, her hand, as if she's a queen. Which I suppose she is, in a way. She's his queen. He often says that. "Look at my queen." Or "What can I get for you, Your Majesty?" Then he bows.

But today he just grabs a piece of toast as it pops out of the toaster, not even taking the time to butter it. "I'm late." A few quick kisses, some ruffling of our hair, and he's gone. I hear her sigh as she picks up his plate and eats his scrambled eggs. Anything we leave on our plates, she eats. There are never any leftovers in our house.

I'M IN A SCHOOL PLAY that morning. A musical written by the students; we're very proud of it. I have the role of a singing turtle. I'm twelve years old, with budding breasts, but still I wear a purple shell. She made the costume for me, and I held on to it for years. Even in high school, I occasionally tried it on. My mother dyed some old sheets purple and made a cast that embraced me. Every mother made her child's costume, and mine was no exception. It was what she did—made costumes, baked for bake sales. She went to every one of Janine's soccer and my field hockey games. She was what people used to call a "hands-on" mother.

In the car, on the way to school in my shell, she makes me repeat my lines and then sing a ridiculous song I've written myself—the words of which have long escaped me. But it doesn't matter. I like to perform. I don't care if I'm good or bad. I don't have stage fright. What's there to be afraid of? "What's the worst that can happen?" she says. I can get up in front of all kinds of people and sing a song or give a speech. I've never really tasted fear. I suppose I'm like the dodo, that trusting, flightless bird that doesn't know fear until it's too late. At the end of the play, she rushes up to me. She hugs my purple shell until I think it will crack. "You were great," she says, kissing the top of my head. "I'll get you after school."

Was there something in that? Some hint of what was to come? Detective Hendricks asked me that over and over. Why did she tell me she'd get me after school? Why did she hug me so tightly? Was that out of the ordinary? I try to recall all the gestures from that morning. The way she reached up and tucked my hair behind my ear and told me, "Love you, Pigeon." But she did this every day, didn't she? Do I remember it because on that day it was out of the ordinary? Or because it was the last time I ever saw her? Love you, Pickle. Love you, Worm. Love you, Puppy Dog. She had all these terms of endearment for us. But "Pigeon" was my special name. Was there anything unusual about "Pigeon"? No, she used it often. I remember the way her eyes looked deeply into mine, as if every good-bye was our last. But did they look more deeply this time? Did she hug me harder? She used to tell me not to go away angry, because you never know if you'll see that person ever again. But we weren't angry. I had been a great turtle. I would see her after school.

None of it was different. None of it seemed out of the ordinary. I've played it in my head a million times, but it always comes out the same. Still, afterward, I searched for signs, as did my father and Janine, for anything that seemed unusual. We picked apart every word, every gesture. Because without clues, without hints that something was wrong, how could any of this make sense? When she tucked my hair behind my ear, was she trying to tell me something? Was she trying to say good-bye?

Later that morning, my mother goes home for lunch. She's a librarian, and we only live a block from the library. That day, she tosses a load of laundry into the machine. Then she goes to her studio and has a cigarette, always an unfiltered Pall Mall—a habit she struggled to give up. She likes her "alone" time. She opens the back door and blows the smoke outside. Then she locks it shut again. In the kitchen, she defrosts a meat loaf for dinner and leaves it in the microwave.

It will be days before we discover it, and only because of the rancid smell. She puts her car keys and pack of Pall Malls on the counter. She makes herself a sandwich—sliced turkey and Swiss cheese on rye. She doesn't eat it all. She takes bites out of the middle, leaving the crusts.

5

PERHAPS THAT SHOULD HAVE BEEN our first clue—if we'd been looking for clues at the time, which we weren't, because we assumed she'd be back soon. But my mother never left anything on her plate. Her hungry lips never stopped moving. When we settled in New Jersey, just after Janine was born, my father cooked big

American meals of pot roast and potatoes, whole chickens on the grill, and corn, and my mother ate and ate, but it made no difference. She was still hungry.

Once I asked her why, and she told me it was because of the snake. When she was an infant and wanted to nurse in the morning, her mother, Anna, never had enough milk. Anna couldn't understand why she didn't have milk in the morning, and why her child couldn't get enough. She was concerned that Viola was failing to gain weight. Anna was always exhausted. She slept like the dead, but one night she awoke and felt something suckling at her breast. She assumed it was her baby and that her husband, Josef, disturbed by the child's crying, had placed the infant there.

But when she reached down to stroke her daughter's head, she did not touch the soft silken hair, the smooth flesh and pudgy limbs. This body went on and on. And the head was bald and the skin dry and scaled. In the moonlight Anna saw a long black snake drinking at her breast. Anna screamed, flinging the snake away, and in the morning made her husband move from the farmhouse where they'd been living, into the town where Viola grew up. Apparently, snakes can smell mother's milk from miles away. When a woman is nursing, the snakes come out of the forests and the hills and wait, hoping.

When I was a girl, I believed that my mother was hungry because of the snake, but as I grew older, I came to understand that it was nothing but a story. Once, when I asked my father, who had an amateur's interest in science, he just laughed and said, "Snakes can't nurse from women." We'd already moved to New Jersey after my father was honorably discharged, and I was only interested in the facts. We lived in a house in a cul-de-sac, where snakes do not wait in driveways to suckle at nursing mothers' breasts.

By the time I was ten, I no longer believed that she was hungry because of a snake. Still, I knew little of my mother's early years. She claimed to have come from somewhere outside of Naples, a place that was once called Malavento but somehow became Benevento. My father liked to joke that she sprouted up in his life like a mushroom. He seemed to have no idea where she came from, either. She was orphaned during the war, he told me. She never had any people. Not that he knew of. All we knew was that in Benevento, on a June summer night, witches came together to make new broomsticks and grind green walnuts into a brew called *nocino* that makes married men dance naked in the town square and widows take boys to their beds.

6

I LEFT NEW YORK SUDDENLY, on a whim. I called two of my clients, canceled appointments, and scribbled a note to Patrick that I stuck under a magnet on the fridge, where we often left messages. I said that I was sorry. I had to leave. Patrick was used to it, I suppose. My comings and goings. But I have never ventured this far before. "Don't worry," I wrote. "I'll call." I grabbed my passport, threw a few things into a bag, and flew to Rome, then came here. I didn't want to wait for Charlie Hendricks to call again. Whatever he has to tell me, I want to find out for myself.

I wonder what Charlie looks like now. How has he aged? Is he fat and bald? He had those tendencies—that linebacker build, the silken brown hair. Would I recognize him on the street? If he's stayed fit, the way he was then, when I first met him, not in uniform, but in that navy suit. It's been years, but for a decade of my life I saw him often. I saw him whenever I could. It was never strange to me at the time, though looking back, I suppose it was. But for years no man, not even my own father, mattered to me more. My mother's detective, as I came to think of him, was my first love.

ACROSS THE STREET FROM WHAT was perhaps once our home, there's a small park with a bench in a grove of trees. I walk over and sit in the shade of two Roman pines. It wasn't until I was grown that I realized these weren't really a type of tree, but, rather, a style of pruning. The lower branches are removed, allowing the canopy to flourish. I know enough about Italian culture for this to make sense. Italians love the light yet crave the shade. The entire Renaissance is based on this notion.

I open the small folder of photos I've brought with me. Mostly faded Polaroids, which I keep in a drawer and rarely look at. But now I flip through them. There are pictures of me and my mother, taken on this very promenade. Pictures from our balcony. Some images of the building itself. These are faint and barely discernible, but I'm fairly certain this is the place. No other building looks like this one.

I peruse these until I come to several versions of my mother's painting of the red house. At least that's what she called it. It's more like a red monolith. It sits in a field, shaded by a single tree, with no other buildings around it. Really it doesn't look at all like a house. It's too big and square, a building with too many windows. Too many rooms. Just a big box of a building that looks as if it had gone to ruin. I can't imagine what it would be like to stage all those rooms.

7

LATE AT NIGHT IN OUR BASEMENT, in a tiny room near the laundry, my mother paints. I'm not sure how she learned, but it's what she does in her spare time or when she can't sleep, which is often. We have a big house and she can paint anywhere, but this is where it seems she wants to be. Sometimes I'll slip out of bed and sneak downstairs to watch her. To spy on her, really. There's often a look on her face. It is as if she's gazing out a window into the distance, but the room where she paints has only one tiny window, too high up to look out. There is something about her that makes me think she's not really here. She's staring somewhere beyond. Looking back, I believe that what I saw on her face was longing. Homesickness, perhaps, though there never seemed to be a home she missed. She grew up near Naples during the war years, but she never talked about it. "Oh, why dwell on that?" she'd say if we asked.

Her paintings are odd, otherworldly, unschooled. She doesn't care what people think of them and she rarely hangs them or shows them to anyone. In this space that's more like a storage closet, she keeps her paints, canvases, and easels. She paints a simple land-scape, but slowly she transforms it, reshapes it. She layers in dark-ness, shadows. Out of those shadows, faces appear. Sometimes miles of faces, staring out from the woods. Trolls hiding under bridges. They terrified me as a child.

"Where does this come from?" I once heard my father ask. "Aren't you happy?"

My mother just shrugged. "You can't tell a painter what to paint," she said. "What am I supposed to paint? Puppies?" But my mother doesn't seem to have any darkness inside of her. She's what I'd call perky. She laughs. She rises early, humming with the birds.

She gets things done. But late at night, when we are supposed to be in bed, she goes down to that little room by the laundry.

She favors confined spaces—the car, a bathroom, or that tiny room in the basement—unless she's out, hiking in the woods or her beloved Pine Barrens. She's a creature who wants to stay inside her cave. In part, I think, because she's always cold. She can never get warm. Despite my father's complaints, she keeps the temperature in the house set at eighty. Even in summer, she wears a tattered sweater or sweatshirt when she paints. She's not a particularly gifted artist, but she's a dedicated one. There isn't anything in her paintings that strikes me as significant or unusual. Though they are rather abstract, and the pattern of people in them deepens and deepens, as if you're looking at yourself in a house of mirrors.

It's not until I'm much older that I begin to wonder why she chose that room as her studio. By then, I'd begun to wonder about a lot of things. There were a number of rooms in our sprawling house. And in summer she could have painted on the sun porch. But she never did.

I'm not sure when it was that she began painting the red house. But she painted it from many different angles—front views and back views—and at different times of the day, the way Monet did with his haystacks. Bird's-eye perspectives. Aerial views. Shadows shifting. I didn't even remember these paintings until I found them among my father's things when he passed away a few years ago. They were hidden in the back of a closet. They were so simple in their design that at first I thought I'd made them as a child, but she'd signed them all. It was as if he didn't want to look at them, but he didn't have the heart to get rid of them, either. From time to time, I imagine he took them out, as I have, and puzzled over them.

He searched for her over the years. Or, at least, I'm pretty sure he did. Once, not that long after she'd gone, he left us with our grandparents and went away for a couple weeks. He returned looking tired and drained. My grandmother hinted that he'd gone to Italy in search of her, but I never knew for certain. I've tried to find her online but have come up with nothing. And I've searched for the building she painted the color of dried blood, but, again, nothing. Was it a place where she lived? A school or orphanage where she'd been sent?

Often, she began her paintings with just an image of a simple red house, but then the building would grow more complex, with wings and rooms that seemed hidden or secretive. She'd paint in trees and fields around the house, until sometimes the house vanished altogether. But each painting had to start there.

On the back of some, she scrawled, in Italian (a language she rarely spoke after we left Italy), "*Non sarò qui per sempre.*"

"What does this mean?" Detective Charlie Hendricks asks that night when he first comes to our house, as he turns one of the paintings over in his hand.

"I will not be here forever," my father replies.

"But what do you think it meant to her?"

My father just shakes his head. "I have no idea," he replies.

8

I PUT THE PICTURES—EXCEPT FOR the snapshot of the building we lived in—back in the envelope. Then I take out the small journal I carry in my bag. It's a place for musings and also serves as a sketchbook. A kind of visual diary. I suppose that, in this, I take after her. If I'm bored or nervous, I doodle. For years I just drew patterns. Repeating shapes and colors. Eventually I started drawing things I saw, the real world—not some maze that had become my imagination. Somehow, to my father and teachers, not to mention my therapist, this seemed like progress.

Now I draw a rough sketch of the building, the trees that line the block. Just some basic strokes, some angles for perspective. After a few minutes, I close the sketchbook. I take a deep breath, walk across the street, and ring the bell. No one comes, so I ring again. A woman shouts, "*Venga, venga.*" I hear the shuffling of feet.

Slowly, the heavy wooden door opens, and reveals a stout old woman. She is dressed in black, a wedding ring still on her finger, though who knows how long ago she buried her husband. I can't help but wonder if she wasn't our *portiere* forty years ago. And when she looks at me with her translucent blue eyes, I realize she was.

"No room," she shouts, as if I've come to rent an apartment. My Italian is rusty, but this much I can understand. I glance at the doorbell and see her name.

"Signora Russo, I am sure you don't remember me, but my family lived here a long time ago. We were on the top floor and my mother was married to a U.S. serviceman." The woman glares at me, trying to understand my poor Italian. "My mother was Viola Wilkins." I have an old picture of my parents, and I pull it out. My father in his pilot's uniform, standing with his arm around the tiny waist of my mother. She has long dark hair and the most beautiful smile. It's as if her entire face is a smile. Even though the photo is in black and white, I know that her lipstick is bloodred.

The old woman squints and then claps her hands together. "Ah, *sì,* Signora Wilkins. Signora Wilkins. Yes. Beautiful lady."

"I am her daughter," I reply, oddly elated, though it is strange to say these words. Can you still be the daughter of someone you haven't seen in thirty years? I am not sure what I expected to find. Yet this woman remembers us. So it must mean that we were really here. At times, everything seems as if it's all make-believe.

"*Sì, sì,* I remember your family. Please come in!"

I walk into the entranceway of the building I haven't visited since I was a child. I was sad when we left. I had friends here, and we played together all day long. We were free to run between apartments and floors, and somehow our mothers always knew where to find us. No one seemed worried that we'd get lost or run away. Now I can't even remember their names. I loved our apartment and all the neighbors except, of course, Greta, whom my mother swore was a *strega*. A witch. When we moved to a housing development in New Jersey, it seemed as if we'd moved to the moon. And though I had friends, I was never free to roam.

Entering the building, it is as if nothing has changed. Even the cooking smells seem familiar—fried seafood, tomato sauce, bread in the ovens. The stairs appear to be crumbling, exactly as they were when we lived here, as if they have remained in an identical state of disrepair. Signora Russo welcomes me into her apartment, which also looks frozen in time. A dark, dank ground-floor apartment that looks onto an alleyway. It has none of the sea views or breezes that we enjoyed. She lived here with her husband, who supposedly did maintenance on the building. I remember him vaguely. As far as I could tell, all he did was drink wine and play dominoes while their four or five children ran wild. The minute I step inside, it's stifling. I feel as if I can't breathe.

"How are you?" Signora Russo rattles off in rapid Italian. "How is your mother? Your father?"

In my limited Italian, I tell her that my parents have both passed away and that I am trying to visit the places that mattered to them. There is no point explaining anything more elaborate than that, and I can't do it in Italian anyway. I also tell her what I've told Signora Piazza. I've come to look at architectural restoration. I am writing a paper about Brindisi. This, of course, is Patrick's field, not mine, but Signora Russo doesn't question me. "I am here on business," I tell her, and she nods, not entirely understanding my purpose but not seeming to care.

"I did not really know your father." She points up to the sky, where he flew every day. "But I am sorry to hear about your mother. She often brought me a loaf of bread or some cheese when she went to the store. She was a good lady. Was she sick?"

I am taken aback by this question. "No, it was very sudden. It has been many years now."

She nods, patting her heart.

"Yes, she had a heart attack," I reply. Did she? Is that what happened? Some kind of attack of her heart? I try to envision where she ran off to, or with whom. And if I am not somehow repeating her pattern. We chat for a while about this and that. Signora Russo drags out a basket filled with postcards, letters, and photographs that other people who lived in the building over the years have sent her. "Do you remember this family?" She holds up a faded snapshot of a bedraggled-looking crew. "They lived right below you."

I'm nervous as she flips through her cards and photos. I half expect to see my mother's face appear with a note that she's alive and well and living in Fort Lauderdale. Did she disappear back into a world as anonymous as the one she'd come from?

"My father didn't ever come here, did he?" He spent years looking for her, until he settled into watching nature shows and drinking gin.

She looks surprised by the question. "No, I never saw him after they left."

Finally, I ask. "I don't suppose that I could see the apartment upstairs, could I? The old apartment." Signora Russo hesitates, making a face. "I've come all this way. I have such fond memories."

"There are people living there," she says.

"I would be happy to pay you for your trouble." I take a twenty-euro note out of my wallet. Signora Russo grimaces again, but she takes the money and begins the slow climb up the stairs. I follow.

WHEN WE REACH THE SIXTH FLOOR, I'm huffing and puffing—though Signora Russo seems quite used to it. How did my mother climb these stairs with me once or twice a day? Signora Russo knocks, waits, knocks again. A cleaning woman in an apron and head scarf answers, and after a flurry of banter and hand gestures, the cleaning woman lets us in. I slip five euros into her dusty hand for her trouble, and she pockets it.

We walk into a darkened apartment that smells of cigarettes and garlic. It seems small and cramped, not at all the way I remember it. There is a crib, hanging from the ceiling, but no baby. I move in and out of the musty rooms. I remember light, ocean breezes. None of this feels familiar, as I assumed it would. Slowly, it dawns on me that there is nothing for me here. Just as people have moved on, so has this building. There is not even a hint of my parents and the life we lived in these rooms—happily, as I recall. As we are about to leave, I ask, "Would it be possible to go out on the balcony? I'd love to see the view once more."

Again, Signora Russo says something to the cleaning woman, who grumbles. "Well, I'm sure the family wouldn't mind if they were here." Signora Russo looks at me and again she shrugs. "Just for a moment."

She pulls back the curtains, opens the door, and I step outside. I duck under the lines of sheets and school uniforms hanging out to dry, until I stand on that wide wraparound terrace where we used to sit. I rest my hands on the railing and take a deep breath. Children are playing in the street. Beyond lies the cerulean sea.

My memories begin to coalesce; those vague first recollections somehow come into focus now. How many mornings did we sit on this balcony, tossing bread crusts to the birds that swooped and caught them in midair? My mother loved this balcony. Every morning after my father left for the base, she'd grab me and her cup of coffee (the first of many) and hold me in her lap while we waited for my father's plane to take off. She knew the sound of his engine and she listened for him to pass overhead before we set out to market, and she listened for his return before she began lunch. It was her unfailing routine. How she knew it was his plane, I'll never know, but she waited for it every day.

9

MY FATHER WAS A PILOT with the Allied forces. He flew top secret missions over Albania. "Top secret" was one of my first expressions. My mother would whisper "top secret" to me, pressing her fingers to her lips, and we'd laugh and laugh. My father never talked about his work when we lived in Brindisi because he couldn't, and he never wanted to talk about his work as a car salesman when we moved to New Jersey because he hated it.

My father's plane was louder than others, and it seemed heavier than the rest. Which it was. It was only much later that he told me what he flew. A Grumman C-45, outfitted with heavy guns and bombs. It was almost as if his plane groaned as it was struggling to rise—a sound I came to associate with my father as he grew older. After, we understood it was because of the cargo he carried and the missions he was on, but back then, all that mattered was that my mother knew his engine, the way you know the footsteps of someone you love.

He looked so handsome in his uniform in the mornings as he gulped down his coffee and pastry, then left for the base. Perhaps it sounds awkward for a daughter to say this, but even at a young age I could see the attraction. They were all over each other, my parents. They were always touching, caressing, in a not so subtle way. It wasn't a big leap for a child to surmise what went on in the bedroom because of what went on in the kitchen or the dining room. My father caressing my mother's backside as she stood at the sink, my father kissing her when she brought him his supper, his hand gliding over her breast.

It was my father in uniform that drew my mother to him in the first place, that taut-fitting olive drab. She loved the way it was snug around his chest and hips. While he was with the army, he wore it every day. He was tall, strapping, very blond, and she was dark, almost swarthy, the way Southern Italians can be. People said that I looked just like her and that Janine took after him. At times our mother joked, "Your father, he had nothing to do with you. It was all me." As if I had just sprouted via spontaneous generation. A mushroom like her.

She liked to tell me about the first time she saw him. It was in a bar outside of Naples. He had been here during the invasion of Southern Italy, and he returned a few years later with the Allied forces. His first mission was on September 9, 1943. Operation Slapstick. My father loved that name. Get it? Slapstick, like Charlie Chaplin or Buster Keaton. The Marx Brothers and the Three Stooges. Slipping on banana peels. Getting a pie in the face. Some kind of cosmic joke. Late in his life, he watched reruns of those comedies. They were the only things that made him laugh.

As the German defense failed in North Africa, the Germans fled via Sicily and Southern Italy. He drew little maps like a commanding officer, complete with arrows, to show me the Allied invasion that meant the liberation of Southern Italy. Sometimes we pretended I was a soldier, awaiting my orders. My mother never liked his war stories. She'd put her hands over her ears and walk out of the room.

"We thought we'd have a big battle on our hands," our father liked to say. "We thought the Italians would be firing at us from the beachhead. Instead, they greeted us with open arms. We met no resistance at all." He liked Italy and he liked being in the air force. A few years after the war, he returned as a reconnaissance pilot. That's when they met.

I don't know what my mother was doing at a servicemen's bar outside of Naples, and I never thought to ask. I can only assume she'd gone to pick up men and she wasn't shy about it. And an American GI was the biggest catch for a poor Italian girl. She didn't speak any English, but Ernie Wilkins didn't seem to mind.

He had a smattering of Italian and she was a quick learner. He loved her thick dark hair, the way it tumbled down her back, and her tiny waist that he could wrap his hands around. Later, in the States, where she grew stout, he still tried to put his hands around her, but she'd bat him away.

We lived right near the airfield, so my father left just before the start of his shift. This is also why he was able to come home for lunch. As soon as he was gone, my mother and I sat on the balcony, smelling the sea and having our breakfast until his plane passed overhead. When it did, she'd point to the sky. "That's him." At times, she swore she could see him in the cockpit. I'd wave and she'd tell me he'd waved back. Then we'd go about our day, but always with that tinge of worry that wouldn't leave, that worry stuck in the back of her brain—what if he never came home, what if this time something happened. She bit her nails. She bit them down to the quick. Even years later in New Jersey, if he had to go to the store or if he was late, she worried that he wouldn't come home—until one day, she never did.

Though she tried, my mother could not quiet that place in her brain where the worry came from. What was he doing up there, and why did his plane seem heavier than others, his engines louder? There was a reason. My father wasn't just flying reconnaissance over the Adriatic. His plane carried bombs. In the Cold War years, these were, theoretically, for deterrence. Once he was in the air, she'd try to distract herself for the next several hours. Most days she'd wrap me up and we'd go off to market or stroll the promenade.

My mother had to get out, in part, because she couldn't bear to hear Stephan's crying. Stephan was the baby who lived on the floor below us. Every morning, my mother listened to his cries. It went on for hours. At first, she felt bad for his poor mother, Greta, a young German woman about her age, who was also married to a serviceman. My mother assumed that Stephan was a colicky baby and now a difficult child.

But one morning we ran into Greta leaving the apartment. We could hear Stephan crying as Greta was locking the door. "Oh," my mother said, "it must be so difficult for you with Stephan crying all day."

Greta just looked at her, shrugged, and walked off in her bathing suit to the sea, where she stayed until lunchtime. Greta was leaving her baby alone in the apartment while she went to the beach. Later, when we'd see Stephan in his pram, my mother would shake her head. She had seen the terror in his eyes, and later I wondered if he'd recognized hers, as well.

10

"THAT MOTHER OF YOURS," our father whines as he drives us home after the school secretary called him. But it isn't really a whine. It's his high-pitched, singsongy voice, which he uses when he's joking. He can never really be mad at her. Not exactly. Though clearly he's annoyed. He had to leave work early to come and get us. He grumbles about her. She can be so scattered, leaving the oven on once when she went to work, and a neighbor, seeing smoke, called the fire department. Even then, he wasn't truly mad at her. He rarely was. Definitely not today, when she's late to pick us up. It's not that unusual for her, really. Not enough to worry about.

It's happened before. Just a few times. Enough for concern but not enough that we feel she's forgotten about us—because how could a mother, who cuts off the crusts of sandwiches and makes costumes by hand, how could she forget about us? We're her life. We know because she tells us all the time, putting her hand on her heart, and sometimes slipping into Italian, which she rarely speaks—"*Mio cuore.*" But she can get distracted and forget doctors' appointments and dinner dates. "Make lists," our father urged her, and she'd try, and then after a while she'd give up. "What good is it if I make lists but never look at them?" she'd say. And then: "I'm just a big . . ." She'd search for the word in English. "Flake," our father would tell her, and she'd laugh.

She always told us to make good use of our time, so we do. I get all my math homework done, and I help Janine with her reading assignment. She struggles with reading. It's about a dog that travels in a balloon. It crosses mountains and lakes until the balloon brings him home. No one even knows that the dog went on an adventure. But Janine has trouble paying attention. She keeps looking at the door.

Still our mother doesn't come. A crossed signal between our parents? *I thought you were getting them. I thought you were, etc., etc.* A dentist's appointment ran late. A meeting at the library, some errand she had to run. *Time just flies,* she'll say.

We could walk home. It's only a few blocks down side streets to the cul-de-sac where we live outside of Short Hills, and we've done it on weekends when we have practice or a game, but Mrs. Partlow won't let us. Our mother came for us every day after school, often taking us back with her to the library, where we'd do our homework until closing time. She loved her job at the library, being surrounded by all those books. Sometimes it seemed as if she could lose herself there.

AT FOUR O'CLOCK, MRS. PARTLOW calls my father. He comes and gets us as soon as he can. "Oh, my wife." He slaps his hand to his head. "She must have forgotten." But she hadn't returned to the library after lunch, either. Later, her colleagues tell the police that, yes, they were concerned, but things happen, and sometimes it's best to let well enough alone.

"That mother of yours," he says again, his thumbs drumming on the wheel. He's still, to us anyway, a handsome man, though he's lost hair and there are pouches under his eyes. As he drives, his belly protrudes a bit over his belt. Our mother used to punch him there, teasingly. "You are not the man I married." He was soft as a pillow. He'd shake his head because she could be capricious (a word I've heard a lot over the years). She was a Capricorn. After she'd been missing for a while, and we began to consult fortune-tellers and psychics, this gave them pause. It seems that Capricorn is the sign of people most likely to disappear. This is, apparently, statistically true.

We pull into the driveway. Her car is there and we park next to it. Again, our father shakes his head. But at least we know she's home. We breathe a sigh of relief. Of course, there's a logical explanation. Some glitch, a missed cue. She took a nap. She lost track of the time. The ground is mushy as we clomp across it. That loamy scent of spring in the air. We're each ready to scold her for her absentmindedness and then praise her for the pasta with seafood she's preparing. The front door is ajar. This isn't a big surprise. She rarely locked the front door and hardly even closed it.

"What do we have to steal?" she'd say.

"Something could happen to you if you're alone here," he'd reply.

"Oh, who would bother with me?"

Our father pushes the door open. "Viola," he calls. There's no answer.

He goes upstairs and then down to her studio in the basement. He comes back, shaking his head, puzzled. "She's not here." Perhaps she's gone for a walk.

The house is quiet, eerily so. On the counter is the plate with the crusts of her sandwich, a glass, half drunk, of apple juice. Our father stands there, staring at the plate. Beside it are her keys, and a wallet with her ID. She has taken nothing with her. She must have run out to a neighbor's house. To the corner store for milk.

We wait. Our father feeds us a snack. We watch TV and finish our homework while we listen to his phone calls. "Is Violet there?" he asks. She long ago Americanized her name to Violet. "We must have gotten our signals crossed." Then he hangs up and dials again.

When it's time for dinner, he takes hamburger patties out of the freezer. Clearly there's no seafood pasta tonight. He burns them in the skillet. We eat them anyway between two pieces of white bread with lots of catsup. We wait for the phone to ring, watching the door while our father paces. "Did she say anything to you, kids? Was she going somewhere tonight?"

Maybe that's it, he reasons. She's gone into the city to see a ballet, a play with a friend. Someone picked her up. It's his fault, he assumes. He can be absentminded, too. Or she'd forgotten to tell him. It's not on the animal calendar on the fridge. It's March, the month of baby birds. In school, we'd learned the difference between a nestling and a fledgling. We are still nestlings, our teacher explained. In a few years, we'll fledge. Our father checks his watch, once more shaking his head. At any moment she'll walk in the door.

11

SIGNORA RUSSO GUIDES ME OUT of the apartment, glancing around as if we'd just robbed it, and leads me back downstairs, where she puts on a kettle for tea. I'm not really a tea drinker, especially on a warm day, but Signora Russo goes into the kitchen to make a pot, and I plunk myself down on the very soft sofa. The apartment is small, just a warren of tiny rooms that seem like closets, but which once housed her children. Now it is filled with clutter. Newspapers, envelopes, photographs of children at sporting events, in front of birthday cakes. Some, I assume, are her sons and daughters, but others are probably grandchildren. Dishes are stacked in cabinets. I hear Signora Russo fumbling around in the kitchen, moving pots and pans while I take it all in.

Her apartment reminds me of the Andersons' house. The project I'd just finished before coming here. It was a tough job. An old Victorian with a wraparound porch. The Andersons, who'd lived there for the past thirty-five years, had filled it with antique couches, old wingback chairs, large, bulky armoires. I had to explain to them that, in order to sell their house, most of their furniture would have to go into storage. They had to move out all those antiques, that bulky furniture that seemed so elegant fifty years ago. And the clutter. Anything that can be a distraction to a potential buyer. It is not easy to convince people that no one really wants to buy a house with a lived-in feel. No one wants the sense that someone else even lives there. No one wants to dwell with somebody else's ghosts.

And the photographs. Poor Mrs. Anderson had so much difficulty taking the photos off the piano and the refrigerator and the walls. How big a family did they have anyway? How many grandchildren? Six? Eight? There were family pictures on every conceivable surface.

Whenever I walk into a home, such as the one where I'm sitting right now, I can't help myself. I'm always asking myself questions. Did people make love in these rooms? Were they happy here? I know the Andersons were. Mrs. Anderson kept crying when I got rid of all that old, clunky furniture and brought in more of the French Provincial style—a lot of bleached pine. I got rid of the weird floor lamps and track lighting. (Who puts track lighting in a Victorian?) When I finally finished, she looked around and said, "Well, it does look better this way."

I want to get up and yank back the curtains. Let the light in.

Curtains are one of the first things to go. Anything that obstructs or blocks the light. Nothing makes a place look more spacious than natural light. And, of course, mirrors, not to satisfy someone's vanity, but to enhance the space. You can do a lot with mirrors. Now, sitting here in this dark, cramped apartment with the curtains closed, I can hardly breathe.

At last Signora Russo appears with her tray of tea. "So, tell me, Laura," she says as she pours, "how you have been? Are you married? You have children?"

I strain to understand her Italian. I took a year or so in college, and it's slowly coming back. When I realize she is asking me these personal questions, I struggle to reply. "Yes," I tell her haltingly, "I am married, but we don't have children."

She looks at me as if I'd just told her I have only a few weeks to live.

"Ah, *peccato*," she replies.

"We couldn't," I lie.

Patrick and I debated whether or not we would have children. Some years he wanted kids. Other years it was me. There was always a patio to build, a room to redo, a trip we wanted to take. Some delay, something that had to be done. We'd put the discussion on the table, then take it off. Then we'd go on an exotic trip—a bike ride through Vietnam, a hike in the Pyrenees—and we'd wonder how we'd do this with a kid. So, we didn't have children. We had miscarriages, which, of course, disappointed us. We were sad at the time. "Perhaps it's for the best," Patrick would say, shaking his head. It's a way he has about him—thinking that things are for the best. Nothing terrible has ever happened to him. He grew up with his parents and brothers in a subdivision in Westchester. They had huge Christmas dinners and family reunions, tag football on the Fourth of July. I gritted my teeth and tolerated these festive occasions. He never had to put up posters of his missing mother on telephone poles, or wear a button printed with her face.

After a couple of miscarriages, we didn't keep trying. No fertility clinics, no drugs. No adoption. It might have made a difference. But instead of children, we've had dogs and trips and projects. All the dogs have slept on the bed. Perhaps it's not too late. We still have a little time. That window hasn't completely closed. But I think we are beyond that. Our marriage has taken a turn. A subtle shift away.

Years ago, a toddler climbed over a fence and tumbled into the gorilla compound at a zoo. Everyone was aghast, screaming, and then mesmerized when the female gorilla took the child in her arms, held him to her breast. She protected him as the male threatened her, and then turned the little boy over to her keeper when he came to her gate.

I became obsessed with this story. I read that mothering in gorillas is learned behavior. An orphaned gorilla won't know how to care for her young. She has to be taught by a mother of her own. So many times, I've tried to imagine that child in the embrace of the gorilla. What if your first memory is of huge hairy arms and a leathery chest? Heavy simian breath. I imagine that child would be able to hold on to such a recollection, whereas I seem to have lost so many of mine.

"Where are your children?" I ask out of politeness. "I remember them."

"*Fuori, fuori.*" She gestures with her hand. "They have all moved away to the north. Better jobs up there," she says with a sigh. She points to an array of photos on the mantel that look like children, grandchildren, and a handsome man. "My husband. He was a wonderful man. He died too soon."

I nod.

"We had four children. Only one is nearby, in Bari, but that is not so near, is it, Laura? It is not that near if I fall. If something happens to me. Who will take care of me?"

I feel for the sadness of her life. "But you could go and live with one of them. You don't have to stay here." She just shrugs. I have the sense that her children do not want her. "I wish I still had my mother to take care of."

Signora Russo smooths down her black linen skirt, picking off a piece of lint. "You must miss her terribly. I can tell how much you loved her, for you to come all the way here."

I gather my nerve. It is the question that has been nagging me. "She never came here, did she? I mean, you never saw her again after we left."

Signora Russo appears stunned by my question. She looks away. "No, I never saw her after you left." Over the years I've come to know when someone is lying. It's a skill you acquire when you can no longer trust the world. I study her face. I can't help but feel as if she knows something that she is not telling me.

I take out my photos. "Do you know anything about a red house?" I ask the old woman as she stirs sugar into her tea. She does not look up at me, just shakes her head. Her lips form the word *no*. I show her the picture of one of my mother's paintings. "Do you know this building? Did she ever mention anything to you about a red house? Maybe she lived there?" I show her the image. A large red building, sitting in a field.

She waves her hands over her head as if batting away a fly. "No," she replies. "*Niente.*" We finish our tea. When we are done, she picks up the cups and ushers me to the door.

12

"LET'S START AT THE BEGINNING." Those are the first words I remember hearing Charlie Hendricks say. Perhaps there were others, but that is where my awareness of him began. Not when he came in or sat down, a notepad open in his lap, pencil poised. It's when he says this. He's wearing a blue suit, which surprises me. I thought policemen wore uniforms the way Officer Duffy, who accompanies the detective, does. But Detective Hendricks looks as if he has a party to go to—except that it's one in the morning. His piercing blue eyes cut through me. Janine is asleep, but I'm curled up on the couch, my legs tucked under me. He was at the time, and for a long time afterward, the most handsome man I'd ever seen.

"Let's start at the beginning." But how many beginnings can one story have?

IT WAS AFTER MIDNIGHT WHEN my father phoned the police. He found her insulin vials in the fridge and her syringes in the little pouch she kept in their bathroom. "This is not normal," he says as he paces in front of us. "Something is wrong." No matter where she might be, this has never happened before. Yes, there were times when she'd be gone for an hour or two. She needed quiet time, she'd say. But she never stayed away. Not like this.

Janine and I sit on the couch, watching a TV show. I can't remember now, but I think it was a comedy. There's canned laughter. We're staring at it when the two officers arrive about an hour later. They stand in the vestibule with our father and listen. They come into the living room. Our father joins us on the sofa, the two of us still in our jeans and T-shirts, while the officers sprawl in two armchairs that seem too small to hold their imposing frames.

It hasn't even occurred to us to get ready for bed. Our father offers them coffee, but Detective Hendricks, the one who isn't wearing a uniform, says that they're fine. Our father apologizes, but he's rinsed the plate and the glass she'd drunk from. He tossed out the sandwich crusts. "It never occurred to me," he mutters to the officers, "that she wouldn't come home."

Detective Hendricks makes our father go over one thing again and again. "Keys, everything where she left them. Car in the driveway. House unlocked, correct?"

Our father nods. "Yes."

"And she required medication that she did not take with her."

My father, his eyes red, barely whispers "Yes."

The officers exchange glances. Officer Duffy hands our father a piece of paper on a clipboard. "Normally," Detective Hendricks says, "we wait twenty-four hours, but in this case . . ." His voice trails off as he looks at us. Our father begins filling in the sheet.

NAME OF MISSING PERSON: Violet Wilkins
MAIDEN NAME: Viola Umberto
NATIONALITY: American/Italian
TYPE OF MISSING PERSON (Disabled, Involuntary,
   Endangered, Juvenile, Disaster Victim):

My father, tears pouring down his face, circles the word *Victim*. Then he scribbles in the margins: *Diabetic. Requires insulin.*

DISTINGUISHING MARKS (tattoo, scars, moles): None
IDENTIFYING FEATURES (body X-ray, dental records,
   footprint):

Footprints. It is mud season, so, perhaps, somewhere in our yard, on the lawn, we'll find a trace of her step. But I don't understand how this can become a clue. Left-handedness. These are all factors used in identification.

My father checks the box for left-handed. She was both proud of it and joked about it. She liked to name geniuses who were left-handed, like Einstein. All astronauts were required to be left-handed. NASA claimed it made them more able to use both hands on the controls. She knew all kinds of facts about left-handed people. They were more creative and more depressed than right-handed people. Whenever a left-handed waitress was writing out a check, our mom would say, "Oh, a southpaw," and the waitress always laughed. My mother would raise her left fist in victory. They were also a higher risk for suicide. They died more frequently in accidents. To me, it meant that sometimes she told our father to turn right when she meant left. And sometimes she turned on the hot water instead of cold. Once, she scalded me in the bath.

There was a quote she liked. "The left hand is the dreamer, and the right hand is the doer." And then she'd shake her head and say, "I guess I'm a bit of both, aren't I?"

I bend over my father's shoulder as he fills out the form, shaking his head. "It's impossible," he mutters. "This cannot be happening to me."

When the form is completed, Officer Duffy takes it back. Detective Hendricks looks it over. "Obviously, she left in a hurry. And no note." Detective Hendricks makes us go over and over how she spent the day. She took us to school. She went to her job in the library. She came to a school play. She dropped off Janine's forgotten lunch. Then she went home, made herself a sandwich, ate everything but the crusts, and disappeared from our lives.

"Did she have any family here?" Detective Hendricks asks.

"None that we know of. They were all in Italy. They died during the war. She only had us." My father now has tears in his eyes.

"Friends?"

My father shakes his head. "Maybe a colleague or two from work. Her family was her world."

Detective Hendricks nods, and then gazes around our neat, well-appointed home, our tidy, spotless life. Then he looks my father in the eyes. "A mother like this, she'd leave a note. Even if she knew she was never coming back, she'd let somebody know."

Then he tells us that he's treating our house as a crime scene.

13

I HAVE A TENDENCY TO collect random facts. All crash-test dummies are male. Fish oil supplements are causing the global anchovy shortage. Female flamingos turn white when they give birth. I hold on to accounts of grim, weird deaths, fluke accidents. The woman whose children gave her the gift of a camel, only to have it crush her in an act of love. I'm obsessed with hikers who slip off trails and tumble into crevasses. Or that poor guy who got his head stuck spelunking. People who have vanished, never to be seen again. Families left wondering for years and years to come. I can spend whole evenings watching marathons of *Law & Order*. I particularly love an episode about a woman who kept seeing her vanished son. For a decade, it almost drove her mad. And finally, she convinces the police that he's alive.

I can't say when it was that I realized that getting myself wrapped up in someone else's tragic life gave me pleasure. I found gruesome stories, especially those involving murder or some heinous crime, incredibly satisfying, if not downright pleasurable. It was a feeling of deep satisfaction, a penetration into another person's misery. I can still watch endless loops of police procedurals and true crime shows. I especially like the subsequent trauma of those who survived. That loss is the most important thing to me. The mother's piercing cry, the lover's inconsolable sob. Long ago, I became a voyeur of grief.

We were, of course, never able to have a funeral for my mother. We had no closure, no way to mark our tragedy. We just kept floating on an endless pewter sea of loss, though every March, on the day she disappeared, my father found a way of commemorating her. He'd bring home a potted plant of violets for Viola. I could never bear seeing those plants beside her picture on the mantel.

Nor could I stomach watching them turn brown and die, as they always did.

THERE WAS A TIME WHEN I attended the funerals of strangers. It happened spontaneously the first time. I was walking by a church and mourners were going in. A nice young man in black, who perhaps saw me hesitating, made a gesture for me to go inside. It was a service for an elderly parent. The mourners were contained and respectful. The person had lived a good long life. I observed the family. How they wiped away their tears, how they leaned against one another. But this was not enough for me.

I grew more discerning. I didn't want to attend services for people who were merely experiencing the sadness of loss. I wanted to view those who felt as if their beloved had been swallowed by quicksand. I wanted to see grief when it became a howl in the dark, unfeeling voice of the universe. The shrieks, the sobs, the tears. Something that had been denied me.

I had my limits. I never went to gravesides. I never went up to the caskets. I sat in the back like an anthropologist, observing this strange ritual. Just as I staged apartments, I staged my own losses. If I was walking by a church or a funeral home where a service or a wake might be going on, I'd wander in. No one ever asked. No one ever stopped me. Perhaps there was something about me that looked as if I belonged.

14

AS I WALK BACK TO THE Monument of the Sailor, I think
I'll spot her returning from the market, laden with groceries. Or
strolling the promenade. I used to look for her all the time. At
the mall when I'd go back-to-school shopping, at the supermar-
ket when I had to grab ingredients for dinner, or after school. I'd
think I'd see her, waiting for me by the gate, at the checkout aisle,
or slipping between the clothing racks. I'd catch a glimpse. Later,
shaken, I'd tell my father. He'd just nod and reply, "I'm sure she's
somewhere, watching out for you."

Now, for the first time in years, I have a sense of her—as if she
is near. At the water's edge, I find the same boatman who ferried
me here. He's smoking a cigarette. As I approach, he spits into the
sea. He doesn't seem to recognize me. Part of me wonders if I have
ceased to exist, if I'm invisible. As I climb on board, he hesitates,
perhaps hoping for another ride to make it worth his while. I sit in
the back in silence. Finally, he unmoors.

As the boat putters back to the center of town, I feel as if I am
passing through a portal from one world to the next, from the living to the dead and now back again. As if I have descended into
some darkness that cannot be known or explained. This darkness
can descend on me at any time. When I go into bathrooms at gas
stations or cafés, I think I'm going to find a dead body on the floor.
Floating on my back in a pristine lake, I close my eyes, and then
open them, startled, afraid that something will grab me and pull
me down.

As the boat chugs across, I feel the mist on my face. We bounce
up and down in the wake of other boats. I close my eyes. I want this
ride to go on and on. I never want it to stop. But moments later,
the motor slows and we pull into the dock. This time, he offers his

hand to help me disembark, though I have no idea why. As I walk along the promenade, I think to myself, What have I accomplished by coming here? I've found the building where we lived. And that is all.

15

"LAURA," DETECTIVE HENDRICKS SAID, "I'd appreciate it if you'd give me a call." Was that all he said? I listened for a sense of urgency in his voice. There was none. But he always was a cool cookie. That was something my father liked to say about the cops who swarmed our house, but especially Charlie Hendricks. A cool cookie.

Now, suddenly, he called me out of the blue. How did he find me? After all these years, how did he track me down?

Laura Smith. I have the most ordinary of names. It's like Jane Doe.

In fact, I once saw my name on a sample customs document. FILL IN NAME OF PASSENGER. EXAMPLE: LAURA SMITH. Who is Laura Smith? Who was Jane Doe? When did that name come to represent the nameless woman in the shallow grave? The body never identified at the morgue. The anonymous, the unclaimed.

16

SIGNORA PIAZZA OFFERS ME DINNER, but I politely decline. I climb back up to my room, where I pull a table out of the way, open the balcony doors to let in the breeze off the sea. Then I flop on the bed. Mosquitoes buzz around me, but I don't care. I want to breathe in this place. I smell the brine, the sea. The air she breathed so long ago. I think I should write to Patrick and explain to him why I am here. Let him know that I'm safe. I don't want to do what she did. Leave without a word. Without a trace. But I'm not sure what I want to say.

I close my eyes, and I must have drifted off, because when I open them, it's dark. Restless, I feel the ocean breeze call to me. I decide to go out. The signora tries to stop me, telling me it is late and dangerous, but I don't care. I explain to her as best I can that I'll be fine.

The evening is warm and the port lively as I stroll. Nothing feels very dangerous. Boys skid by on rickety bicycles. Children play ball with their parents. Orange moonlight shimmers at the crest of the sea. Suddenly I'm hungry. I slip into a small restaurant up Via Montenegra, where I order a glass of rosé and the squid ink linguini with clams, shrimp, and mussels, all pulled from the sea. It's delicious, but I barely touch my food. However, I drink my wine. Then order another. But I leave most of my meal. The waiter seems disappointed when I ask for the check. I'm a little tipsy as I go for a walk along the sea.

A huge white yacht named *Sweet Secret* is being scrubbed down by its crew. They are swabbing every inch of it, and I stop to look. Moored around it are ferries, bound for Greece. It's from here that my mother swore she could see Albania. To me, it's just a narrow strip of sea. The night grows cooler, and I sit on a bench and take out my journal. I think I'll sketch this *Sweet Secret,* but instead I just sit, the journal closed in my lap.

Couples stroll hand in hand, families are still out eating, even as children slump in their chairs or emit wide yawns. Their parents chatter on, ignoring them. A man guides his elderly mother out for a stroll. Teens practice their soccer moves. An old couple staggers along, whispering in a language only they can understand.

17

I READ SOMEWHERE THAT PEOPLE tend to buy houses that remind them of their childhood home. They will buy a house with rooms or vistas or some configuration of what they recall, even unconsciously. One morning, they wake up and realize that they've re-created the place they left so long ago. It's true of the house I live in with Patrick—a fixer-upper we bought in Brooklyn almost twenty years ago, for a song. A real DIY job. I suppose we were urban pioneers. We bought it cheap in a neighborhood that everyone said was crazy. But it was what we could afford and, as Patrick liked to say, it had good bones.

But there was nonstop work to be done. The rooms had been divided, and it seemed as if at least two and maybe three families had occupied the house. For a while, Patrick and I lived on the third floor while he ripped out bathrooms and an outdated kitchen. He studied old plans, searched for archival photos. We took endless tours through other people's houses. We'd walk through a stranger's home and say things like "Let's strip all the paint off our banisters" or "I bet there's original tin under that drop ceiling." For a long time we were nomads in our own home, moving from floor to floor while Patrick stripped moldings, banged out walls. Once we uncovered a nest that mice had been building for years. It was filled with all kinds of string, rubber bands, plastic ties. It was beautiful, in its own way. I was sorry to see it go.

While Patrick tackled the inside, I dealt with the outside. It was my preferred place to be. We had a small front yard with a tree pit. I fenced in the yard and the tree pit and planted bulbs. I ordered tulips and narcissi and hyacinths. The backyard was shady, so I learned about shade plants. I bought all varietals of hosta—ghost white, August moon, purple passion. And then I decided to build the pond.

Patrick was opposed. It would be a nesting ground for mosquitoes, he said, and, given all the trees around, including, at the time, a soaring oak, leaves would keep falling in. I didn't care. I wanted a pond with fish. The pond was not so simple. It required demolition; then we had to bring in rocks and create a plastic lining and a water source. It was much more complicated than I'd imagined. Finally, I was able to add the fish. I went to Chinatown and purchased eight koi.

I named them after tragic lovers. Patrick found this strange, but it seemed fitting to me. Romeo and Juliet, Othello and Desdemona, Anna and Vronsky, Tristan and Isolde. Not that I could actually tell them apart, but the names seemed to stick. They made it through the first winter but fared worse the second. I lost Romeo that spring, and Isolde didn't make it past June. By the third year they were not doing well at all, so I moved them to an inside tank, where they died off one by one. The pond filled with leaf debris in the fall. Eventually we drained it and I planted azaleas. They bloom every spring.

Slowly the house came into its own. I loved its dark wood paneling, the white walls, and windows with paned glass. The sitting room with the chaise longue, where I like to read. And then, one morning, it occurred to me that our home was eerily similar to our house in New Jersey—the one I couldn't wait to get away from. It had that old-world feel. The dining room with the crystal chandelier and the Biedermeier furniture. The dark wood everywhere. Those clean white linens and fluffy duvets. My mother opened all the windows on the first days of spring. She loved to let the freshness in. It was as if she couldn't get enough air. In winter she never drew the curtains. She had to let the light in. I tend to do the same. But I take little comfort in these similarities. The house I grew up in was the one she left. Or had to leave. Just as I may be leaving mine, as well.

I MARRIED PATRICK BECAUSE I wanted to have a life. Or what you'd call a normal life. Something different from what I'd known. Someone who phoned or came home when he said he would. I cannot say that reliability is the human trait I admire most, but it is the one that has come to matter the most to me. If he is even a few minutes late, I panic. My heart starts pounding. I don't have a problem with leaving. I just don't like being left.

Not that long ago, I read about a woman who was in a plane crash over the Amazon when she was a girl. She was sitting next to her mother, who clasped her hand as the plane blew apart. This girl fell two miles to earth, and managed to survive. No one else did. Finding herself in the middle of the jungle, she recalled the advice her parents—both biologists—once gave her. If you are lost in the jungle, find a stream and follow it. It will lead to a river, and the river will take you to people. So she walked for eleven days, until she found it.

Follow the stream.

Years later, in an interview, she was asked if she was terrified during her time alone in the jungle, and she replied that it was not fear she felt. It was a bottomless sense of abandonment.

18

I RISE EARLY, HAVING BARELY slept. Patrick hasn't returned my call. I'm not surprised, and maybe I shouldn't care so much. I've hardly been an ideal wife. Recently we've talked about separating, though neither of us has taken the first step—beyond sleeping in the spare room from time to time. Still, even an angry call would be something. Either he isn't awake or he has nothing to say. Or perhaps he's moving on. There is much we've never discussed. I'm not sure if I can bring myself to have that talk now. It's true I've been having an affair, a fling really, but it's not just that. I cannot explain the wedge between us. I leave another voice mail. "This is something I had to do." And then I add, "I haven't run off with someone. It's not like that."

I have no idea how this last part will land, but it's too late for regrets. I'm also wondering why I can't just tell him the truth. I've come looking for my mother. I'm not ready to talk to her detective. I need to do this alone. But that seems too difficult to say.

I EAT A QUICK BREAKFAST of a doughy pastry and coffee, and then head out. I have no plan for today except to wander. I cannot help but feel as if I am following threads that lead to a dead end. Once more, I follow the sea. It's another warm, blustery day, and I stoop to pick up a smooth, polished stone, some scallop shells. I slip these into my purse. Of course, this is what she did. Perhaps we are both crows, my mother and I. I look for objects that might have some interest for me, but like Hansel and Gretel, I have lost the way.

I stop to buy an espresso and then slump onto a park bench. It's not long before an inchworm appears beside me on a silken thread.

It's a green, translucent creature, so tiny yet full of life. It makes determined strides as it pulls itself up, and then drops back down. It lights on the bench where I am sitting. Then it rises again.

I have long had an interest in ephemeral art. Ice sculptures, butter sculptures, sand castles. I'd planned to make enduring work, but things kept getting in my way. I'd start a painting, but there was always something wrong and I couldn't correct my mistakes. I never finished anything. After all, my life exists in snippets, scraps, shards. Bits and pieces, discarded things. This is why I do well with the found, the fragment. Objects not intended to last. I loved building sand castles as a kid. And I loved watching the sea come and wash them away.

My studio at home is a converted garage. It was a study in incompletion until I finally gave up on the idea of making art that was perfect or permanent. That was when I came to the transient. Driftwood, moss, ice, and snow. I made sculptures out of icicles, but that was too ephemeral, even for me. And the feather phase became arduous when I constrained myself to the stipulation that all the feathers had to be foraged.

A few years ago, I stumbled on snails. I read an article about a veterinarian in Poland who painstakingly repaired the damaged shell of a snail. It was a long, detailed piece about a snail that had been stepped on and how the veterinarian glued it back together. After that, people began bringing him their snails. I learned that a snail can go dormant and sleep for three years. If it crawls without stopping, it will cover only a kilometer in a week.

Snails are born with the tiniest of shells. You cannot separate their bodies from their house, or they will die. They are always home. Suddenly, snails seemed like excellent material for my next project. Art intended to endure, like the mandala of the Buddhist monks. I bought a few dozen snails at the pet store. They are sitting at home in a terrarium, sleeping, waiting for me to decide what to do.

Sitting in the shade, watching the inchworm and contemplating dormant snails and the swirls in a leaf, I see some pattern here. An organizing principle that I have yet to understand. Then I know what I must do. I return to the dock, where I find the ferryman who rowed me across the day before. Again, he doesn't seem to recognize me. There is no nod. No hello despite my exuberant *"Buongiorno!"* He shepherds me across—still in silence, not acknowledging me in any way. I get off at the monument to the fishermen. Then I walk along the residential streets until I come to the building where I grew up.

I knock on the old *portiere*'s door, and she opens it. She glares at me as I stare back at her, trying to smile. "I need to know more," I tell her.

I think she's going to close the door in my face, but instead she looks at me, long and hard. "Go to Castellobello," she says.

"What about Castellobello?"

"The Red House. It's there."

Then she closes the door, more gently this time.

19

THE ROAD FROM BRINDISI to Bari is a highway that follows the sea. It is beautiful along the Adriatic, and I am happy to be driving. Happy to be away from it all. I've got the windows down. The sea breeze engulfs me. To the right is the Adriatic, and to my left are hills that seem to rise into mountains. The median is thick with shrubs that bloom white and pink. I struggle to remember their name. Terraced along the side of the hills, grapevines and olive trees grow. For a moment, I forget my mission. I forget where

I'm going and why. I just like to drive. I put the radio on and tune in some silly Italian rock station and try to sing along. I can pass hours this way. I tend to drive on service roads. I avoid the highway. I am ambling along, windows down, smelling the sea.

Oleander. The name comes to me suddenly, just like that. I am driving along miles and miles of oleander. A word from my childhood. What did she tell me about the oleander that grew everywhere in the blazing Mediterranean sun? That it was a beautiful plant with colorful flowers. But never taste the petals because they are poisonous.

My mother knew a lot about poisons. She was fascinated by plants that could harm you. Hemlock, mushrooms, oleander. But oleander was the most dangerous because it had beautiful flowers. It was a plant that could betray you.

20

THE PINE BARRENS IS A mysterious place—one that fascinates my mother endlessly. Its mysteries seem to hold sway over her. Every chance she has, she wants to go. It isn't that far from our house, just twenty minutes or so down the road. My mother is obsessed with the underground streams, the purity of the water that flows there. "It's the cleanest water in the world," she boasts, as if she's had a personal hand in it. She loves to take us on long hikes or bike rides even as we complain about the heat or the bugs in summer. She never wants to go in winter. She hates the cold. But in summer, we're there all the time.

There's a ghost town in the Pine Barrens that consists of buildings in ruins. An old mining town. Now there're just the shells of facades with no windows. Doorways leading into rooms with no walls. We find the place creepy, but for my mother, it has an endless allure. She walks among these abandoned buildings with their skeletal frames. She seems to be oddly at home here. I never understand it.

There's a lake where we like to go to picnic. No one knows how deep it is. We aren't allowed to swim there. "You can look," she tells us. "But never go in the water."

There are many legends about the area, but the one she seems the most drawn to involves a devil—the infamous New Jersey Devil, for which the hockey team is named. It is said that in 1735, a woman named Mrs. Leeds gave birth to a son. He was her thirteenth child, and therefore cursed. In one version, she abandoned him in the woods, to the mercy of the elements and predators. For years, there were rumors that a feral child who walked on four legs roamed the woods. In another version, he was born a monster and attacked his own mother just after his birth. Then he flew up the chimney and over to the Pine Barrens.

Whatever its origins, the child who grew up to be the Jersey Devil is still said to wander the Pine Barrens. And whenever a child disappears, the old wives' tales say to look for it there.

The devil child becomes a scary bedtime story my mother tells. She warns us not to wander off. On weekends, whenever we can, she wants us to go to the Pine Barrens. She taunts us with a wink. "Maybe we'll meet the devil this time."

21

I STOP AT A VILLAGE BY THE SEA. In the car, I slip into my bathing suit. At a cabana, I rent a towel, lounge chair, an umbrella, and order a lunch of *crudo,* which seems like a safe bet, given that I am at the sea. *Asciugamano, sedia da spiaggia, ombrellone.* I am surprised at how quickly my Italian is returning. The seafood is fresh and briny from the Adriatic. I sip a glass of white wine. Then I lie down on my lounge chair. Around me children shriek, dogs bark, and people chat. I get up and run into the sea.

Gulls soar overhead, perhaps mistaking me for a fish. Two boys play with paddles and a ball, knocking it back and forth. They keep tumbling into the surf. I smile at their antics and float on my back. I close my eyes. The lapping waters hold me aloft. I am here inside this moment, this present, a place I can rarely be. I drift, floating; everything is just so.

Suddenly I hear a child call, "Mama, Mama." All around me, it seems children are suddenly calling Mama. My eyes snap open and I lie there, staring at the sky. A vampire in her coffin. Then the darkness envelops me.

22

"WAS THERE ANYTHING UNUSUAL about your mother? Any distinguishing marks? A mole, a scar, a tattoo. Anything about her that you think might help us find or identify her?" They ask the same questions every time they come. They show up at dinnertime, which usually consists of mac and cheese and canned vegetables, not the elaborate meals she'd make for us. It's unnerving the way they suddenly appear. Our father grows anxious. He says they're trying to catch him doing something strange. Burning stained laundry, scrubbing the floors with bleach. None of which he does, of course. They've gone over every inch of the house and the yard. They've dug up all the bulbs and left gaping holes where hydrangeas had been. My father pleaded with them. "Those are about to bloom."

"Was your mother suicidal?"

It's true that some nights, she did run off. She did disappear without telling us, but not for long. No, she was never gone for long. An hour, maybe more. Just wanting some "alone" time, some "mommy" time. It was never anything that we worried about. It's not like she came back with liquor on her breath. She'd be gone for an hour or two. Never more. Just enough to clear her head, she'd say. It didn't happen that often. And besides, she always came home.

"Oh, no, she wasn't like that at all."

23

CASTELLOBELLO RESEMBLES A TOWN designed for hobbits. Sitting in the midst of Murgia's rocky terrain, it is a medieval village of gray conical-shaped houses that resemble the hats of dwarfs. The houses, I learn from the guidebook, are called *trulli*. No one knows why they were constructed in this way, though the theory is that they could be built and broken down quickly if the tax collector arrived. It remains a mystery.

Now it's a tourist destination. A town filled with souvenirs,

T-shirts, snow globes. Tour buses are everywhere, and the smell of diesel is in the air. I find parking on the outskirts, and drag my suitcase into the center of town, where I find the tourist office. A German tour guide and a large group stand there, sifting through travel brochures. I push past them to the desk, where a woman with long red fingernails is engrossed in something on her desktop. She is young and bored. She's sipping a can of soda and barely looks up at me. "How may I help you?" she asks wearily.

She's ready to pull out the usual maps and brochures, when I say in my broken Italian, "I am looking for the red house." The woman makes a face as if she doesn't understand what I am saying.

"La Casa Rossa," I repeat slowly, this time with emphasis, but she still just shakes her head.

She stares at me blankly. "I don't know," she replies, and she hands me a map and a brochure. "Perhaps you will find it here." Then she goes back to whatever was occupying her interest before I walked in.

I walk out into the blazing sun. It is very hot and there are many tourists wandering around this city of conical houses. I follow the throngs as they snap pictures and buy postcards and key chains. I wander up and down the side streets, but nothing presents as a red house, and certainly nothing looks like my mother's paintings of it.

Weary after a while, I buy a gelato and sit in the shade in a small park in front of a church overlooking the city. The Belvedere. It's a dry patch of land with a couple of scrawny trees, but it is a respite from the heat. And it has a vista from which I can see everything.

From here, I think I will be able to spot a red house, but all I see are the gray conical rooftops. I sit on my bench in the shade, licking the gelato as it drips down my hand.

IT'S GETTING LATE AND I'VE HAD a long day. Too tired to hit the road, I take a room at a small boutique hotel, overpriced, with tacky décor. Plastic flowers, chrome and black leather chairs in the parlor. My room has a lumpy mattress and bad art. Opening the curtains, I gaze down into a courtyard, where women are doing laundry. All of the window boxes are filled with geraniums. After a long, hot shower, I dry my hair and dress slowly. I resist the temptation to flop down on the bed. I force myself to step outside into the evening.

It's still light out, but most of the tour buses have left. I'm still looking for what might be a red house, but all I see are the gray *trulli*. The air is much cooler and fresher, and now that the beating sun is gone, it is bearable to walk these streets. I climb uphill and down, past these strange medieval hobbit houses. Painted on the roofs are symbols that seem to be from long ago—some appear to be crosses, the others evil eyes. There's a heart, a swastika, a six-pointed star, and a candelabra. I assume that these are intended to seem ancient, and perhaps they once were, but I can't help wondering if they're just painted for the tourists.

I pass an old man, sitting on a stool, in front of a house. He's squinting in the sun. I smile at him. He smiles back, and then cocks his head, as if he's puzzling over something. He has a shock of white hair and piercing blue eyes. He leans on a cane perched between his legs and he's wearing a wool jacket and pants too warm for the season. He doesn't take his eyes off me as I walk by, but he starts to rise. "*Scusi*," he says.

He's staring at me now, with those marble blue eyes open wide, as if he's seen a ghost. I smile back at him but slip out of the way. He calls out to me again, "*Signora, scusi.*" I am wary of getting involved in a conversation with an old man. It's a stereotype about Italian men, I know, but still. And besides, I probably won't understand a word. I duck down an alleyway. When I turn, he is nowhere in sight.

24

"I KNEW SHE WAS THE ONE for me." My father snaps his fingers. "I knew it right away." Our father likes to tell this story and, when he does, if she's there, perhaps at a party or function or some annual office picnic for the car dealership where he works, she'll smile demurely, with exactly the smile that he fell for in the first place when they met outside that bar in Naples. That was the smile he eventually put on the buttons, the ones we had to wear when we were searching for her. It was the smile that lit up her face, and showed her dimples and pearly white teeth. She had beautiful teeth. They were very straight. She was proud of them. She never wore braces, she claimed.

Our father was right. Her smile could light up a room. Set it on fire. "Your mother's a pistol," our father liked to say. For him, it was love at first sight.

They used to joke about it. Right in front of us. "Weren't sure if we even wanted kids, after the war and all, but then boom. For a while we called her Efie." He'd point at me. "For equipment failure." That always made people laugh, though it made me blush. Mainly because I always knew that I was a mistake. Janine showed up five years later. Still, my parents never hid things from us. If they were in a fight, they fought at the kitchen table or in the car. They never fought behind closed doors. We never heard them hissing at each other in the dark. And they kissed in front of us, too. Long, deep kisses that hinted at other things—things they did in the dark. And then it was early to bed or an afternoon nap. Or, if we were on vacation, a quick trip back to the room.

They fought and bickered and made love and laughed at dirty jokes in front of us all the time. Friends of ours used to comment, "Your folks are so cool. I wish mine were like that." Our parents used to say, "We love each other. What is there to hide?"

I was proud of the fact that we were a family with nothing to hide. They showered an abundance of love on us and on each other, and that love spilled over into charity. We often spent Thanksgiving serving food in a soup kitchen. "It will teach them good values," our mother said. All the clothes that no longer fit were given to nearby churches, especially winter coats. "There is no reason to hold on to something that another person can wear."

This love included animals, as well. Violet liked to rescue things. Stray dogs and cats, and birds. She didn't like keeping anything in a cage, though. It made her sad, and she rarely clipped the wings of our many birds. From time to time, we had canaries and parakeets, and once we even had a small cockatoo, which in a prior life had been kept alone in a dark room and plucked all of its feathers out, even from its wings. But under our mother's care the bird grew back its feathers, and we had her for a long time—until we found a good home for her in a senior center.

Often there was a bird or two flying around the house. Somehow she trained them, because they rarely soiled the countertops or our shoulders or heads, where they landed. If a bird was in flight, my mother had only to hold up her hand and it would land right on her fingertips. We were careful to close the screen doors, but still one of our birds escaped. It was November, and the cold was upon us. Our mother sent us around the neighborhood with printed posters that read "Missing: Green parakeet. Answers to the name of Petie. Last seen in the company of sparrows."

We never saw Petie again.

Later, we'd put up other posters, but with my mother's face.

25

I'M NOT A FAN OF EATING ALONE. It's hard to know what to do with my hands, my eyes. I pretend to be busy reading a book, but often I'm lonely or bored. Tonight, I'm hungry, so what choice do I have? I stop at a wine bar for a glass of a local vintage and a plate of cheese and figs that are the best I've ever eaten. I'm not that hungry, and don't think I could eat or drink more. Suddenly, I'm exhausted.

Asking for the check, I feel as if I can't even get up and leave. My body seems heavy, weighted down. It's as if someone poured cement in my limbs. I'm not sure when I've ever felt so exhausted. I'm dragging myself back to my hotel when I hear someone behind me. He's shouting something. It sounds like *"Aspetta, aspetta."* Wait, wait. But I have nothing to wait for here. I hurry along.

Looking behind me, I can make out a figure, yelling something, and as he comes closer, I realize it is the same old man I ran into earlier and he's calling out to me. He's calling a name and seems to be almost running, huffing really. Now he's shouting and calling out to someone, but there's no one else on this street. I keep going. He must be crazy. If he weren't so old and frail, I'd be afraid.

But why is this old man brandishing a cane, chasing me, a stranger, up a hill? Despite his age, he keeps gaining. I walk more quickly, wondering if he means me harm. Have I in some way offended him? Or does he think I have? Perhaps I should run, but it seems foolish to run from an old man with a cane. He's shouting, *"Signora, per favore."* He's calling out, *"Aspetta, aspetta."* Even as I slip down an alleyway, I still hear him begging me to wait.

26

I DREAM ABOUT HER AGAIN. She's sitting on the bed, looking at me. She takes my hands and speaks to me in Italian—a language she rarely spoke once we left for America. She talks for a long time, and I listen carefully. I know that what she is telling me is important and, in my dream, I understand every word. But when I wake in a hot sweat, I can't remember a thing. It's one of those dreams you want to grab on to and not let go, but you can't. It's so much sand through your fingers.

I try to go back to sleep. But I just toss and turn, so I get up. Still nothing from Patrick. Now I'm starting to panic. He is ignoring me. Who can blame him, but he's never done this before. I try calling him again, collect, from my room phone. It's just past five in the morning. Only a little after 11:00 p.m. at home. But he doesn't pick up. I leave a long, rambling message. Then I decide to go for a walk. I get dressed and wander through the lobby, which is empty. There's not even a desk clerk in sight.

It's a brisk, almost chilly morning and a shiver runs through me. I hesitate. Perhaps I should get a sweater. But I don't feel like going back. I turn right outside my hotel and head up a narrow street, into a warren of shops that opens onto more alleyways. As I wander, I contemplate the puzzle that stretches before me. Why did Detective Hendricks call now? Why did old Signora Russo send me here? I cannot help feeling as if she knows where my mother is. Is the red house she painted really here? Did she come to live in Castellobello? In this town? And what about the writing on the back of her paintings. *Non sarò qui per sempre.* "I will not be here forever." What does the "here" actually stand for? My head is spinning with questions, and I long for answers.

I reach a dead end and head back, assuming I am returning the

way I came, but the streets do not look the same. They were lit
when I began my walk, but now, except for the occasional light in
a home, they are dark. I am uncertain which way to turn. I keep
going down alleyways that open onto yet more narrow streets. Or
I come to another dead end. I find myself wandering through an
Escher-like maze. I take stairwells that lead to the darkened front
doors of strangers, then turn around and head back into the night.

There seem to be so many ways to get lost in this city. My heart
is pounding as I struggle to find my way back to the illuminated
streets. I hear footsteps. A man walks behind me, then past. A cat
darts in front of me. I'm startled and give a little shout. The man
pauses, as if he has forgotten something, then continues on his way.
Though there isn't a tourist in sight, the shopkeepers are opening
up. They are putting out for display T-shirts and key chains shaped
into little *trulli*, endless carousels of postcards. I hear the sound of
grates going up to welcome the tourists. I walk through the town in
the quiet of the morning, wondering if I will find something familiar, something as austere and lonely as the red house she painted.

But there is nothing like that here. I pause at the conical houses,
but in the end, I know that there is no large red square house
among all these cones. I am starting to assume that if such a place
existed during the war, it has been torn down to make room for all
the tourist bus parking lots, new hotels, and apartment complexes
that line the outskirts of this town. I do a loop until I come once
again to the Belvedere.

I am stuck in a labyrinth, perhaps of my own making. Every
turn takes me to a dead end. The proverbial wild-goose chase.
But why would the old *portiere* send me here? Just to get rid of me?
Or for some other reason? Did my mother talk to her about this
town? It seems I will never know the answers to the questions that
have plagued me these many years, but I also know that it's time to
leave. And, I suppose, face what I have been avoiding for so long.
All the things I've been running away from for all these years. My

flailing marriage, the foolish nature of my work, my empty life, and, of course, what propelled me on this journey in the first place, Detective Hendricks's phone call.

Maybe some woman has pressed charges against him. Perhaps he's calling to be sure I won't do the same. But I doubt it. At any rate, it is time for me to stop running. Face the music, as my father used to say.

Strangely, I feel closer to my mother here than I have anywhere else. It is like that child's game, when you're looking for something. You are getting colder, warm, warmer. I am getting warmer, but there remains something elusive, like the rainbow's end, always just out of reach. Meanwhile, my mother, the elusive ghost, keeps slipping away.

Finally, I come to a small café that has just opened, and I ask directions to my hotel. The barista, an older woman with hair dyed the color of oranges, starts speaking to me in rapid-fire Italian, pointing in different directions. Finally, she stops pointing and grabs me by the arm, walks me to the corner where the streetlights begin again, and in the light of dawn I see my hotel. I have been walking in circles all along.

27

THEY ARE ALWAYS SORRY, the police officers. They shake their heads. They seem to feel bad that they have no news. What more can they say? It's their job. And so they ask over and over again. Was there anything strange? Anything suspicious about our mother before she disappeared? I've learned over the years that it is one thing when a person dies or goes away, but it is another altogether when that person disappears. It is a magic trick. Some sleight of hand. Except it just goes on and on. A road trip that never ends.

I imagine her coming home for lunch. Making herself a sandwich, a cup of tea. Then she walked out of the house, and left all of us behind. The next part is harder to imagine. Was someone waiting for her, or did he make her leave? Did she just do this on her own? "No sign of forced entry," Detective Hendricks says over and over. No sign of a struggle. Not an errant fingerprint.

The person waiting. Her lesbian lover. Her secret best friend. Did she have a second life? An enemy? Did my mother have a whole side to her that I never knew and could never imagine? Did she run off to Florida? Is she living near a sinkhole on a cul-de-sac?

It happens every time there's a news flash—a terrorist attack, a plot foiled, remains discovered. What are remains anyway? I've asked myself this a lot. Because, ultimately, nothing remains. I find myself trembling, afraid to look. I don't want to know. I don't think I could bear it if I turned on CNN and saw her staring back at me.

FOR YEARS I ASKED MYSELF, What did I do to make her leave? Did I disappoint her in some way? Was it because I fought with her about my homework, my hair? Because I started mocking her accent? She had one of those mellifluous Italian accents that sounded as if she were singing arias. When I was little, I loved her voice, but as I approached my teenage years, it became a source of embarrassment. My friends would ask if my mother was the nanny. Once, my mother overheard me mimicking her in an exaggerated Italian accent, and she sat down in front of me and my friend and cried. A couple years after she was gone, I got up the nerve to ask my father, "Did I do something wrong? Is that why she left?"

And he replied impatiently, "Laura, not everything is about you." Then he poured himself a drink.

After that, I was silent in my belief that somehow this was my fault. I kept it inside of me, like those mantras you're given at an ashram when you're twenty years old and get on a Zen kick. You're told never to share your mantra, so I never did. Not with any therapist I ever saw. Not with a lover. Not even with Patrick. Still, I'd stay up at night and roll the thought around in my head like a hard candy in my mouth. Certainly, she wouldn't leave my father. She loved him. And not Janine, who always did what she was told. I'm the one who was stubborn. I'm the one who got caught in her crosshairs. I'm the one who was leavable.

28

MY SOPHOMORE YEAR OF high school, I take a class called Survey of English Literature. It's required and it's boring. I sit in class doodling, as I do in most of my classes. I draw patterns of endless lines that weave in and out of one another. The drawings cause the guidance counselor to have some concern. We've gone through Chaucer and some medieval tales. Now it's time for Shakespeare, and the teacher assigns *Twelfth Night*. She vaguely describes the plot. It's the story of a brother and sister who arrive in Illyria, a distant land. It is a story of immigration and exile, the teacher says. I'm not paying much attention as she starts to read out loud.

In the second scene, my ears perk up. I put down my pen. The scene opens with the sister arriving in Illyria. Her name is Viola. "What country, friend, is this?" Viola asks.

"This is Illyria, lady," the Captain replies.

"And what shall I do in Illyria?" Viola asks. "My brother is in Elysium." She goes on. "Perchance he is not drowned; what think you, sailors?"

And the Captain responds, "It is perchance that you yourself were saved."

"O my poor brother!" Viola replies. "And so perchance may he be."

I am frozen in my seat as the teacher assigns parts. I put my head down. I cannot read this out loud. I cannot even read the words of the play, about two siblings in exile who will never see their home again, who must invent new lives for themselves, who change their names and wear disguises. Who is this other Viola who has fled? And why?

I raise my hand. The teacher smiles, thinking I am volunteering to read a part. Instead, I ask if I may go to the bathroom. She looks, as she often does, disappointed in me. I race out of the classroom to the girls' lavatory.

I throw up in the sink.

29

I HEAD BACK TO THE HOTEL. I've decided to pack and check out. I want to be on the road before the tourists arrive, but I'm too late. The buses are pouring in, and the hordes are filling the parking lots and side streets, following their guides, who sport umbrellas to make sure each group follows closely behind. I try to grab a sandwich at a nearby shop, but there's already a wait. My plan is to drive back toward Rome, maybe spend a night outside of Naples, a few nights in Rome. My flight home is at the end of the week. I have no more business here.

I order a panini with tomato and mozzarella. I'm nibbling on it as I wheel my suitcase, dodging in and out of tour groups, to the parking lot where I've left my car. I turn down a narrow alley to avoid some of the tourists, when I hear someone shouting at me, the way he did the night before. That gruff man's voice telling me to wait. "*Signora, aspetta, per piacere.*"

A stranger is calling out as if he knows me, but how could he? I'm dragging my suitcase, and then I see him again. It's that same old man who has been stalking me. I'm almost at my car. My street Italian is coming back. "*Lasciami in pace,*" I shout, but he keeps on coming. And he's still yelling, but now he's calling out a name, something I vaguely recognize.

I walk faster, trying to get away from this madman, but he keeps calling. And then when he has almost reached me, I hear what he's saying. "Viola, *aspetta,*" he yells. "Viola. *Sai tu?*"

I stop dead in my tracks.

"My name is Laura," I tell him.

"You are not Viola?" he asks, not believing me.

"No," I tell him. "I am not Viola." I am trembling as I say this. He appears crestfallen—until I continue. "I'm her daughter."

The old man fixes his watery eyes on me. They seem to swell as he approaches. Then he smiles. His blue eyes sparkle, and he has neat white teeth. He scrutinizes my face. "Ah, yes," he says. "Of course. She would be old, like me."

"You knew my mother?"

He is staring at me as if he can't believe it. "You look just like her."

I can't move. I know that I resemble my mother, but it never occurred to me that our similarity is enough for someone who knew her decades ago to think that I am she.

Now he stands before me. "Yes, I knew her."

I am shaking my head, trying to make sense of this. "But you knew her only as a girl."

"But, you see, for me she never aged. She has always stayed the same."

For me, too, I want to tell him.

"Anyway," he says with a heavy sigh, "I would know her any-where." He holds out his hand. "My name is Tommaso. Tom-maso Bassano." He speaks with a silky, clear Italian, like a radio announcer, and I find myself understanding much of what he says. More and more, my mother tongue is coming back to me. Tom-maso looks down, shaking his head, and I catch a glimpse of the young man he must have been, with his deep blue eyes and pitch-black hair, his sharp, carved features and his muscular limbs.

"You knew her well?"

Again, Tommaso nods, smiling at me sadly. "Yes. I knew her." He stares down at his shoes.

"How?" I ask. "How did you know her?"

He looks down as if he doesn't understand, though I'm fairly certain he does. He ignores my question. "How," he goes on, "how is she? Is she . . ."

I stand in the sun, thinking I might faint. "It's complicated."

For a moment we stand in stunned silence. He seems relieved that I don't ask him to explain, and I'm grateful that he doesn't ask me to elaborate, to tell him if she is dead or alive. Perhaps we are both afraid to know the truth.

Suddenly, he opens his mouth and pulls back his cheek. His breath is stale, but it is such an odd gesture I don't know what to do except stare into the dark cavity of his mouth. He points to a gold tooth near the back. "Your grandfather," he tells me, "he pulled this tooth. And he made this new one for me, sixty years ago."

I stare into his open mouth as he shows me his gold tooth, which glistens in the morning sun.

"My grandfather was a dentist?" I don't know what else to say. I can't believe my luck. This old man knew my mother. He must have, to call me by her name. So the old *portiere* did not send me on a wild-goose chase after all. "Did they live here?"

He shakes his head. "No, not here. Not in the town."

"So where?" I ask. "Where did they live?"

A cloud comes across his bright blue eyes. "They lived at the Red House."

"The Red House? I am looking for that house."

He nods solemnly. "Come," he says with a wave of the hand. "I will take you."

30

THE ROAD OUT OF TOWN is cratered from the trucks that barrel by. Cement mixers, trucks carrying steel beams, lumber. Produce trucks loaded with the sweetest strawberries, tomatoes, arugula. We drive along an industrial landscape—tire stores, gas stations, loading docks. Tommaso keeps his eyes on the road, squinting, and every few minutes he suddenly points to the left or the right. He's asked me to drive. "My eyes," he tells me, "they aren't so good." I make sharp turns, dodge a garbage truck.

The road is dusty and it's hot, and the air-conditioning isn't working very well in my rental car. Still, we cruise along until we reach a dirt road filled with potholes. It is surrounded by trees on both sides and fields of wheat, olive groves, vineyards. And then suddenly, Tommaso points. "*Alla sinistra, sinistra,*" he says, almost shouting, and I make a sharp left. He points again. "*Alla destra.*" I turn again. "There," he says.

And suddenly I see it. Tall, red, looming. A solid block of a building. Not a house, not a home, not a place you could ever live. It's a barracks, a warehouse, a prison. It stands alone in a field on a hill, exactly as she had painted it. "Tommaso," I ask, "what is this place?" But he is silent. He shakes his head as we turn up the dusty drive.

We pull up in front and get out. We stand in the shade of a tall oak tree. The building before me is abandoned, padlocked. It is huge and desolate, and a shiver runs through me. A cold I cannot account for. For a long time, I just stare. "Tommaso, where are we?"

He shakes his head, looking down. "This is not a story I planned to tell." He speaks softly and I lean in to listen. "They came from the north."

THE

SECOND STORY

31

TURIN, MILAN, FLORENCE, ROME, NAPLES. The train clatters along the Italian countryside. Towns and cities zip by. There are brief stops in Florence and Rome, time to get out and stretch legs and sore backs, but that is all, then back inside the hot, dusty compartment with the windows closed because the porters don't want the dust to get in, and the guards don't want the people to jump out. But who would jump from a moving train? Only crazy people, Viola thinks. Still, it is hot, stifling. And then there's the stench of bodies and something stronger, more pungent.

A woman not far from her faints and keels over. An old man clutches his chest. All around her, mothers clasp their children, fathers slump, heads in their hands. Her father sits straight, his back pressed against the wooden seat. He sways to the movement of the train. Rudy is crammed against him. For now, he sleeps, his forehead glazed in sweat. Viola rests against the window beside her mother. She watches farmlands slipping by. Her mother, Anna, clasps Viola's hand. Anna is a woman who bathes daily in lavender water, who brushes her hair a hundred times before bed, but she, too, reeks of sweat.

It's September 1942. Though it's a warm day, her father, Josef, is wearing wool trousers and jacket, the best clothes he had for this journey. In his lap he clutches his satchel of dental instruments— probes, picks, tartar scraper, a hand-operated drill. He sighs and looks at his wife. Reaching across he puts his hand on her knee. "Anna," he whispers.

She shakes her head, closing her eyes.

He leans forward, stroking her. Viola presses her face against the glass. Farmlands slip away. The land grows hilly, almost mountainous. Her mother's dark eyes are red from crying. Her normally round features look thin and wan. And her lush, thick hair, which she usually wears neatly in a bun, is greasy and disheveled. "It will be all right. I promise." He reaches up, touching her face.

Anna sighs. "You don't know."

"You didn't have to come."

Anna nods. It's true. She didn't. The children, either. Anna's family have been Italian Jews for centuries, and thus far, no Italian Jews, except for agitators, have been sent into exile. But Josef had no choice. He has the word ALIEN stamped across his passport, as do most of the other Jews in this convoy, but not his children. They were born in Italy. It doesn't matter that Josef moved here from Romania over twenty years ago. Any foreign Jew naturalized after January 1, 1919, has had his citizenship revoked, and must be sent to a detention camp. Josef tried to bribe officials, but his efforts failed. He knew that eventually he'd be sent away.

He didn't expect his family to accompany him. Others have been separated. His friend Bruno was sent to the south and his wife somewhere else. Their three-year-old daughter remained in Turin with distant relatives. Josef shakes his head as the train rattles south. He looks pleadingly at Anna, then at Viola, who stares at him with her huge dark eyes, which match her mother's. "It's just for a time. Until this madness is over."

Anna softens, her fingers touching his. "I don't blame you." Her eyes well up like those of a lost child. "It was my decision." Josef runs his hands over the smooth leather case that houses his instruments. This was the one thing he refused to leave behind. He flicks the latch. Inside, the metal and mirrors gleam. His tools rest on a bed of velvet in narrow grooves. He fondles his probes and explorers, the picks for getting between the teeth, under the gums, into

THE RED HOUSE · 75

the tiniest spaces, the miniature mirrors and extraction forceps. It was foolish to bring them. He closes the lid.

THERE'S A STOP IN NAPLES, where they're allowed to stretch their legs. An armed guard stands nearby, smoking a cigarette. Around them is rubble. The city is in ruins after several years of Allied bombardment. Whole blocks have been obliterated. Children and dogs pick through the trash heaps. Anna grimaces at the streets filled with garbage. People are using entryways as their toilets; laundry is strung up everywhere. Starving cats fight with street urchins over a morsel of bread. A man tries to sell Josef his sister, who appears to be younger than Viola. Josef shakes his head as Anna turns away. She ushers the children back on the train.

Naples, then farther south. Pompeii, Benevento, Foggia, Bari. Viola crouches against the hard wooden seat, curled up, knees to her chest. Her hair tumbles over her shoulders even as she tries to pin it on top of her head. Sweat pours down her neck. She has just begun to bleed. Her stomach aches from the cramps. When it began, just before they left, Anna had shaken her head. "Of all the times," she'd said. But then she hugged her daughter. "I started early too," she said. And she'd told Viola what to do.

Now blood flows into the cloth she stuffed between her legs. Viola is sure that if she stands up, her dress will be stained. She doesn't think about where they are being taken, or what awaits them. All she can think about is the shame if there is blood on her skirt. And the soreness of her swollen nipples, the ache in her breasts. The hair sprouting between her legs. She thinks she will die if her father sees that she has become a woman. But her father, who is so prim and proper, who washes his hands before every meal, and wears his suit to dinner on Sunday afternoon, doesn't notice anything. He just stares straight ahead.

32

IN BARI, THE TRAIN STOPS, and they are told to get off. There are perhaps fifty, sixty of them altogether. But where are they headed? There is no point in asking; they've learned that no one will answer. In Josef's opinion, the people who guard them don't even know. They are just being handed off to the next and the next. But at last, after two days in the hot, stifling train cars, they stagger down with their belongings. The bright sun blinds them. Hungry children weep. But they stretch their legs.

In front of them is the sea—blue and shimmering. Boats and barges sail by, and it all looks so normal. Josef takes a deep breath of the briny air. "It isn't so bad here," he whispers to his wife. He points to the sea. "Perhaps we will stay nearby."

She squeezes his hand. "Perhaps we will."

Rudy is whimpering. Viola clasps him by the hand. "Look, a beach." She points toward the water. "You love to swim." Rudy tries to drag his sister toward the sea.

But on a tree-lined street, yellow buses idle. The kind that take children to school, but today they are the passengers, being taken elsewhere. Nothing is explained. They do as they are told. They board the buses. On the buses, they are once more greeted by the raw smells of sweat and urine, of bodies that have not been washed in days, and breath. Bad breath. Viola longs to brush her teeth. And remove the soiled cloth between her legs. Throw it away and stuff a new one in its place, because she feels blood seeping. The closeness of the bus, the bodies, the stench as if they are dying, the smell of her own blood overwhelms her.

The buses pull away in a slow procession, a caravan, and soon they are driving through the city with its harbor and drydocks and naval ships lined up, and then they turn away from the sea. Her father keeps looking back, as if the water held a promise. He twists his body for a final glimpse and then it is gone—all that shimmering blue. Now they are bumping on the dusty roads in the heat, the driver careless on the turns, honking as cars come around the bends. Driving farther and farther away from the coast, an area where it is now hilly and there are fields of wheat and vineyards and olive groves.

Viola presses her face to the window. It steams up with her breath. She rubs it away. The road is rough and lined with repair and auto mechanic shops. There are stretches of rugged, rocky terrain that open up into fields of wheat. The bus climbs as the road rises toward the nearby hills terraced with olive trees. They pass a sign. Castellobello. There are murmurs on board. Some think they have heard of it before. They nod in recognition. But that's only because the name sounds familiar, as if a town named "Beautiful Castle" couldn't pop up anywhere. "Oh, yes," some say knowingly. "I've heard of this place." They haven't.

The bus makes a sharp left and the inhabitants packed in the back swing to the side. Some topple over, and Josef shouts at the driver, "Be careful." The driver scowls. An old man who smells of his own urine falls on Viola, who scrambles out from under him. Anna reaches for her, tugging her back into her seat. When Viola looks up, there it is on the hill in the middle of a field of golden wheat, the wheat waving. On the crest sits the large red building, a squat structure with stucco walls. There are whispers. Her father drops his head into his hand. They turn up the long, unpaved drive.

The giant red block of a building perches on a barren hill in a field. There is nothing around it. Nowhere to go. Just the four-story structure with all the character of a cube. It looks like a place that houses animals and criminals, not a place to live. The passengers stare in silence. The Red House looms. Birds fly in and out of barred windows. The building is a husk, a shell, the skin that a snake has shed and left behind.

The buses pull up in the shade of an oak tree. It is, in fact, the only tree in sight. The doors are opened, and one by one the families tumble out. A young soldier with cobalt blue eyes helps them disembark. One at a time, he offers the passengers his hand, as if they have arrived at a spa on holiday. When it's Viola's turn, he looks at her with a sad smile. His eyes are blue like Rudy's special marbles. She sets her foot on the ground. She can breathe again. She totters beneath the oak, happy to be in its cooling shade. It is actually two trees, conjoined, their trunks braided. She thinks she will come here during the day and sit in this shade.

When she looks back, the young soldier is helping the next person down.

33

FOR THE PAST FEW YEARS, Viola has watched her world shrinking. All the things she's done freely for so long—going to the school across the street, playing with her friends, getting a Saturday gelato with her father, listening to the radio with her grandmother—one by one, they have been taken from her. She remembers the day when her parents called her and Rudy into the living room. Fall 1938. She's getting ready to leave for school. They rarely sit in the living room—a space reserved for guests and formal gatherings. It's the only room in the apartment where Viola isn't comfortable.

When she walks in, her parents are waiting. They sit stiffly in the winged armchairs. On the table is a plate of biscotti, but it seems as if they are more for display than to be eaten. No one ever eats in this room. Rudy, who is only six, plays with a toy train on the floor. They motion for her to join them. Then they eye one another, and Anna begins to speak. "We have gotten a notice." She struggles to find the words. "You are going to attend another school." Viola doesn't understand. She has gone to one school her entire life. The one across the street from where they live. "We think . . ." Anna hesitates. "A change might be good for you and Rudy."

Viola shakes her head. "But all my friends are there."

"Well," Anna replies, "you will make new friends."

But Josef waves his hand. "Let's just tell them the truth."

"I don't think . . ." Anna protests, but her Josef goes on.

"Jewish children are no longer allowed to attend public schools." She can't comprehend what her father is telling her. She is only eight, and being Jewish is hardly something she's ever thought about. Even her grandparents barely mention it.

"So what if we are Jews?"

Josef folds his hands in his lap. "There is a new law. You can no longer attend the school you've always gone to, but your mother and I have good news for you." Viola drops her eyes. She knows when her father is lying. "We have found you an even better school. It's just a short bus ride away." In fact, it's almost an hour away, and requires two transfers. But it is a Jewish school. The only kind that Jewish children can now attend.

Viola is even more perplexed. She knows that they are Jews, but she doesn't know what that really means. They go to temple twice a year with her grandparents; they don't keep kosher—though they avoid pork. They sometimes celebrate a holiday that their Christian friends don't keep, but that's about all. Otherwise, there's no difference. No one has ever mentioned to Viola on the playground or at school that she's different from the other children. Indeed, several other students at her school are Jewish. No one cares. "Some of your friends will probably go to the new school you will be attending," her father says.

Then her mother picks up the plate and offers her a cookie.

RUDY GOES UPSTAIRS TO BE with their grandparents and Viola stays in her room. From her window she looks down at the schoolyard. She sees her friends playing outside at recess and later racing home. They walk in tight clutches, laughing, whispering among themselves. All except for Leah and David. They are not at school, either. Watching her friends leaving the schoolyard, she thinks they might ring her bell to see why she isn't at school. And Natalia, their housekeeper, will feed them cookies and snacks. But no one does. None of them ever rings her bell again.

34

BEFORE IT WAS A PRISON, the Red House was an orphanage that housed blind children. The children ran their hands along the walls to find their way. The greasy smudges of their fingerprints remain. Before it was an orphanage, it was an agricultural school, where boys learned how to raise sheep and harvest olives. But it sat idle and abandoned for the past decade, until someone decided that it would be a good place to intern Jews. No one thought to make repairs. No bathrooms were added or beds brought in before sending them here. The birds weren't banished. Shutters that once covered the window frames weren't reinstalled.

The families mill in the shade of the conjoined oak trees. Some of the men have removed their jackets. Women fan themselves with their hands. Children whimper. Some men step away to relieve themselves in the bushes. Some of the women timidly raise their skirts, as well. A little boy soils himself and screams as his mother tries to wipe him off with a dirty handkerchief. They hope for water or something to eat, but nothing is offered.

Instead, soldiers motion for them to follow. The new "residents" shuffle into the giant stucco building. Never mind that they are in enforced exile. They walk into a dark, cavernous, windowless room. Once they are all assembled, they are led down a stark concrete corridor, then up one crumbling stairwell and then another, until they come to a hallway of spare, unadorned rooms, no bigger than cells. All Josef can think is that he has traded one prison for another.

A soldier points into a filthy room of rusted sinks and toilets. There are two shower stalls with no curtains. Cold water trickles from the spouts. "You may bathe here," the soldier says. "But not at night." At the end of the hallway, a man with a clipboard shouts out names. Families disappear into the rooms. When Josef and Anna hear their name called, they file into a dingy cell with gray walls. There are four straw pallets, without bedding, and a window frame with bars, but nothing to protect them from the wind, the rain, and, eventually, in winter, the cold. A family of doves flies out of the room. Anna sobs. "We'll freeze."

"It is still summer." Josef pats her arm. "Don't worry about what might happen later. We won't be here that long." She gazes at her husband.

"How can you know?" Anna trembles.

Josef tries to comfort his wife. "It's just a feeling." He wraps an arm around her shoulder. "All will be well." And then he adds softly, "You did not have to come."

Anna scoffs, pulling away.

Viola stands by the window. She gazes across the fields of wheat. Except for a few copses of trees on the hillside, there is nothing for miles—just the grain that blows in the breeze. Overhead, storm clouds gather. A light rain begins to fall. She closes her eyes. The rain on her face feels good. Her stomach growls.

Rudy comes and stands beside her. "I'm hungry," he whispers. He slips his hand into hers. They have not eaten a proper meal since they left. Anna had hastily packed cheese and sardine sandwiches, but they were soon gone.

Viola holds her brother's hand. He's small for his age. She remembers the first time she held him. It was like holding a puppy.

His fingers clasped hers. She had to uncurl them. "I'm hungry, too," she says. "I'm sure there will be something to eat soon." And she pulls her brother near.

DESPITE THE RAIN, THEIR ROOM is stifling, with only its small window and so little breeze, even on the top floor. Something smells rancid—a dead animal, perhaps. The birds, nesting in the rafters, fly in and out of the open frames. There are droppings everywhere. Still, for a moment, Anna is relieved. At least there are the four straw pallets in the room. That is something, isn't it? She wonders where the linens are. Surely they will be provided. And perhaps this is just a stop along the way, not where they are really headed. She will move two of the pallets closer to the window for the children to get fresh air, and she will push the other two together so that she and Josef can be near each other in the nights ahead.

Suddenly, a grim-faced woman appears in the doorway, followed by a man who seems confused. Two young boys hide behind their parents. The new family chatters among themselves in a language Viola does not understand. But her father does. He stands up and walks over to the man, who is perhaps a few years younger than Josef, though his hair is pure white. His wife looks away. Josef extends his hand and the man takes it hesitantly. Josef speaks quietly to the man, who nods. Then he mumbles something back.

Josef walks back to his wife. "We have to make do," he says. "Their names are Rivka and Reuven. They are Romanian." Anna motions toward two of the pallets. The new family takes the ones that are offered. Then they go back to muttering among themselves.

In the hallway there is grumbling. Some of the Jews are Germans, who managed to cross the border into Italy. Others have come from Eastern Europe, like Josef.

The soldiers begin to leave. Anna rushes after the one with the blue eyes who'd helped them off the truck. A handsome young man, Anna thinks, not so unlike her Josef when she first met him all those years ago. "But where are our blankets, our pillows?" And the soldier looks at her with that sad smile as he turns away. "And food? We have nothing."

"I am sorry," the young soldier says. "Tomorrow."

"Tomorrow?" Anna asks in disbelief. "My children have not eaten in days."

Viola stands trembling next to her mother. "Please," Viola whispers.

He glances at her again with those sad eyes. "Tomorrow," he says, and he walks away.

35

THEY COULD HAVE STAYED, OF COURSE. They could have ignored the ruling, as many did, but Josef felt it best not to. "We will be safer in the south," he told Anna, meaning farther away from Germany and the fighting in the north. "Perhaps they will forget about us." He's heard stories of others—antifascists who had been sent to obscure outposts in Sicily and Basilicata to wait out the war. There were worse fates. And besides, who knew what would happen to them if they remained in the north? He had done his best to reason with her. "We will be safer," Josef said.

"Or," Anna argued, "we'll be sent farther away."

Josef had shaken his head. "I don't think so." His argument was not baseless. Mussolini had never hated the Jews. His mistress was a Jewess—though he had abandoned her when he allied himself with Hitler. At least, Josef reasons, they are together—except for Michele, their elder son. He dropped out of university shortly after the arrest of the Jews in Turin in the antifascist plot. Since then, Josef watched his elder son grow more and more remote. At first, they fought about it. Josef warned Michele to stay away from politics. "Italian Fascists," Josef told his son, "are idiots. They won't amount to anything."

But Michele wasn't so sure. "You'll see. They are taking over." Josef shook his head. How could his son be so naïve?

Long ago, he stopped asking Michele where he was going or whom he was seeing. They had an understanding. Or, rather, they had drifted into a silence that neither cared to break. Josef left a hall light on when he went to bed, and in the evening, whenever Michele returned, he turned it off. This was how Josef knew his son had come home.

In fact, Josef had had trouble taking the fascists seriously until they arrested him and threw him into prison. For weeks he languished at the Nuove Prison—several of them spent in solitary confinement. He never understood why he was there. Or why they released him. They never tortured him, or even asked him anything. He had never been political. He assumed it had to do with his Michele. When he was told he was being sent into internal exile, he did not hesitate. He reasoned that it had to be better than where he'd been. He packed his bag.

But Anna had struggled with the decision. She did not want Josef to go alone, nor could she bring herself to leave the children. Then there were her elderly parents and, of course, Michele. Her oldest—her love child—had long ago broken her heart. He'd vanished into a world neither of his parents understood, one he refused to share with them. They rarely met his friends. He almost never brought them home. Nor did he discuss the meetings he slipped off to in the evenings. Still, Anna could not bear to leave him.

Josef had assured her. It is good if he stays behind. Perhaps he will take care of things. Their house, their cat. Perhaps he will be waiting for them when they return. But return when? And from where? Already in her head, Anna is writing letters and postcards to her son. Letters that will never be answered.

36

THAT AFTERNOON, THE WOMEN SEARCH the Red House for provisions. Rivka, the Romanian woman who shares their room, mutters to herself as she opens and slams cabinets shut. There is a stove and some pots in the mess hall, and that is all. There are no potatoes, no bread. No milk. There is nothing to cook or feed their children—some of whom can't stop crying from hunger. "We must look for food," Anna says, taking her children by the hand. Other women follow. They head out into the fields as the soldiers guard them from the towers above. They forage for dandelion greens, mushrooms (Rivka, it seems, knows about mushrooms), and whatever grains of wheat they can find. They cook it in a cauldron with water from the bathroom sink.

"Eat," Anna tells her children. "They will bring us something in the morning."

A tear trickles down Viola's cheek. Her father wraps his arm around her. "Please, Pigeon, you must eat." He calls her by her pet name when he wants to comfort her. He nicknamed her Pigeon as a toddler because she fluttered around. From the time she could walk, she ran. She could barely sit still. One Saturday, when she was just a toddler, they walked along Via Roma, where pigeons flocked in the square. She darted away and ran after them, then tossed her head back and laughed as they scattered. "Pigeon," he called her as she ran back.

The word just popped out. He hadn't said it in years. But suddenly, he recalled his father's dovecot—an old shed out back, and a flood of memories came with it. His father was an expert in homing pigeons. He'd restored the dovecot himself. He built shelves for nesting and holes so that the birds could come and go, though they never went far. His mother never liked them. They were dirty and messy. They weren't pets. They were never eaten. They served no purpose. They banged at the kitchen window when they were hungry. But his father loved them. They soared in circles with a wave of his hand, as if he were conducting an orchestra.

After school, Josef mucked out their cages and fed them seeds. Their coos soothed him. The iridescent blue-green of their wings tucked inside all of that gray sparkled. And they mated for life. Once, a pigeon in their dovecot was killed by a stray cat. It lay in the yard while its mate walked around it, nudging it, perching in a branch above until night fell. Then Josef's father gently removed the dead bird. In the morning, the mate returned to its nest.

Josef gives his daughter a hug and then tickles her under her chin. She bats his hand away. But she can't refuse him. She eats the tasteless gruel.

37

AFTER THEIR MEAGER MEAL, THEY RETURN to their cells. Though there are no doors on the cells, they are told to remain for the night. "You may not leave before dawn," the residents are told. The doors are locked. The only toilet is a bucket in a corner, already putrid. Without a word, the Romanian family lies down. The two little boys take one pallet. The parents lie on the other. They seem to fall asleep immediately. Reuven starts to snore. At first it is a low rumble, but it soon cannonades. Rivka shoves him and he rolls over. For a time, it's quiet again.

But Josef and Anna sit up. They listen to the soldiers' footsteps as they patrol the halls. The soldiers chatter, joking about a girl. They talk about sharing a beer. Anna sits on her pallet and weeps silent tears. Josef kneels before her. He strokes his wife's hand.

"I didn't think it would be like this." She looks at him with her dark, sad eyes, shaking her head.

"I promise," he says, kissing her forehead. "I will get us home."

She motions toward the Romanian family. "They're unfriendly," she says.

"They're just as frightened as we are," he replies.

After some discussion, Josef and Anna decide that she will sleep with Viola and Josef with Rudy. "The children are too old to share a bed," Anna says. Then, not knowing what else to do, they lie down on their pallets. Viola is desperate to bathe. To wash the blood clotting between her legs, but instead she must rest in her mother's arms and wait until morning.

They try to find a place where the straw does not scratch their skin. Despite the heat of the day, the night grows chilly. They have no covers. Only the clothes on their backs. Perhaps the soldiers do not think they need blankets yet. Josef stares at the open windows. After the weeks he languished in prison, he is grateful for the night breezes and the stars. In the morning, he will explain to whoever is in charge that the wind is already harsh.

In the corridor the soldiers walk on, their footsteps receding. Except for the wind and the distant barking of a dog, there is only silence.

38

THOUGH JOSEF HAS LIVED IN Italy longer than he lived in Romania, he never changed his name to Giuseppi. He has always been Josef. And his last name, Malkin, he could have changed that, as well. It might have been easier for him, and for his family. A simple change. No one would have known. No one would ever have suspected that he wasn't Italian, if not for his name. But it was something he'd held on to. A piece of the past. Anna had never asked him to make the change, and it had never mattered until now.

Almost everything else has faded. The village where he was raised, its mud-soaked streets, the sojourns into Bucharest to see the lung specialist when he had asthma. Even his parents' faces. They have all slipped into memory. He just held on to his name. His parents were small, dark people. His father ran a leather goods shop, and his mother kept everything clean. She sewed such tiny stitches; he could never see when she repaired an old shirt, a hole in his trousers. He had brothers and sisters. They all came to the train station to say good-bye when he left for school in Turin. He was a hero. They waved until he was out of sight.

He never saw them again. He never thought that war would divide them, but it did. By the time he could return, he heard there was nothing left. He supposed he could have gone to see for himself. The guilt has eaten at him for years. Anyway, they are long gone and all he holds is this image—hands waving, small bodies receding as a train pulls away.

He recalls snippets of his early years. A dog named Alfredo, who followed him everywhere. The breads and pies his mother set on the windowsill to cool. And, of course, the pigeons. His father spoke more lovingly to the birds than he ever spoke to him.

Once, not long before Josef left his village for good, he and his father carried a pigeon into the mountains. His father blindfolded the bird and put it in a box. They set out early in a cart, through forests and hilly terrain. When they reached their destination, his father opened the box. He stroked the bird and removed its blindfold. The pigeon turned around in circles like a weather vane. Then it flew home.

39

AT DAWN THEY FILE INTO the mess hall, lined with wooden tables and benches, where tin bowls and spoons are stacked on a table. They are bleary-eyed and dirty. And they are all hungry. Those who slept have slept poorly. Most are still in their filthy traveling clothes. They have not been able to bathe. Each prisoner—for they are really prisoners now, aren't they?—takes a bowl, into which thin gruel is ladled. The children put a spoon to their mouths. It takes like paste. Rudy spits it out and Viola puts her spoon down in quiet refusal. Anna shakes her head, tears rising, while Josef trembles with rage. He stands up and walks over to the soldiers. "We need something more to eat. The children need milk."

"You will have more to eat when you have completed your work," one of them says.

"Work?" Josef asks. "What work? My children have not eaten."

But the soldier turns away. The officer in the room explains in a loud voice. They will have to work to pay for their food and lodging. Chores will be assigned based on previous experience. Those with no experience will be assigned to cleaning the quarters, latrines, and working in the fields. Once they have earned some money, they will have better food.

Josef can hardly look at Anna as he returns to the table. "We must eat what we have." He shakes his head, resigned.

"Eat this?" she hisses. "How? This is not food."

"Be quiet," he tells her. "Do as I say."

But Anna folds her arms across her chest.

Nothing could have prepared her for this. Until her marriage, Anna came from a world of privilege. She had always lived with her parents, Bernardo and Sara Levi, and they took care of her and her brother impeccably. So much so that both children never moved out of the building they were raised in. They were kind and loving people, well-to-do, as Anna's father had been quite successful in helping develop the typewriter for Olivetti before branching off into a factory of his own. He was a good businessman, known for his kindness to his workers. He gave them ample vacations and allowed them to stay home for two weeks when there was a new baby. They were devoted to him.

Anna has never been away from her parents before. They live in a spacious apartment off a quiet residential street, away from the wide boulevards and bustling traffic, not far from the center of Turin. When Anna and Josef decided to marry, they purchased the apartment two floors below. It wasn't as large as her parents' apartment, but Anna knew that she and her children could always go upstairs, which they did several times a day, and for lunch. Anna can almost taste Natalia's eggplant Parmesan or her mother's kosher chicken sausage.

Gently, Josef touches her arm, pointing to the gruel in the bowl before her. "Please," he says to his wife. "You must eat."

40

CAPTAIN EMILIO CASSINI IS A SMALL, stout man with a thick gray mustache and a hearty laugh that seems to come out of nowhere. He strides into the mess hall on the second day, sporting his cape and uniform. "Welcome to the Red House," he bellows in a heavy Apulian accent. He chuckles nervously. More Jews have arrived by buses in the night, and now about two hundred stand, pale and trembling, before him. Men and women, small children, grandparents. No one knows what awaits them.

Captain Cassini goes on. "While you are our guests, you will be expected to work." There is muttering among the residents, many of whom do not speak Italian. The whisperings of translation can be heard like a strange echo. The captain continues: "Not the small children or the elderly, but the rest of you. Soon, my lieutenant will ask each of you your profession, and assign you tasks. Some of you will be assigned work in town. Others here. Food will be provided, but you must work for it. You will receive a small stipend."

One of the residents raises his hand. "How much of a stipend?" the man with a thick accent asks. Beside him, his wife tugs at his sleeve.

"Thirteen lire per day per person," the captain replies.

The residents grumble. It is not much.

"But, sir," one of the residents shouts out, "what about food now? And bedding?"

The captain ignores their pleas. "You must be patient" is all he says.

For how long? He doesn't explain. For now, they will have to make do. Most have brought very little with them. Many fled to Italy seeking asylum, and left everything behind. "You may walk out into the fields," the captain goes on, "when you have completed your work, but you may not go beyond the outer fence or down to the road. For now, please share your professions."

Anna clasps her children to her as Rudy whimpers. His forehead is sweaty. Viola runs her hand over his brow. The blue-eyed soldier is there, watching her. He cannot be much older than she, maybe fifteen or sixteen. Perhaps too young to be a soldier. But he already looks like a man. Viola is afraid of him, a soldier, in uniform and with a gun, but she feels something beyond fear, too. She feels his eyes on her. He looks at her in a way that makes her want to hide.

She wears the same thin summer dress she's worn since leaving Turin days ago. She is hot and sweaty and dying to bathe. They have only been able to rinse off in the filthy sinks. They may take showers once a week, on Friday, and it is only Tuesday. In the sink, she rinsed the bloody cloth from between her legs but then had to stuff it back in place again. Everything is dirty. Viola thinks she must smell. Still the boy's eyes are on her.

One of the soldiers begins roll call, reading off the long, tedious list of "guests," as they are designated, not prisoners or hostages, but guests. As each name is called, the person is asked to approach a table and state his or her profession. Another soldier, sitting at the table, writes down what they say. Those who are doctors, lawyers, or engineers are told to stand to the right, while their wives and children tremble. A tailor and a cobbler are also told to step to the right. Some of the women are nurses. They will also be sent into town to work. The others will remain in the fields, or care for the children.

Anna, Josef, and the children shuffle ahead in the line. When they reach the front, Anna speaks up first. "I am a clothing designer," she says proudly. "I could work in a tailor shop." The soldiers grumble, shaking their heads. One draws a line through her name. She is told to step to the left.

"You will be more useful here," the captain says. He turns his beady eyes to Josef.

"I am a dentist," Josef says, and the captain nods, then points an imperious finger to the right.

"We are in need of a dentist," the captain says. Josef steps to the right.

One woman says that she is a teacher. She is told to set up a school in one of the windowless ground-floor rooms. "But what will we use for books and paper?" she asks.

Captain Cassini replies, "It will be provided," and then he laughs.

Reuven and Rivka are next. Reuven explains in very rudimentary Italian that he was a lawyer in his country but has been a street vendor since coming to Italy. Captain Cassini makes a face. "We will find you something to do."

"My wife is a cook," Reuven says, "but she speaks very little Italian."

Captain Cassini considers this. "She will be useful in the kitchen."

A few more residents state their professions. Then a balding man with a grim expression approaches the table. "My name is Angelo," he says in halting Italian. "I am an artist."

"An artist," the soldier at the table says, looking perplexed. "What kind of artist?"

"A painter," Angelo says.

Another soldier laughs. "So you paint walls?"

"I paint saints and angels on walls," Angelo replies.

"Ah, Angelo paints angels." The soldiers laugh again as Angelo stares straight ahead. The soldiers aren't sure if he understands their banter. Captain Cassini cocks his head. "We will find something for this artist to do, as well," he says with a flick of his wrist. And the balding man steps to the left.

When everyone is assigned a task, Captain Cassini takes Josef aside. "You will come with me," he tells him. He points to his satchel. "Bring your instruments."

Josef trembles. "But I am not allowed . . ."

"You are allowed if I say you are. We need a new dentist. Many people have bad teeth. Lately, the barber has been pulling them."

It has been four years since Josef has been allowed to practice his profession on non-Jews. Four years since he locked his office because he had so few patients. Since the racial laws were passed in 1938, not even street vendors have been allowed to peddle their wares. Jewish generals have been expelled from the army. Teachers have gone to schools, only to find their classrooms locked. A respected Jewish publisher in Modena jumped off a roof.

Josef stares at the Fascist Party pin on the captain's lapel. Then he mutters, "Sir, the children need milk. And we have no food." Even when he was in le Nuove prison he received food. Anna was allowed to deliver it to the prison, along with clean laundry, twice a week. The only restriction was for fruit. No pits.

"All of Italy is starving," the captain replies. "We must tighten our belts. Come with me. There will be food when you have done your work." And he walks away.

41

IT IS A WARM FALL DAY as they drive down the bumpy road. Josef clasps his dental tools in his lap as the car careens in and out of potholes. Josef stares outside. He has never been to the south. He is stunned by the vineyards, the rolling hills, the olive groves. Orchards of orange and cherry trees. Fig trees and caper shrubs grow wild. Fruit hangs ripe, just out of reach.

The captain drives too quickly, racing around the bends as trucks barrel down on them. At each turn, Josef braces himself against the door. He tries not to stare at the captain's Fascist Party pin, but he can't help himself. It was the fascists who arrested him and threw him into a dark, barren cell at Le Nuove. Probably they wanted Michele. After three weeks they released him. He never knew why. "We are all fascists and Catholics," Captain Cassini says, perhaps sensing Josef's gaze. "It goes hand in hand. You are not a fascist, I assume?"

Josef shakes his head. "No," he mutters, "I am not." And then he adds, "I am not anything." The captain nods, not seeming to care. The countryside rushes by, too fast now for Josef to enjoy. The fields of waving grain. It is as if the captain is late for an appointment, but it is barely seven in the morning. As they speed along, Josef glimpses mothers sending children off to school, fathers heading to work. Women tote bags to the market to shop for the midday meal. How strange that life goes on while his children are hungry and his wife weeps.

As they bounce along the pitted roads, Captain Cassini chatters about songbirds. "They are messy, you know." He keeps several in his home, but his wife complains. "She is right about that," the captain concedes.

Josef nods. "Yes, birds can be messy."

"They require so much cleaning and tending. They're always tossing their seeds onto her freshly cleaned floors. It's becoming a pain to keep them," Captain Cassini says. "Not a pain to me," he adds, chuckling, "but to my wife."

He drives with one hand, gesticulating with the other as he weaves around the potholes. Morning dew glistens on the ground. "I don't know about songbirds," Josef says. "My father kept pigeons. But my mother complained about them, as well."

"Pigeons? Why?"

Josef wonders if this is a trick question. He isn't sure what the right answer should be. "I don't know. He loved them." As Josef says this, he thinks, Perhaps more than he loved me. He pauses, and then says. "They can find their way home."

"But they don't sing."

The captain says little more. He focuses on the road. Soon they are driving along the narrow, winding streets of Castellobello with those odd, conical-shaped houses. Josef has never seen houses like this before. He imagines that trolls must live here, or creatures from fairy tales. He expects to see tiny men and women, but normal people come and go. A widow sits in front of her door, snapping peas. Two small children play with a stick and a ball. Men in snug vests and caps stand on a corner, smoking cigarettes, holding steamy cups of coffee in front of a café.

The captain pulls over. "Here we are," he says.

Josef looks up and sees a plaque down the street in the shape of a tooth. The sign reads EMILIANO CASSINI—DENTAL SURGEON.

"You are a dentist?"

The captain nods. "Yes, of course. Everyone must be something. I was only recently conscripted," he says, and motions for Josef to leave the car.

42

THE DENTAL OFFICE IS DOWN a narrow side street. As they walk along, Josef peers into the dark conical houses. Inside, they are more like caves. From the Stone Age, Josef thinks. They clearly have no running water or electricity. How can people live like this? And then there is the stench. Gazing into one of these hovels, Josef sees a woman with a stricken face. She holds up her child, who is quivering with fever.

Josef shakes his head sadly. The child appears to be dying from malaria. There is nothing he can do. In another doorway, a boy sits, his eyes crusted with pus. Flies buzz around him, but he doesn't bother swatting them away. These are diseases he has not seen in the north.

They continue until they come to the entrance of a house, and what seems to be a waiting room. Josef is struck by the antiseptic smell of the dental office, still familiar after years away. Already three patients—all of them old women—are waiting. The captain sighs. "It's as if they live here," he says. The captain leads Josef into a room with a dental chair. "This will be your chair. When patients come, treat them here." Cassini sighs at the tedium of his life. "At the end of the day I will drive you home."

Home. Josef shivers. Back to Turin? But, of course, Captain Cassini doesn't mean that. Josef understands that the Red House is now his home.

"I must wash," Josef says, and the captain, now Dottore Cassini, for here he is to be called Dottore Cassini, laughs that odd laugh that seems to come out of nowhere, and points to a sink in an alcove. Dottore Cassini points to a white coat on a hanger. Josef understands that he is to wear this coat and be a dentist here. He goes to the sink, removes his wool jacket, puts on the white coat, and washes his hands.

It has been so long since he has been able to practice real dentistry that his hands shake. What if he can't remember what to do? What if he injures a patient? Perhaps, for the moment, he should tell the captain that he would be better suited to cleaning teeth. He is not sure if he is capable of more. He washes his hands over and over, as if he can rid them not only of the filth but of something else—something darker, dirtier. Something he fears may never go away.

He sterilizes his instruments in boiling water, lays them out on a tray covered with a white cloth, and waits for his first patient.

A woman arrives without an appointment, tugging a small boy. She is a tall, stately woman, dressed in a navy skirt and blouse. She wears a scarf draped around her neck, and Josef senses immediately that she does not wish to speak with him. She is waving her hands as she explains that he has a baby tooth that won't come out and now another tooth is growing in right behind it. "I must see the doctor," she says. Already the boy is trying to drag his mother away. Josef bends down, trying to coax the boy, who is hiding behind his mother.

"Dottore Cassini is busy," Josef says, "but I can help you." He is on his knees, playing a game of peek-a-boo. The little boy smiles.

"I don't mind waiting." The woman glares at Josef, wrapping the scarf more tightly around her throat. Then she slumps into a wooden chair, the boy squirming in her arms. She does not look Josef's way again.

A gentleman, sporting a fedora and wearing a tight vest, arrives, but he, too, only wants to be seen by Dottore Cassini. The man has crooked yellow teeth. "I wish to see the doctor," he sputters. Josef tries again to explain that the doctor is busy, but he can tend to him if he wishes. But the man just shakes his head. He leaves rather than having to wait.

In the afternoon, an elderly woman staggers in, clutching the swollen side of her face. She is dressed all in black, the way widows dress in the south. Around her thick silvery hair, she wears a somber scarf. "Oh my God," she says. "I need to see Dottore Cassini."

Josef is in the reception area. "Do you have an appointment?"

The woman groans. "It's an emergency," she pleads, pointing to her swollen jaw.

He must repeat what he has told the others. "I'm sorry," Josef says, "but there are other people waiting. I could take care of you. . . ."

Perhaps sensing the commotion, Dottore Cassini pops out of his office. "Ah, dear Sofia Bassano, I'm so sorry. What seems to be the problem?" She points to her swollen jaw. "My colleague, Dottore Malkin, will tend to you." She looks up. With her watery blue eyes, she takes in Josef's beard, his dark eyes.

"If you prefer to wait . . ." Josef offers. He knows this will not be a simple cleaning. The woman is in pain.

"I can't wait," she says, clasping her jaw. Groaning and muttering to herself, the woman follows Josef. She is a stout woman, and Josef must help her into the chair. "You are from where?" the woman asks as she settles down. He organizes his instruments.

"I am from up north," he explains, "but I am living for now outside of town."

Sofia nods, pursing her lips. He knows what she is thinking. She has heard about the arrival of the Jews. It is not a secret that they are being detained at the Red House. She obviously wants to leave, and if she were not in so much pain, she would. She keeps staring at Josef. She has likely never seen a Jew before. She thought they'd be different. Horns and a tail. Drinking the blood of children. Perhaps she thought they would emit a sulfurous smell. She did not expect him to be a person, such as herself.

"If you would prefer to see Dottore Cassini . . ." Josef is gentle, kind to her.

She groans again, putting her hand to her cheek. "Oh, no, it is all right."

"Please open wide," he says. She sits back and opens her mouth.

Josef closes his eyes and smells. Her mouth has a putrid odor, like death. But from the looks of her robust cheeks and the color of her skin, she is far from dying. He picks up his probe and mirror. He looks inside. "This might hurt a little." He moves the probe to the back of the tooth, but she doesn't flinch. He sees an abscess on the gum and two badly decaying teeth. "You must take better care of your mouth," he scolds her gently. He feels his fear draining out of him. He knows what to do. All of his knowledge returns.

She moans and waves her hand. "I know. I know."

"I might have to pull this tooth," he tells her, "but I will try to save it. I will try not to hurt you." Josef gives her several injections of Novocain and waits while it takes effect. Now he tests Signora

Bassano's gums and gives her two more shallow injections. Then he drains the abscess and cleans out the tooth. She stares into his dark eyes with her shiny blue ones. Blue is the color of truth, Josef recalls his mother telling him once. "I'm hoping we won't have to pull it now, but we must wait for the infection to heal." He smiles at the old woman, but as he does, he suddenly feels faint, clammy. He has not eaten anything but gruel for two days.

"Are you all right, Dottore?" she asks, still staring into his eyes.

His stomach grumbles and he is ashamed. "I am so sorry," he says. "I skipped breakfast."

"You must eat," she scolds him, as he scolded her about her teeth.

"Yes." He smiles sadly. "I must."

When he is finished, he tells her to rinse her mouth for two days with boiled salt water and an analgesic he gives her for the pain. "Come back at the end of the week. Hopefully I won't have to pull that tooth. There are also two cavities, but they can wait. If the pain returns, come right away."

When she reaches into her purse, he waves her away. "You may pay Dottore Cassini," he says.

43

ANNA SITS ON HER PALLET, staring at her hands. They are almost unrecognizable to her. Brittle nails that are usually trimmed and polished. Veins she's never noticed before. She never had time to notice, really. Until four years ago, her hands were always busy, pinning, sewing, cutting patterns. If she was not working in her couture shop, she was at home, straightening pictures, tidying up. Then, after the racial laws, she homeschooled her children when it became too much for them to take the long bus ride to the Jewish school, which they didn't like anyway. She learned how to cook and clean—tasks that had never been hers to perform before.

Now she has nothing to do. With Josef gone and the children attending their "lessons," Anna is at a loss. She wishes she'd said she was a teacher, because it would not have been a lie. If she'd said teacher, at least she would have some occupation. She likes to be busy. She likes to use her hands. She has a nervous nature that only sewing seems to soothe.

She decides to straighten up their cell and settle in as best she can. It is small and stuffy, not much bigger than their pantry at home, but if she can just put away the few things they have been able to bring with them, it will feel more tidy. She starts with Rudy's satchel. He has only brought a pair of trousers and two shirts, short pants, and a light jacket. She folds and smooths them out. There are small cubbies in the corner. She dusts these out with her hand-kerchief, leaving half of the cubbies for the Romanian family. Then she stuffs Rudy's clothes in.

She takes Viola's things and spreads them on the pallet. An extra dress, a summer sweater, stockings, a pair of dress shoes. Nothing practical. Why didn't she bring a warm jacket like Anna told her? A wool dress. Did she think it would be summer forever?

She gazes around the cell, wishing she had something to brighten it up. A colorful spread or shawl. Flowers. She makes a mental note to gather some wildflowers from the fields. But then what would she put them in? She shakes her head. Anna is resourceful. She will find something—even a tin can.

As she is sorting their clothes, Rivka comes in. "Good after-noon," Anna says with a smile, but Rivka doesn't look at her. She scowls. She has an unfriendly face. There is water dripping from her hands onto the floor. Rivka has come in with a handful of soak-ing wet underclothes. She mutters as she drapes them across the narrow windowsill. Anna feels herself grow tense. It is bad enough having to share this small space; now this woman is hanging up her wet intimates.

Anna likes a house neat and tidy. Since Natalia stopped working for them, she has become a bit of a housekeeper. She spotted a clothing line downstairs when they arrived. She's not sure if Rivka understands Italian, but she tries to explain to her that there is a clothesline down below. Rivka just shakes her head.

"People steal," the woman mutters. So at least Anna knows she understands.

Anna tries to hide her annoyance and wonders if the woman means to steal from them—not that they have anything worth taking. She banishes such thoughts and goes downstairs, out into the fields. She is searching for flowers. As she walks across the barren fields, she laughs at herself. How foolish, she thinks. There will be no wildflowers until the spring.

44

AS SOFIA MAKES HER WAY HOME, her jaw begins to throb as the numbness wears off. Though her mouth is not nearly as painful as it was before, it is still sore. Her thick legs are heavy on the cobbled streets, but she almost feels a bounce to her step. She is old, but not that old. She's barely fifty, yet she moves like an old woman on swollen legs, which she elevates at night in order to sleep. She was not always portly. Once her husband swung her on the dance floor. He lifted and twirled her around. She smiles as she thinks of them dancing. "Carlo," she mutters. "It's been so long."

Giovanni Gaglioni, the butcher who has taken over from his

father, greets her. He's brandishing a bloody knife. "Signora Bassano, I'll just be a moment. Please, sit. Sit."

He tells her to sit as if she's an old woman, but she prefers to stand. She just waves him away. She is afraid to talk, fearful that her numb mouth will drool. And he knows she never likes to sit—though it could be a wait. Signora Massina is ahead of her, and her order always takes a long time. She talks a lot.

Giovanni grins, and his white teeth shine. He's too familiar, she thinks. She preferred his father, who was more respectful. And the son tends to give her more than she asks for. Just a few extra grams, rounding off her order and then overcharging her for what she didn't want in the first place. Then there are leftovers to deal with, which make her sad. Still, there is no other butcher on her route home, and she doesn't have the strength to argue. She'll give the leftovers to her grandson.

"Just some mortadella." She's hoping that Signora Massina will offer to let her go ahead, but she doesn't. Giovanni is tying up a pork roast for Signora Massina. "Ah, you must be making your eggplant parmigiano." He tightens the string on the roast. Sofia smiles grimly. It is difficult for her to talk. She's afraid she'll bite her tongue. She just gives him a nod. Who would she make the eggplant parmigiano for now? It's hardly a dish you make for two people, let alone one. The question swirls in her head as she listens to his endless prattle and knife waving and mindless greetings. He is a harmless man, though full of himself.

"I'll be with you soon," Giovanni repeats with his broad smile.

Signora Massina looks at her pork roast. "Giovanni, is that enough? You know how they are. I think I'll need a chicken, too." She shakes her head and then says to whoever is listening, "Ah, they come for dinner. All they do is eat." She shakes her head, laughing. "I never know who will turn up. And they don't lift a finger."

She says this as if she is supposed to be pitied because she has a big, rowdy family, but Sofia knows that it is just the opposite.

Signora Massina complains about her life to make others, who are less fortunate, feel even worse. Sofia tries to drown out her chatter about her children, who arrive empty-handed and won't rinse a dish. Yet Signora Massina likes nothing better than to tell anyone who will listen about her grandchildren, who come to dinner every night. "Oh," she complains, "I never stop cooking for them."

In fact, if Sofia felt like being compassionate, she'd admit that Signora Massina has a rather sad story—though not an atypical one. She was married to one of the men who disappeared. He left for America, taking their oldest son, a decade before. For two years, he wrote to her, and then his letters stopped. She was left to raise four children alone.

Many men have left Castellobello. They went to fight in the Great War. They went to fight in Abyssinia. They left for America. And now they are fighting this new war. One by one, their wives declared themselves widows. They dressed in black and hung death pennants above their doors. They knew what lay ahead. Many men never returned. Perhaps they died. Perhaps they met other women and started new families. Occasionally there are sightings. A husband spotted in the Garment District of New York, a child who has grown into a man at the stockyards in Chicago. Rumor and innuendo. Sometimes they come back, maimed, shadows of their former selves.

The widows of Castellobello live with this weird uncertainty. One such widow was carting a jug of water from the well a few years ago, big with another man's child, when her missing husband, whom she'd married in her youth and had not seen for twenty years, suddenly appeared beside her. He slid back into her life as if he'd never been gone, no questions asked. He raised the child in her womb as his own. Stranger things happened. In Signora Massina's case, the husband did return with the child, who had grown into a tall, sturdy man. He did not seem to mind the two extra children who had been conceived in his absence. But Sofia's Carlo never left. Carlo stayed with her until the day he keeled over while changing the oil in a farmer's truck.

Sofia sighs. Signora Massina wants something more, but she isn't sure. Perhaps a piece of liver. Sofia could leave and come back later. Instead, she sinks down into the wooden chair that has been in the corner of this shop since she began coming here. It's just as uncomfortable as it always was, but she's in no rush to return to her two empty rooms. She listens to the gossip. A priest seen staggering home drunk from a visit to his mistress. The daughter of the deputy mayor who ran off with an older man, then mysteriously returned. "You should have heard the shouting," one of the customers says.

"That woman has never been able to control her children," Signora Massina replies as she scrutinizes Giovanni's wrapping of her pork roast and chicken. Sofia chuckles. It is a well-known fact that one of Signora Massina's sons had to marry his pregnant girlfriend. One of her daughters had her marriage annulled. Still, there is no story that Sofia won't pause to listen to. She is a kind-hearted lady, and means no harm, but she's been widowed for so long and has no one to talk to. The townspeople know she is lonely.

Signora Massina isn't sure about her order. "Is it enough, Giovanni?" Sofia sinks deeper into the chair. She rubs her jaw as the medication wears off. A strange despair settles over her, as it does most evenings at this time. The empty house, the long night alone. Her other children have moved away, though they visit from time to time. Were it not for her grandson's visits, what would she have to look forward to? He comes to see her almost every evening after work. She always feeds him.

Poor fatherless child. He was just a toddler when Luigi, her youngest, was killed in a farm accident. His death almost killed Sofia. And Beatrice, Tommaso's mother, couldn't handle all the children at home, so she sent Tommaso to live with Sofia. For weeks, he cried into his pillow. Sofia would sit at the edge of his bed, trying to comfort him. She did not know what he cried for more—his dead father or his lost mother. He cried until it seemed as if he had no more tears, and then he settled in. Sofia and Carlo raised him as they had raised Luigi, and all their other children.

After school, Tommaso worked in his grandfather's auto shop. One day, Carlo collapsed to the ground. Tommaso kept shaking him to get him to wake up. He'd been a strong, youthful man who'd made love to his wife the night before, and now he was gone. Carlo was hardly in the ground when Beatrice decided that it was time for Tommaso to come home. "He will be too much for you alone," Beatrice said.

"But he's no trouble. He's a help," Sofia pleaded, to no avail. Beatrice would hear nothing of it. So Sofia explained to Tommaso, "You do not live far. I will see you often." Once more, the boy sobbed as he was dragged away.

Sofia waves her hand in the air as if swatting a fly. Who needs to think about such things? For now, he comes to her at the end of the day. That is something, isn't it? It's for him she shops and cooks. "Signora Bassano." She hears her name called. Giovanni is slicing her mortadella. Perhaps, if Tommaso will slice the eggplant, she will make that eggplant Parmesan after all. Giovanni wraps it carefully. "Nothing more? Signora? A nice cut of beef?"

She shakes her head. "Tomorrow," she says as she pays for her cold cuts. It costs more than it should, but she doesn't have the strength to argue. She stops at the baker for bread, then at the wine shop for a local red that comes out of a spigot. They like to sip it with their evening meal (and she's been known to have a nip or two after Tommaso heads home). A quick stop at the cheese monger, and her errands are done. Balancing her parcels, she continues down the narrow street to her house.

45

HER PATIO IS CARPETED IN tomatoes and figs. They ooze in the sun, and the air is redolent with their smell. Soon Sofia will preserve them in olive oil and herbs. Flies swarm around the desiccated fruit, sucking whatever juice they can. There's no point swatting them away. They just return. The flies are everywhere in Castellobello, as are the mosquitoes at this time of year. It is malaria season, and Sofia is careful not to be outside for long.

As she walks up her path, laden with parcels, her jaw throbbing, she shoos her two chickens and itinerant rooster out of the way. Her courtyard is lined with geraniums, and, as she passes, she deadheads a few. She pushes aside the black pennant that has been draped across her lintel since Carlo's death. Many of the houses in Castellobello have these black pennants. Even if the men in question come back to take over a failing business, care for an aging parent, the black pennants of death remain hanging over their lintels.

But Sofia and Carlo had a happy, loving life until Luigi was killed. They were happy and then they were not. It was that simple. Only Tommaso's living with them seemed to assuage their grief. Sofia often thought that Carlo died of a broken heart. She tries to banish such thoughts. Still, each time she enters and leaves her two rooms, she must push the black pennant out of the way. Now she lifts it up and gives the heavy wooden door a hard shove with her hip.

She enters the dark rooms she inhabits. Blinking, she adjusts to the light. Sofia puts her parcels down on the kitchen table and pauses to rub her jaw. Sofia lives in one of the *trulli* that she and Carlo lovingly restored. It was little more than rubble when they claimed it, and the town, which had once been almost abandoned, was in ruins. No one wanted to live in these strange conical-shaped

houses, so peasants came in to claim them. No one even wanted
to live in Castellobello then, and property was dirt cheap. They
bought wisely. Carlo and Sofia were frugal, and eventually scraped
together enough money to buy the auto-repair shop, as well.

Over the years they rebuilt the walls, opened the rooms, and
raised their three children here. But now, Luigi is gone and only
her daughter Isabella lives nearby. Their plan was to sell this house
one day and move to the seaside. Then Tommaso came to stay with
them and, after Carlo died, Sofia did not have the heart to leave.
At least in Castellobello, she has Tommaso. In the dim light on
the mantel, her wedding picture shimmers in its silver frame. The
statue of the Virgin looms over the room.

She places a kiss on her late husband's forehead. It is lucky that
the picture is covered in glass, or it would have been worn away long
ago. Then she straightens the Virgin and halfheartedly makes the
sign of the cross. The house smells like a barnyard. Her two chickens and rooster, despite her best efforts, more or less live inside. She
has been known to let the chickens sleep on her bed.

As she sorts out her parcels, Sofia winces. Her jaw is throbbing
in earnest now. But it is still nothing compared to the pain she
had endured before going to see the dentist. Jews, she thinks. She
knows nothing about Jews. She thought they would look different.
She thought they would be different. Rubbing her cheek, she goes
back outside to check on her plants. Bending down, she touches the
soil, making sure that none of them are thirsty. She talks to them,
coaxing them along. She plucks a handful of the basil that grows in
abundance near the door. To the side of the house, there is a veg-
etable patch where she grows yellow squash and zucchini. Though
it is late in the season, the tomatoes are still plentiful. Squeezing
them gently, she chooses the ones that are almost overripe and
good for sauce.

"Ah, Carlo," she says, "I think these are just right." Pursing her
lips, she kisses the air. Sofia often finds herself talking to her dead

husband. She tells him about her day. She talks about rising prices and whose children moved away. She speaks about her worries for their daughter Giulia, whose husband can't earn a living. Sofia doesn't think of Carlo as gone; he has never been gone to her. It is as if she can feel him with her when she lies down at night, or in the garden, where they worked side by side.

She never talks to him in front of her children when they visit, because they will think she has lost her mind. Sometimes, she'll be at dinner and she'll get a strange, distant look because Carlo is speaking to her, complaining about the food or what a poor house-keeper their daughter is, and then Giulia will say, "Mama, are you here? Are you even listening?" But it brings her comfort to talk to him. For years after he left—that is how she prefers to think of it—she still made dinner for the two of them. When Tommaso noticed this, he began coming around for supper. He has been coming ever since.

BACK INSIDE, SOFIA PUTS ON A POT of water. She will cook the orecchiette that she and Tommaso made on Sunday. Sofia is proud of the fact that she has taught her grandson everything he knows about cooking. She would never allow any of her children or other grandchildren into her kitchen, but even as a small child, Tommaso had a knack for it. He asked questions about how much flour the pasta needed. He gazed as she chopped onions and diced tomatoes. One day she let him taste her soup. "Add lemon," he said, and he was right. He was only six. After that, she'd let him stir as she ladled water into the sauces. She'd hold him up as he dropped in the rind from the Parmesan. One morning, she came into the kitchen and found him wielding a sharp knife that was as big as his arm. He was slicing the eggplant paper-thin. His knife skills remain the best she's ever seen.

Now she chops an onion and dices the tomatoes and tosses

them into a pan. They sizzle as she stirs with a wooden spoon. She adds a bit of water. She has plenty of jars of her tomato sauce, but while she still has tomatoes growing on the vine, Sofia prefers to use them. She will ration the jars all winter, until she can start to can the tomatoes again. When the sauce is simmering, she throws in the basil.

While the sauce simmers, Sofia goes into her bathroom. She takes out the clasp that holds up her long silver hair. The clasp is tortoiseshell, a gift from Carlo, years ago. She washes her face and brushes her teeth. She brushes her hair for a hundred strokes as she does every night. Then she leaves it long and flowing.

Tommaso should be arriving soon. She adds another cupful of water to the saucepan, and a pinch of salt. While she waits for the water to boil, she puts the meat into the small refrigerator one of her daughters purchased for her. She has two surviving children who live nearby, and many grandchildren, but Tommaso remains her favorite. Even though it has been years since he moved back in with his mother, he is always stopping by to help her with small tasks—fixing a shaky table leg, bringing her firewood. And to share a meal with her. She cannot help but think that he has never been happy anywhere else. Poor fatherless child.

As she stirs the sauce, he comes up the walk. "You're late," she says without looking up. He laughs because she always says the same thing. "Where have you been?"

"It's only five o'clock, Nonna." He hands her the sack that contains his soiled uniform. She puts it into her washing sink and hands him the fresh one, neatly washed and ironed, which he will wear the next day.

"It seems later." She sighs.

The kitchen fills with the savory aroma of tomatoes and onions simmering on the stove. The freshly cut basil. He tries to take the wooden spoon from her hand to taste the sauce, but she bats him away. "We will eat in a minute."

"Just a taste?" It's a game they've played since he was a child. He tries to take the spoon from her, and she bats him away. As she drops in the orecchiette, he grates the cheese and then adds spoonfuls to the sauce until it is thick and creamy. Now she lets him taste it as she stands back with her arms folded. He nods. "It's good. A little too salty." He scoops out a cup of pasta water, which he adds, and then increases the flame. When the pasta is al dente, he drains it and adds some chopped basil. He tastes the sauce again. "It's better now."

Sofia chuckles but doesn't say a word as they sit down to their meal. "How was the dentist?" he asks.

"I saw a new dentist. One of the Jews who lives outside of town."

Tommaso nods, rubbing his cheek. He has a tooth that's been bothering him for a few days now, but he doesn't want to go and see Dottore Cassini. He knows who the new dentist is: the father of the girl with the dark eyes.

Sofia spoons the orecchiette onto their plates, then covers it with the sauce. But before Tommaso takes a bite, she places a hand gently on his knee.

"Tell me about the Red House," she says.

46

ON THE CAR RIDE BACK to the Red House, Josef is smiling. It surprises him. He isn't listening as the captain rambles on. He isn't watching as the vineyards and olive groves zip by. He's trying to remember when he last smiled. And he cannot. He has been unhappy for so long. He is searching for the word for what he is feeling. He can see the old woman, moaning as she climbs into his chair. He sees the relief on her face as he drains the abscess and gives her medication for her pain. Her efforts to pay him, the lift in her step as she left his office. It all brings a smile to his face.

It had been four years since he had seen a patient. He did not know if he could still fill a cavity or pull a tooth. He did not know if he'd ever gaze again into the mouth of someone who was not a Jew. As he hugs his box of instruments to him, he finds himself swelling with gratitude, warmed from within. He almost wants to hug the captain to thank him. For so long now, he had wanted to work. And now he has.

"It's been such an ordeal," the captain is saying. Josef nods. But he has no idea to what the captain refers. He thinks it's about his canaries.

As they pull up to the Red House, Josef gets out. "Thank you for today," Josef says. "I enjoyed the work."

The captain nods. "I needed the extra hand." He points to Josef's instruments. "You can leave those at the office. No need to carry them back and forth."

Josef appreciates the offer but hesitates. What if they are sent somewhere else suddenly? He might be forced to leave his instruments behind. "Thank you, sir. But I like to keep them with me."

The captain shrugs. "As you wish."

47

VIOLA IS BEING WATCHED. As she works in the fields, she can feel it. She glances around to see who might be there. She looks up at the turrets where the soldiers guard. But she sees no one. Still she senses it, as animals do. Her tangled hair falls across her shoulders. She runs her fingers through to unknot it. She'd give anything for a comb and brush. In her haste, she forgot to pack them. Sweat runs down her neck. There are grain and olives to harvest. While their husbands and fathers go into town, the women bend, gathering grain for bread they will never eat. They shake the olive trees until the olives fall into nets, which are carted away.

Rudy works alongside her. He doesn't know what he is looking for, but he follows his sister's lead as she claws at the earth. Even the smallest children must forage for whatever roots and wild plants they can find. Rivka, who knows her mushrooms, shows them the ones that are safe, and the ones to avoid. She holds up a mushroom with a white cap, shakes her head, and hurls it away. She teaches them what wild ramps look like and where to find tubers.

At the end of the day, tired and aching, Viola returns to the Red House. The blue-eyed soldier stands at the entrance. He takes a step in her direction. "I just want to talk to you," he says. "My name is Tommaso."

"Ah," she says, "so it's you. You've been watching me."

"I've been looking out for you," he replies.

"I am Viola." She lowers her eyes.

"Viola," he repeats. She cannot bring herself to look at him. It would be like staring into the sun. He motions toward the conjoined oak trees. "Here," he says, "walk with me." They walk toward the shade. The wind blows through the branches. The breeze feels good. "How are you doing?"

"We are trying to settle in," she tells him.

"It must be difficult," he says, looking up toward the building.

"Yes, it is. They give us very little to eat." She hesitates. "We are very hungry."

"What do you need?" he whispers.

"Everything," she replies. "We have nothing."

He touches the dark hair that falls across her shoulders, pushing it out of her face. His hand is warm and soft. Viola doesn't flinch. He points to a grove of trees across the field. "Meet me there tomorrow," he tells her, "at the same time."

He touches her cheek again. Her face is hot and flushed.

"I have to go," she says.

"I'll see you tomorrow," he whispers.

Viola races back to the Red House so fast, she has to catch her breath.

ON THE STAIRWELL, SHE RUNS into a girl who lives a few doors down. They are about the same age. The girl has strawberry blond hair that flows down her back. She pauses as Viola is about to run past her, afraid that her mother has noticed her missing. "You like that blue-eyed soldier, don't you?" the girl says, laughing and tossing her curls.

Her name is Leila. Viola laughs with her. "What makes you say that?"

"Oh, the way you look at each other. He likes you, too."

Viola looks at her askance. "But how do you know that?"

Leila points to her head. "I can tell."

48

"THE CAPTAIN WOULD LIKE TO SEE YOU," the soldier says. But Angelo isn't paying attention. He has been given the task of repairing a wobbly table in the mess hall, and he's concentrating on that. He has the table turned upside down and he's hammering the joints. But his mind is elsewhere. He's dreaming of angels. His namesake. His calling.

Once, long ago, he saw them for the first time on the frescoes of churches. His father was a stonemason. He would sit in the pews while his father worked, gazing up at the plump bodies of the putti or their gossamer wings. At some point, he began drawing and painting them. He scribbled sketches in notebooks intended for school. Once, his father saw one of his notebooks and tried to take it away. "Jews don't draw. And we don't draw angels."

Then, his name was Malach, which means angel in Hebrew. His parents couldn't decide which of the archangels they should name him after, so they named him after all of them. When he came to Italy, he changed it to Angelo. But even as a boy he wondered why they'd named him Malach if Jews didn't draw angels. And why did his father work in churches?

His mother knew that the only thing her son loved to do was draw. And he was good at it. She made his father relent. She saved the money she scraped together from the mending she did and bought him a set of colored pencils. Once he began drawing, it was all he ever did. He never went to art school, but taught himself the techniques of oils and pastels. He sold them in the town square in Budapest.

Eventually, he began carving angels from stone, as he did for the headstones in the cemetery where his wife and stillborn son lie. When he couldn't leave grief behind, he made his living this way. Angels have always weighed on him. Now they enter his sleep. They come disguised as beggars or thieves. They are not only benevolent; they can be mischievous, as well. Sometimes it seems as if he is soaring with them above the earth on gossamer wings.

He has taken to talking to them. Never when anyone else is near, but on the long walks he takes in the afternoon in the fields, when they are allowed fresh air. His fellow exiles try to make small talk with him about the food or the guards. But he has no interest. He nods as if he is listening, but he's not. His mind is elsewhere, listening to the voices inside his head. The ones that tell him what to draw. He scribbles on any surface he can. Belligerent angels, sad devils. He knows that something is passing through him. He is the mere conduit.

He thinks it is one of his angels talking to him, not a soldier in uniform. But the soldier says more firmly this time, "Please, come with me, sir."

Angelo looks up and sees the soldier standing there.

"Why?" Angelo asks. "What have I done?"

"Just come," the soldier repeats.

Angelo is used to twists and turns of fate. He has lived through wars, the death of his parents, his wife, and his only child. Only the angels have stayed with him. Has he already done something wrong here? He follows the soldier down a flight of stairs, then another, into the subbasement of the Red House. He envisions what awaits him. Imprisonment. Deportation. Torture. Perhaps worse?

They wander down to a dark, musty corridor. Angelo follows the soldier until they come to two large barn doors. The soldier pushes them open, and Angelo walks into an empty room, lit by a bare bulb. It looks like a granary. The captain sits on a chair in the middle of the room. Around him, in the shadows, are buckets, but Angelo cannot see what is in them. Angelo's heart sinks.

The captain motions for him to step closer, and he does, slowly. When he is almost beside the captain, he looks down and sees what the buckets contain. He almost weeps. He gazes around the dark, dank space. Though it has no natural light, it boasts an arching ceiling and smooth, narrow walls. He stoops down. The buckets are filled with brushes and paints, tools for carving and mixing.

"I would like this room to be a chapel." The captain scrutinizes him. "Is that something you think you can do?"

"A chapel?" Angelo looks around the room. This is the last thing he was expecting to be requested of him. He nods. Then he walks over and runs his hand across the wall. The plaster is bumpy, but the walls are dry. "Yes, I can do that." Angelo swallows.

"Good," the captain says.

"Do you know what you have in mind?"

The captain shrugs. "You decide. You may begin whenever you wish. If there is anything else you require," the captain says, "please tell one of my men." And he leaves Angelo to his work.

49

RIVKA WALKS AROUND THEIR CELL, gathering up the clothes that she has laid out to dry. She still refuses to hang them outside. She folds them and places them in their cubby. Anna tries to tolerate her, but it is difficult. Rudy plays marbles in a corner with their younger son, Dovid. Reuven takes Josef by the arm and says something to him. Josef motions to Anna and the two men step out of the room.

In the hallway, Reuven speaks softly to Josef. "Please don't mind my wife," he says in their language. "She has had a difficult time." Josef nods as Reuven continues. "It was very hard for us to come here. We had to leave everything behind. She weeps for her parents. It has been some time since we have had any word."

Josef nods again. "I understand. It is hard on all of us." Then, more gently, he touches Reuven on the arm. "Hopefully this will be over soon."

Reuven continues. "You are a dentist, correct?"

"Yes, I am."

Reuven runs a hand through his prematurely white hair. "Perhaps you could look at my children's teeth. They have not been to a dentist since we left Romania."

"Yes," Josef replies. "I'd be happy to." Josef looks at the boys playing. It is almost time for lights-out. He claps his hands together. "All right, children, everyone in the bathroom." They gaze up at him, surprised. "It's time to brush your teeth." Josef made sure they packed their toothbrushes. The Romanian boys have theirs, as well. The children take their toothbrushes and march single file down the hall to the bathroom.

Josef is a stickler for hygiene. And teeth are very important to him. He can tell from their smiles, their shine or the lack thereof, how healthy they are. Josef reads teeth the way a fortune-teller reads tea leaves. He sees things in them. Illness, sadness or joy, the future. Clean, shiny teeth mean that all is well. He's always reminding them to brush carefully and avoid sweets. He encourages flossing with a piece of silk thread. At times he stands behind his children in the bathroom and coaches them as they brush and floss.

Some days after school, Viola showed up at his office. It was always a surprise, and he was always delighted. Though he would never tell anyone—not even Anna—Viola is his favorite. Michele was too angry and Rudy too frail. Michele, even as a young boy, was always ranting about something that was wrong in the world. And Rudy always seemed afraid. But Viola was curious about everything. She would come to his office after school with her homework and sit at his desk as he saw patients. He had a chest of many narrow drawers—each drawer containing innumerable shiny instruments—probes, tiny mirrors, explorers.

He had a plaster of Paris cast of an anatomical mouth, complete with jawbones and tongue, and another of a tooth that could be dismantled; the enamel came off the tooth, exposing the inner workings—the root, the nerve. Viola knew all the different teeth. She could tell an incisor from a canine. She understood the complex structure—how the root holds the tooth, and how the enamel protects it. Like a tree, her father said, with its roots and bark. Once on a beach they found a tooth that belonged to an animal and Viola held it up. "Canine incisor," she said.

In the back of one of the drawers, Josef kept three small boxes. Each box was labeled with the name of one of his children. The boxes contained all of their baby teeth, every single one, which Josef had saved over the years. A full set. Sometimes when she was bored, Viola assembled them. It fascinated her to see them lying there. It made her feel as if they were already dead.

Her father also collected the teeth and jaws of animals. He had those of a dog, a cat, a small shark, and a wolf. His office was like a miniature natural history museum, and he loved those late afternoons when his daughter came to browse. She exhibited the same meticulous curiosity he possessed. He was hopeful.

Josef stands at the sink behind the children as they brush their teeth. He nods in approval. "Good," he says. "Now up and down." When they are finished, he lines them all up.

"Let me see your teeth." He looks in their mouths.

He turns to Reuven, who stands in the doorway. "They have good teeth, your boys."

Reuven smiles as he ruffles his sons' heads, and they return to their cell.

Suddenly, a soldier shouts, "Lights out," and the Red House goes dark.

ANNA SITS BESIDE HER HUSBAND on his pallet. Everyone else is asleep. She runs her hand over his thigh. Then she laughs. It is a laugh Josef hasn't heard in a while. He reaches across, clasping her hand. "This is so silly," she says to her husband, "isn't it?" Then she tilts her head back and kisses him deeply on the mouth. He pulls her more tightly to him.

She gazes into his gray eyes. It was what drew her to him in the first place—those eyes that seemed to light up and flicker. All his emotions showed there. His went from a dark, somber gray to light and sparkling as the stars. Perhaps Josef could hide his secrets, but never his moods.

And now Anna senses a sadness. Maybe nostalgia. When they first touched, so many years ago, it was as if a strange heat emanated off them. But for a long time now, it has cooled. The excitement drained out of their marriage. Suddenly, perhaps because it is impossible, it returns with a vengeance. They want each other again. Josef runs his hands across her back, grazing her breasts. The touch is electric. He threads his fingers through her hair, and Anna thinks she is on fire.

"We can't," he says.

"Why not?" she asks, her voice husky.

"Because we can't. Not here." He extricates himself from her clasp. He helps her as she settles into her pallet beside their daughter. He kisses her deeply. The children stir, then settle again. Anna and Josef sleep with their fingers entwined. He blows kisses to her. She tries to catch them.

50

NOT LONG AFTER HE ARRIVES in Turin, Josef meets Anna by chance at a cafeteria near his dental school. He goes to the cafeteria often, because it's cheap and serves good pasta with thick sauces and hearty stews that can satisfy him for the entire day. Also, it is run by Jews who serve no pork. Besides, he likes to speak to people, and customers often leave behind their newspapers, which he studies. He can improve his Italian there.

He's nineteen and he's only been in Italy a few months. The Great War has just ended. His parents scraped together all they could to send him to medical school, but after a year, he realized that it wasn't enough. But he could afford to go to dental school.

He never told his parents. At first, he found dentistry tedious. It wasn't like studying the heart or the brain. But in time, he came to love teeth. The enamel that protects them. The nerves that run through them. Just like people, he thinks.

The first time he sees her, he's struck by her soft brown eyes and her dark, lush hair, which is pulled back by two tortoiseshell barrettes. He's drawn to the curl of her lip, which he envisions kissing—a thought he tries to banish but cannot. He stares at her, but when her gaze meets his, he looks back at his food. When he looks up again, she's gone.

For the rest of the week, he returns to the cafeteria, hoping to see her, but she doesn't come back. He's never wanted anything more than to kiss her. Perhaps because he assumes that she is lost to him. But two weeks later she's back. This time, he doesn't look away and he doesn't hesitate. He approaches her. "I am a dental student," he says. "I saw you a few weeks ago."

"Do you think I came back for the food?" she replies boldly.

Josef's face grows flushed. He doesn't know what to say. He can't stop staring at the curl of her lip, the slight irony of her smile. He looks at her hand-stitched sweater, her wool skirt. What could he, a poor dental student, offer her? Perhaps she is making fun of him. He gathers his nerve. "Shall we take a walk?"

"I was hoping you'd ask." She takes his arm and they stroll from the cafeteria near the train station up Via Roma, which is crowded with shops and pedestrians. As they walk, he tells her about Romania. His childhood there. He tells her that he never intended to become a dentist. He's shy to tell her, ashamed of his choice. But Anna doesn't seem to mind.

They cut over to the less crowded Via La Grange, until they come to the Caffè Mulassano. Discreetly, Josef checks his wallet. He only has a few hundred lire. He will have to skip his meal tomorrow, but it's enough to buy them coffee and a pastry, which they enjoy under the arcade.

After that, they begin to meet in the afternoons. She takes his arm, and they walk. They stroll all over the city. Some days they wander on the main boulevards. Other days, they wend their way along the tree-lined residential streets. On warm, sunny days when they have more time, they walk over to the Po and follow its banks. Once or twice, they rent a small rowboat and go out onto the river. After several weeks of these strolls, Josef grows bolder. One day, standing under chestnut trees, he leans over and kisses the curl of that lip, long and slow. Anna is hungry for more.

Their walks become less innocent. They seek secluded benches, isolated groves of trees. When the weather turns colder, Josef sneaks Anna into his dorm. He sees her naked body for the first time. Her round hips, her full breasts. She touches and caresses him as if she has pleasured many men. Josef doesn't ask. She's his first. But he seems to know what to do, where to touch her. He's stunned by the suddenness of her climax, her animal cry. He wonders if his housemates can hear.

Soon, they're always together. There's nothing they won't do for each other. One afternoon in his room, they make love three times. Afterward they lie together. He strokes her hair. She's eighteen. Just old enough. They keep their romance a secret. They enjoy the sense that they are engaged in something clandestine, furtive. It is not until Anna realizes she's pregnant that she tells her parents about Josef. "So you see," she informs them, "I must marry him."

Her parents are appalled. "Who is this young man? What do you know about him?" her father asks. Though Josef is terrified, Anna makes him come over in person to ask for her hand in his thick Romanian accent. Her father can barely contain his rage, but soon he softens. The boy is Jewish, after all, and training to be a dentist. Never mind that he comes from Romania and they may never meet his family. That afternoon, the two men shake hands and it is settled.

The wedding is a small, private affair. Just the immediate family and a few close friends at home. A rabbi presides. For their honeymoon, they go to the shore—a place she tells him she loves. During the day they walk the beach and splash in the waves. At night she's so tired that all she does is sleep.

"There was so much to do," she explains when she refuses him in bed, "with the wedding and all." But even after Michele is born, the tiredness seems to go on and on. It never leaves her.

After the birth, Josef assumes their lives will go back to what they were before. The passionate embraces, even in the middle of the day. But now with a child suckling at her breast, she wants Josef even less. When she is nursing, Josef hears her cooing as she once did with him in bed. He has to leave the room. If they do make love, she seems rushed, as if sex is a chore she must tend to. She seems relieved when it is done. He wonders if her orgasms are real.

By the time Viola is born, they make love rarely—only on special occasions, after dinner parties when there's too much drinking— and then, after Rudy, their lovemaking comes to a halt. Anna is always tired. She has many excuses. Josef wants her as much as when he first saw that curled lip. But, not a man given to conflict, he, too, lets his desire subside.

51

TOMMASO IS UP BEFORE DAWN. It is five miles on a dusty road to reach the Red House, and it takes him about an hour on his bicycle. He must leave at first light. But it is not his alarm that wakes him today. Rather, it is the dull aching in his jaw, his tooth sore to the touch. And the thoughts of Viola. He knows her name. He will look for her in the afternoon.

The dirt road is pitted, and trucks pass, spewing exhaust and dust in his face. In his saddlebags, he has packed his neatly folded uniform, which his grandmother washed and ironed for him the night before. His tooth is still bothering him. He touches it with his tongue. He makes a mental note to visit the dentist.

Six months ago, when he enlisted by lying about his age, against his mother's wishes, he wasn't sure what he wanted out of life. He had not yet seen a path to his future, unlike his brother, Alfredo, who has a passion for machines and their workings, and always wanted to be a mechanic. Or his sister, Isabella, who got pregnant at sixteen and has happily produced a baby a year for the past three years. Her husband works in a tire factory.

But Tommaso has no such ambition. He was three when his father was killed in a farm accident. He has little memory of him, except for a dark shadow that passed over his crib at night as he drifted to sleep, or in the morning before dawn. He recalls thick, rough hands, the smell of smoke and straw. More like a scarecrow than a man. He never saw his father in the light of day. And even then, he wonders if the shadow was really his father or a cloud floating across the moon.

When he went to live with them, Sofia and Carlo were mourning the loss of their youngest child. Sofia spoiled Tommaso with huge bowls of tortellini in savory chicken broth, her orecchiette with the tomato sauce she canned every summer and that lasted until spring. Before he was five, Tommaso could taste a hint of basil. He loved the rich aroma of roasting garlic. He knew when the milk had soured. "He tastes everything," Sofia said.

He lived with his grandparents for four years, until his grandfather died suddenly, and, just as suddenly, his mother appeared, as if she'd awakened from a long slumber. "It's time he comes home," she said. She'd barely tried to see him in the years he lived with Sofia, and suddenly this stranger was tossing his toy soldiers and comic books into a bag and emptying his drawers into a suitcase. Despite his protests and those of his grandmother, she took him away.

Tommaso never settled back into his old house. His mother didn't have basil growing in the windowsill or a saucepan always on the stove. Her house wasn't filled with the rich aromas of her kitchen, but, rather, the stale odors of cigarettes and wine. The meat she bought was tough and, when she cooked it, became, somehow, even tougher. Tommaso offered to go to the butcher for her, to bring home the finer cuts of meat, and pan-sear them, sealing in the juices. But his mother gazed at him with scorn. "So now you're a sissy?"

It wasn't long after his mother took him back that he began showing up at his grandmother's house after school. He helped her pluck tomatoes and dice onions. He stood beside her as she stirred her sauces. She'd blow on a spoon, and when it was cool, he would taste the sauce. He had a perfect sense of what a dish needed, the way some musicians have perfect pitch. "A pinch of salt," he'd say. Or "more lemon." It's a gift, his grandmother used to say, her arms folded across her chest as she praised him.

Tommaso never grows weary when his grandmother hands him her sharpest knife and tells him to slice the onions. He minces the garlic and then chops it even finer. He knows he is a disappointment to his mother, who had hoped that if he did not become an engineer, he would at least train as a mechanic. Her disapproval is why he does not put on his uniform before he leaves the house—though his ostensible purpose is to keep it clean on the road to work. She cannot stand to see him dressed as a soldier. And it's why he goes by his grandmother's every evening—to let her wash and iron one of the uniforms he rotates every other day.

But now he has found a reason to go to work. He has found a reason to help his grandmother in the kitchen. Everything is for Viola. A truck rattles past him, almost sending Tommaso into a ditch. He rights himself and pedals on. His tooth throbs. Ahead of him, he sees the glow of the purple dawn. The horizon illumines the way Viola's eyes do when she sees him. That is something he has never experienced before—someone's eyes lighting up at the sight of him. He knows her name.

As he makes his turn onto the road that leads to the Red House, dawn is breaking. A purple strip of light fills the horizon. Violet like Viola. He will never see another dawn without thinking of her.

52

SOFIA IS UP EARLY. THOUGH SHE doesn't have an appointment, she's going to see the dentist. She wraps up a parcel and carries it with her as she makes her way to the office. She's waiting when Josef arrives. He's surprised to see the widow sitting there, all in black but with a grin on her face. She is younger than he first imagined. Perhaps no more than fifty, though the years haven't been kind to her. The shopping bag rests at her feet. "Signora Bassano, are you feeling all right?" Her smile tells him that she is. "Let me check you," he says.

Gently he guides her to his chair, and she opens her mouth. He probes the tooth. The putrid smell is gone. As he checks her gums, he nods. He might even be able to save the tooth. As he examines her, Sofia cannot help but think about what Tommaso told her. That the Jews in the Red House have no blankets, no warm clothes. Already the nights are chilly, and soon it will be cold. They have little to eat. She is pleased with the package she has prepared. "Well, it is healing nicely," Josef says.

When he is finished and they have made an appointment for cleaning and to fill her cavities, she hands him the sack. Inside are tomatoes from her garden, a freshly plucked chicken, and two wool blankets. "You know, no matter how warm the days, it can be cool at night. Your children must be chilly," Sofia says. "And hungry."

Josef is so grateful, he almost cries. "Thank you," he says, "my wife will be so pleased."

"It's nothing," she mutters. "I will tell more people to come and see you." With a wave of her hand, she hobbles away.

At the end of the day, Josef gathers up the parcel and tucks it under his coat. When he gets into the car, the captain, who doesn't seem to notice him, is waiting to drive back to the Red House. For a while, they drive in silence. Then the captain pulls over. "I must get some things for my wife." As Josef sits in the car, he tries to hide the sack under his feet. A few minutes later the captain returns with bread, wine, cheese. "I can't go home empty-handed," he jokes, and Josef laughs along with him.

"Oh, I know," Josef replies.

The captain points to the sack tucked at Josef's feet. "What do you have there?"

Josef tries to push the sack deeper under the seat. "One of my patients," he replies sheepishly. "She gave them to me in payment for curing her abscess."

The captain smiles. "Oh, Signora Bassano. That was very kind of her. She's a nice old lady." He pulls out the sack and gazes inside. "My men will be grateful. They often complain of the cold." When they arrive back at the Red House, Captain Cassini—for he has become a captain again—takes the blankets, and the chicken, too.

53

VIOLA OBSERVES THE FLIGHT OF BIRDS. In the morning, she watches them from the pallet, where she lies beside her mother. They dart and dive in and out of the cell. The early light catches their wings, and they shimmer purple and gold. Their flight seems like a dance—planned, choreographed, not random. Sometimes, she fears they will crash into one another, but they never do. They leave as quickly as they arrive.

She watches other birds, as well. Tiny brown songbirds that perch on the windowsills, chirping away, and fat white birds whose plaintive cries wake her, and who seem too heavy for flight. Yet there they are, soaring. Her father tells her that these birds mean the sea is near, though there's no other proof of nearby water from her vantage point at the Red House. She loves that his term of endearment for her is "Pigeon." Pigeons are not beautiful or grace-ful, though their coos are soothing. But the small, darting birds capture her attention. She can watch them for hours. She has begun to dream of their flight.

The birds are not the only things that have entered her dreams.

Viola can't get the blue-eyed soldier out of her mind. She is ner-vous to say his name. She knows that this is somehow wrong—that her father and her mother would be ashamed of her—but she can-not help it. The way he looked at her when he helped her off the bus. His sad smile. The way his eyes skimmed her body, her arms, her legs, her small, swollen breasts. It was almost as if he could smell that she was a woman, the way dogs sniffed in the alley behind their house in Turin. Or cats that howl and scratch. Once she asked her mother why they did this, and Anna replied, "They're in love."

Is that what love is? Sniffing, howling, scratching, screaming? Viola doesn't know. Her parents love each other. She is sure of it.

But she has never heard them make these sounds or look each other up and down the way the blue-eyed soldier does with her. She feels something different. Something she's never quite felt before.

But she is his captive, isn't she? Not at all like the swooping birds that her father calls swallows. They are free; she is not. And perhaps she will never be. Perhaps when they were packing (only one bag to take on what her father referred to as their "little vacation"), or later, on that train, she came to understand that the life she had known was behind her, and even if she returned, even if someday they were told that this episode was over and it had all been a mistake, even if they went back and resumed the life they had known, in their house and on their street, with their friends and Michele and her grandparents, at the school where she was an outstanding student, it will never be the same life, but always a different one. Even if she could just open a door and walk back inside all they'd left behind, what was waiting for her would never be the same.

THAT AFTERNOON WHEN SHE RETURNS to the grove, Tommaso is waiting. He smiles and his teeth are bright and white. He motions to her to walk with him into the shade. He puts his rucksack on the ground. Opening the snaps, he hands her a cloth bag. She hesitates, thinking she should not take it from him. What if she gets into trouble? What if he does? And part of her wonders if this is a trick. A way to get something from her, as her mother has often said, that men want.

But then she smells what's inside the sack and it makes her mouth water. Inside are a loaf of fresh bread, still warm, and a hunk of cheese. "From my grandmother," he says.

She tears a chunk of bread, wrapping it around the cheese. She promises herself that she won't eat it all. She should save some for Rudy. But she doesn't.

54

IN THE CLASSROOM ANNA HAS FOUND paper and an envelope. She borrows a pen. Sitting in the mess hall, she writes.

Dear Michele,

I do not know if this letter will reach you. I'm not sure if you are even stopping by the apartment, though I hope you will—if nothing else to check on your grandparents. It is very difficult for me to be away from them, and from you. I miss you, as always, though I know you are working on important things.

We have been at Castellobello for a few weeks now. The ride down was long and tiring, but since arriving, we are adapting nicely. We are staying in a large building where there are many olive trees. The weather has been a bit warm. Much warmer than in Turin, but the nights are cool. I know it will get colder soon, and we are bracing ourselves for that, as we did not bring much in the way of warm clothing. Perhaps, if you think of it, you can ask Mama to mail something to us here? We would be so grateful.

Your father is doing well. He is working in a dental office in town. And Viola and Rudy are attending school. There are in fact two teachers among us, so the children are still studying.

Once I know that you have received this and I hear back from you, I will write more and often. I think of you always, and send you all my love. Please hug your grandparents for me.

Your loving Mama.

There is a box for letters in the entry hall. Though they are given no stamps, they drop their letters in there. It is emptied every few days. The soldiers promise to mail them.

55

"NO MATTER HOW MANY TIMES I tell her," Captain Cassini says, "it's always dry." The captain is chatty as they drive into town, complaining about the meal his wife made the night before. She overcooked the fish.

"That can be a problem with fish," Josef replies.

"Yes, but how many times must I tell her?" He reaches into a basket on the seat beside him. "But my fruit trees." The captain holds up a small, shriveled fig. "This is the best they're producing. How can I share these with my patients? The oranges were even worse." The yield has been small this year, though Captain Cassini laughs. It's just a hobby. "I couldn't live on what I grow. I don't know how farmers do it."

"Yes, I imagine it must be difficult," Josef replies.

The captain takes a bite, then grimaces and puts the rest of the fig on the dash. He prides himself on his apples, but even they are turning out small and sour. "Not even good for tarts," he complains, "though Esmeralda tries to sweeten them." Josef assumes that Esmeralda is his wife, though perhaps she is a servant. He thinks that even a small, tart apple would be delicious right now. He stares at the half-eaten fig.

And then there's his son. "He seems lost," the captain says. "Perhaps I am too hard on him." Josef listens in silence as the captain skips around, talking about dry fish, shriveled figs, and his wayward child. He isn't sure what he is expected to say. He thinks about his own son Michele, whom he doesn't dare mention, and with whom he has been at odds for years.

His oldest child is a mystery to him. He meets his friends clandestinely. They never come to the house, but there are quick phone calls and sudden meetings. And the pamphlets Michele keeps in a suitcase in his room. Josef worries that he will get himself into trouble. But Michele has been mostly silent as to his activities. Josef hopes he is safe, staying with friends or perhaps his grandparents. "Boys can be difficult," Josef replies.

The captain laughs. "How would you know? Yours is so little."

Josef catches himself. He is about to tell the captain about Michele, but he thinks it best not to mention that he has an older boy. "Yes, that is true."

"The only thing that brings me real pleasure," the captain says, "is my birds."

Josef is taken aback. "Your songbirds?"

Captain Cassini chuckles. "Yes. My canaries. They make me happy," the captain says. "I like listening to them sing."

Josef thinks about his father's dovecot. His father kept hundreds of pigeons on the roof. They didn't sing. They just made that low cooing sound. Josef was tasked with cleaning out their little cages. The work was endless, yet he was happy there. The pigeons seemed to know their names. He loved it when his father let all the pigeons out to circle in formation. His father was quite good at it, and Josef learned, too. He could twirl his hand in the air and the pigeons would dip and dive.

The captain shrugs. "Do you know why canaries sing, Dottore?"

Josef shakes his head. "No, I don't."

"Only the males sing. They are trying to find a mate. Just like all men." The captain laughs at his own joke. Josef attempts to laugh, as well. The captain gestures with a wave of the hand. "Once they have found one, they stop singing. That is why the male songbirds must be kept in solitude."

"Oh," Josef says, lying, "I didn't know that."

They drive the rest of the way in silence.

56

ANNA LOOKS FOR THINGS TO DO. There are no beds to make because there are no linens. There is little food to cook. Only pots of soup to stir, made from what the women forage in the fields or the meager provisions they can purchase at the commissary. Now that people are working, they have money to make some purchases, but never more than a few carrots or potatoes.

After meals, she washes the pewter plates with the other women, but after that they sit, idle. These hands are strangers to her. She has not seen her nails like this since she was a girl, because every week she went with her mother to the manicurist, and, later, after the Racial Laws, the manicurist came to them, sneaking up their stairs, her purse filled with emery boards and the bright red polish both women preferred. On the train, she peeled off the polish until they were bare. Now the only thing Anna does with her hands, aside from washing plates and digging in the dirt, is bite them. She bites her nails and cuticles until they are raw.

Anna heaves a sigh. She feels herself sinking. Disappearing down a dark cavern. If she keeps falling, if she does not stop herself, she fears she will disappear altogether. She forces herself to rise from her pallet and goes downstairs. Captain Cassini has already left with Josef, but there is another soldier in charge. Officer Petrucci is a tall, thin man with a stubbly beard. He appears close to Anna's age. She approaches him slowly. "May I speak with you, sir?"

He nods for her to go ahead.

"I am a couturier," she tells him. He looks confused and she realizes he doesn't understand the word. "I have made dresses for some of the finest women in Turin. Is there not a dress shop in town that could use my services? I would like to work."

He meets her dark eyes with a silent stare.

"I need to be useful," she says.

"I will think about it," he tells her coldly, and turns away.

The next morning at breakfast, he finds her in the mess hall. "I have found work for you. Please come with me."

Anna follows him down the stairs. She expects a car will be there, waiting to take her to town with the others. Instead, they follow the long, dank corridor of the soldiers' barracks. In the corridor, they pass that odd Hungarian man who paints angels. He nods at Anna but doesn't say a word as he slips into a room with large barn doors.

Anna continues to follow the soldier until she is led into a windowless room. It smells of mold and mice. In the middle of the room sits a sewing machine. "You will sew uniforms for the men. We will get you wool and anything else you need."

She feels tears well up. This is not at all what Anna had in mind. She wants to leave the Red House in the mornings with the others and work in the town. She feels as if she will die if she has to work in this room. Anna starts to protest, but she sees the look in his eyes. In the corner is a pile of uniforms that need to be repaired. There is also a pile of scratchy wool to be made into winter uniforms. "I will need a dress form," she tells him.

He nods. "I will see what I can do."

When he closes the door, Anna picks up a piece of tattered cloth and begins to sew.

57

TWO DOORS DOWN, ANGELO SITS in a folding chair in the middle of what will become the chapel he is supposed to create. He has spent his days priming and smoothing the surfaces. Sanding down the walls. Then he meticulously swept the dust. The room is spotless, pristine. He has spent hours just sitting in the chair the captain left in the middle of the room, staring at the walls. What is it that the captain really wants him to paint? It was one thing to restore the churches and carve headstones in Budapest. It is another to do it here.

He has decided to paint images of flight. Along with paintings of Jesus on the cross, and his various disciples, which Angelo assumes is required, he had drafted sketches of the Jews leaving Egypt, the Red Sea parting. He draws angels soaring, Jesus rising. Anything that implies escape.

Now he gets up. He picks up a piece of charcoal and starts to draw.

58

WHEN JOSEF REACHES THE DENTAL office, a woman is waiting to see him. She holds a trembling child. Josef looks at the child and sees the ravages of malaria. "I am not a doctor," Josef says.

"Please," the woman begs, holding up the boy. "You can cure him."

Josef knows where she lives. In that hovel just along the walkway to the office. "Go home," he tells her. "I will try to get you some medicine for the boy."

The woman makes the sign of the cross over Josef, blessing him. When she leaves, Josef sighs. He goes into Dottore Cassini's office. "I need some supplies," he tells the doctor. "Quinine if you can find any, or let me order some from Turin. And antibiotic cream. For the children's eyes."

Dottore Cassini shrugs. "It is impossible to get supplies. What can I do?"

"There must be someone you can try."

Dottore Cassini sighs as if he is being inconvenienced.

Josef returns to his office. He is there for over an hour, but no patients arrive for him. All he can think about is the boy who is going to die and his desperate mother, begging him to save her son. He tries to get her pleading eyes out of his head. He keeps busy, cleaning his instruments, polishing his chair, when a young man comes in with a toothache. He looks vaguely familiar. Josef looks at him more closely. "You helped my grandmother," the young man says.

"I've seen you before," Josef says as he prepares his instruments.

"I am doing my military service," he replies, "at the Red House. My name is Tommaso."

"Ah, yes." Josef wants to add "You have eyes for my daughter," but he resists. Perhaps he is wrong. He doesn't want to put any ideas into this boy's head that aren't already there. His name is Tommaso, he says, and he is not more than sixteen or seventeen. He has thick black hair and a set of perfect white teeth. Josef can often forget a face, but he always remembers a mouth, and this young man's mouth is exceptional. Straight, pure white, and when Josef gazes inside, his miner's lamp shining, he doesn't see a trace of decay.

Still Josef examines the young man as he sits in the chair. He probes every tooth, digging into the crevices, searching for the source of his pain, and finally Josef says, "Yes, I see some swelling in the gum. It may be an abscess."

"So perhaps you must pull the tooth?" Tommaso says.

"Well, I don't know if that's necessary. . . ."

"Look again." As Josef leans down, Tommaso whispers to him. "I am here to help you. Please tell me or my grandmother what you need."

Josef is stunned. "I don't think it has to come out. I could give you some antibiotics."

Tommaso stares at Josef. "Pull it."

Josef nods and administers a small dose of lidocaine. The boy does not grimace or struggle as Josef pulls his tooth.

"Thank you, Dottore," Tommaso says upon leaving, vigorously shaking Josef's hand. "I'm sure I'll feel better now."

59

AS WE STAND IN THE SHADE of the conjoined trees, Tommaso wipes his brow. "You do strange things for love," he says with a chuckle. He rubs his jaw, as if he is experiencing some phantom pain. "I didn't really need for him to pull that tooth, but I did not trust Captain Cassini. He could be . . ." Here his voice trails off. "He seemed jovial enough, but he could be a dangerous man." There is a bench not far from the tree, and we make our way there. We sit in the shadow of the Red House. "You know, they were trying to turn this place into a disco until someone in the historic landmark department realized what had happened here."

A disco? I nod, still trying to process all that he has told me. "They were Jews? My mother, her family . . ."

The old man nods. "You didn't know, Laura?"

"I didn't know anything." I shake my head. "Why didn't she tell me?" What was there to hide? She never said a word about being Jewish. We had bacon for breakfast on the weekends. "My mother took Communion at church. How is it possible?"

Tommaso shrugs. "Obviously," he says, waving his hands, "she did not want you to know. We didn't know any Jews until they were brought to the Red House. It was an orphanage, before."

I stare at the enormous red block of a building. Tommaso takes me by the arm, leading me to the car. "There is more you need to hear, but this is enough for now."

"How much more?" I start to protest.

He keeps walking. "More," he says. "But another day."

I'm not sure how many more days I have here, and I'm over-whelmed with questions. "I'm leaving soon."

Tommaso shrugs again. "Perhaps you should delay." I breathe a heavy sigh as he stumbles along in his labored way. He has grown weary. "I will take you back to your hotel."

I clasp his hand. "Tommaso, I need to go inside."

"I know." He nods. "I will find the keys."

60

WE HEAD BACK THE WAY WE CAME and drive mostly in silence. Finally, Tommaso drops me off at the same guesthouse I checked out of that morning. "May I invite you to dinner?" he asks. "Or if you like, I can cook."

"I'm not really very hungry," I reply. It's almost dark and I'm starving, but I don't think I can listen to another word. "I'm very tired," I tell him. I don't tell him I feel as though I've been dropped down a dark well and I'll never be found. "I think I need to rest."

"I have given you a lot to think about, haven't I?"

I nod wearily. "Yes, you have."

"I'm tired, too," he says, his voice filled with regret. "It is hard for me to remember. It's a vault that hasn't been opened in years." He shakes his head. "I will be back in the morning."

I thank him and shut the door. As he speeds away, I drag my wheelie back into the lobby. The desk clerk looks up with an ironic smile. "I see that Signore Bassano found you."

I am taken aback. "What do you mean?"

The desk clerk points at his head. "*Pazzo,*" he says. "He's a crazy old fool, full of stories. I wouldn't take anything he says too seriously." This gives me pause. Is he a crazy old man? Are these made-up stories? Clearly he knew my mother, but what if the rest of it is all in his head?

The clerk hands me a key. "I take it you would like your same room?"

"Yes, that would be fine."

"So you like it here?" he asks as I am turning to head back to my room.

"More or less," I reply, not knowing what else to say.

BACK IN MY ROOM, I OPEN THE CURTAINS. The room looks down on a quaint little courtyard. There are geraniums everywhere. I am sitting on my bed, staring at a picture of two cats. The fibers on the bedspread are scratchy, not cotton. I find myself missing Patrick. Though we haven't really been lovers in a while, he is my husband of almost twenty years, and my friend. And I have been unkind. I pick up the phone and call him. It's late in New York. He answers on the first ring. "Laura," he says, his voice soft, almost a whisper.

I start to cry. "I'm sorry," I tell him. "I had to leave. It's too complicated to explain. . . ."

He clears his throat. "That detective keeps calling. What do you want me to tell him?"

My heart is racing. "Don't tell him anything."

"He keeps leaving messages."

I'm clutching the phone. "Erase them."

There's an awkward silence. "Are you going to come home?" he asks.

And I say the most honest thing I have said to him in a long time. "I don't really know."

61

WE MET IN GRADUATE SCHOOL at Pratt, when I was doing my PhD in art history, though I never wrote my dissertation. I was planning on doing it on the sister-in-law of Vincent van Gogh— Theo's wife. Theo died not that long after Vincent, and his wife, Jo, a simple, uneducated woman, devoted the rest of her life to Vincent's legacy. It is because of Jo that the letters have been preserved. It was Jo who relentlessly pushed Vincent's work out into the world. She fascinated me and yet, as is often the case with me, I let her go.

Patrick was studying architecture, but in the end his interests gravitated to restoration. He liked creating facsimiles of moldings and brass fixtures. He was more interested in the past than in the future. He had a sense that things were better then.

We crossed paths often in the library. Our schedules seemed to coincide. At the time, we were both night owls, and Patrick was often *en charrette* with projects that needed to be completed. We each liked a room on the third floor, part of the music library, which was rarely full and very quiet; everyone listened to the music in silent booths. It was odd, sometimes, to watch a student conducting music from inside one of those booths. Once, a young man was particularly engrossed in the music, gesticulating wildly, silently, and for the first time, Patrick and I looked at each other and started to laugh.

I had seen his serious face, but his face when he was laughing was completely different. He could barely contain his deep, throaty laughter. We were both tired; we'd been studying too long. He wanted to take a coffee break and asked if I would like to accompany him. It began like that. Coffee, study dates, sometimes a glass of wine. It was weeks before we started having dinners and going out. And months before we slept together. Late one night, I mentioned that I had a bottle of wine in my room. Patrick came back to the dorm where I lived. We drank the wine and told each other things about our lives.

But it was much later that I told him about my mother.

I had learned from previous experience. I'd go out with a man three or four times, sleep with him, and then, when he asked, I'd tell him my story. I'd gotten better at telling it over the years. I'd developed ways of narrating it to hold the listener's interest. Someone wrote once that telling a story is like a striptease. You don't want to walk on the stage naked and you also don't want to take too long to take off your clothes.

The way I'd learned this wasn't easy. I'd had several tumultuous relationships in high school and one or two destructive ones in college. Some men tended to evaporate when they learned that I came from the home of a mother who'd gone missing. Perhaps they'd been warned off by their own mothers. Perhaps this just sent up a red flag that I was some kind of trouble. Just before I met Patrick, I was seeing a guy named Roger. He was a lovely man—a music student who went on to have his own jazz quartet. Roger had complexities of his own—an alcoholic mother, an absent father—and I felt comfortable when I told him my story. I told it to him over a few days, most of which we spent in bed. And I came to trust him.

I told him that my mother vanished, that she was never found. I told him how our lives changed. I told him about Detective Hendricks, though I didn't tell him everything.

I liked it when Roger asked me to tell the story again, and then again. I enjoyed recounting it, as if somehow each time I retold it, I was releasing some gas into the universe, as if the waves of it would spread out and release me from its grasp. But by the fourth time, I began to wonder if something wasn't right. I was growing weary of the repetition. On that night, Roger said, "You left out something. About the crusts of bread."

I never saw him again.

But Patrick wasn't like that. He never pried. What interested Patrick was how I saw the world. How we saw the world together. I think of the way he once so admired the door knocker on a man's house in Belgium that the man ended up selling it to him; the way he walks through a museum, never reading what's written on the walls, only looking; the way his eyes seek out beauty; the way he reads long books on overnight flights, the journals where he scribbles everything. I can see him scribbling away.

62

THE MOON IS ORANGE, AND SLEEP eludes me. It offers a promise, and then the minute I lie down, it escapes. I have to sneak up on it like a thief in the night. But still it slips away as I toss and turn. After a while, I fling the covers back and decide to go for a walk. I'm hungry and I could use a drink. I get dressed and head downstairs.

It's almost midnight and the city is asleep. I step out into the dark, warm night and turn right. I follow a narrow street that leads to a warren of shuttered shops. I reach a dead end and head back. The street branches and I assume I am going the way I came, but the streets don't look the same. They were lit before, but now, except for the occasional light in a home, they're dark. I'm uncertain of which way to turn. I find myself wandering through a maze. I take stairwells that lead to the darkened front doors of strangers, then turn around and head back into the night. My heart is pounding as I struggle to find my way back to the illuminated streets. I hear footsteps. I turn and see a man walking behind me. A cat darts from behind a trash can and I shout. The man pauses and continues on his way.

Something is bothering me beyond what Tommaso has just told me. Slowly it comes to mind. A painting of my mother's. Strange gray hooded figures with featureless faces. No eyes or mouths, just the dark shape of bodies, like those Halloween ghosts we'd hang in our trees every year. But those paper ghosts never frightened me the way her painting did. *The Progression of the Souls,* she called it.

She worked on it for years, and when it was done, it hung over our mantel like a shroud, something guests turned away from awkwardly. Who were those faceless souls? people would ask her. I wondered, too, but she'd give a wave of her hand. "I just don't do faces" is what she'd say. But it was as if everyone who came into our living room was making a condolence call. And then, eventually, they were. One day, I'm not sure how long it was after she was gone, the painting disappeared. For a while, the space was empty. Eventually our father hung a mirror in its place. A mirror we were all afraid to look into, for fear of what we might see.

I find myself back at the Belvedere. It's one in the morning, and the churchyard is deserted. There's not a café or bar open in sight. A pair of doves coo, pecking at the ground. I sit on the bench, staring at the dry, dusty earth, trying to make sense of what I now know. My family was Jewish. They were sent here. My grandmother came from an established family of Italian Jews. My grandfather was an immigrant from Romania, but he, too, was once an Italian citizen. Still, they were sent into exile. Why did I never know this? Why didn't she tell me? And what happened to them? Is this where their journey ended? What more can a crazy old man who says he loved my mother sixty years ago have to tell me? What more do I even want to know? Yet I sense that whatever happened to them lives in me.

And that place. That Red House. I cannot go back there. I can't go inside. If I do, I fear I will descend into a darkness deeper than any I've ever known. One I may never come out of. Suddenly, I can barely breathe. My heart pounds. I feel as if something invisible is chasing me. It occurs to me that I am about to disappear, as well. I am staring down an abyss and there is no exit. I cannot stay here. In the morning, I will get up early and drive back to Rome. I will return to my life, such as it is.

I head back to my room, dragging my feet. I lie down on the bed, under the painting of the two cats. I must leave this place. Even if Tommaso comes in the morning with the keys, I cannot go inside. I fear that if I walk into the Red House, I will never walk out again.

63

FOR A TIME, I BECAME OBSESSED with disappearances. Famous, not so famous, people who walked away from their lives, never to be seen again. Agatha Christie vanished for eleven days upon learning that her husband was having an affair. The promising twenty-five-year-old writer Barbara Newhall Follett took thirty dollars and left her apartment and was never seen again. Or Virginia Woolf, who wrote a love letter to her husband, put stones in her pockets, and walked into the river nearby.

If only we'd had such a letter. We might have had some closure. This always disturbed my father. My mother left a note, complete with kisses and a smiley face, if she ran to the store for ten minutes. Why did she leave nothing for us? It made him believe more and more that she was abducted, taken by aliens. She could not have gone, he reasoned, of her own free will.

It is interesting to note that all the disappeared I read about were women, and most were writers. Maybe because a writer's life is part of her narrative. Or perhaps because a writer can carry her work with her in a notebook; it's not so easy for a painter. But why do women disappear more often than men?

I have been obsessed with these accounts, reading in detail. They are mysteries, often without resolution. Agatha Christie kissed her sleeping daughter and got into her car. It was later found at the edge of a chalk quarry, the key still in it, in the back seat a bottle labeled "Poison Lead and Opium," as if Christie had set up a mystery of her own to be solved. In the end, she was found in a hotel, where she had checked in under the name of Miss Teresa Neele (the surname of her husband's mistress). And, despite her grief, she managed to dance in the hotel bar every night until she was found.

I have never had a good answer. Did my mother stage her own disappearance? It's not that easy to do. One needs help, as Detective Hendricks pointed out on several occasions. A supply of cash, an alias, and accomplice to collect you. Was she kidnapped? Did our father murder her? Was she having an affair? Was he? He always said no. He was baffled, and I never doubted him. Yet these niggling questions remain.

When I was a teenager in French class, we read *The Little Prince*. How I wept at the end, when the little prince disappears. And then there was his creator, Saint-Exupéry, who disappeared over the Mediterranean during World War II. Years later, a fisherman found a silver bracelet engraved with the name of Saint-Exupéry's wife, Consuela, and his publisher. But this only seemed to increase the mystery. How could they find a bracelet and not a fragment of his plane?

The Little Prince was a book I read over and over again. But the part that got to me the most was near the end. Page 84. After the Little Prince falls over silently into the sand, and it seems as if he is dead. But in the morning, when the narrator wakes, he says, "I know that he did get back to his planet, because at daybreak I did not find his body." The sadness of his body's not being there weighed on me more than I thought possible. I would have given anything to find her "body" at daybreak. At any moment, really. Her body would have meant closure. Her body would have meant we could move on.

Many people don't understand why it is so important to have "remains." To have DNA or dental records to prove that it is your beloved who is gone. I was so struck by that after 9/11. The search for remains when there were none.

Perhaps Leonard Woolf should have been grateful to have Virginia's letter to him. We would have given anything to have such proof. "You have given me the greatest possible happiness," she scrawled. "I don't think two people could have been happier than we have been." Then she put stones in her pockets, took a short walk down to the river, and drowned.

64

IN THE MORNING, WHEN I GO DOWN to tell the desk clerk, once more, that I'll be leaving, Tommaso is waiting in the lobby.

Again, the clerk gives me that odd look. "*Buona fortuna,*" he says under his breath. Tommaso is dressed in a wool blazer, too hot for the season. Perhaps he is crazy. The desk clerk seems to think so. But he has shaved, and looks tidier than he did the day before. "I am sorry," he tells me, taking me by the arm. "I couldn't sleep."

I walk with him. "I couldn't, either."

"Perhaps we could have run into each other. Were you wandering about?"

I nod. "Yes, I was. How did you know?"

He shrugs.

I do not know where he is taking me, but I allow myself to be led. Does the love we once had for my mother connect us in ways I can't understand? "I can't find the person who has the keys," he tells me, "but I will. May I get you an espresso? Come." He takes me by the arm.

We go into a café and order two espressos. We sit down at a small table in a corner. "I will find them," he tells me. "But first I must ask you . . ."

I feel myself trembling, certain of what is coming next.

"Please, you must tell me what became of her. I have been afraid to ask, but I need to know."

I sigh. "It's complicated." I take a deep breath. It's a question I never know how to answer. Tears well up in his blue, rheumy eyes, and as I watch this seventy-six-year-old man about to break down, I reach across and touch his hand. "The truth is, I don't really know. That's why I came here."

"You don't know what became of her?"

I shake my head. "I have my theories. But no, I don't know."

"I've been married for over fifty years." His voice is barely a whisper. "I have three children. Seven grandchildren. I love my wife. And yet I still think of Viola." He points to his head. "She is always in there, somewhere, in the back of my mind."

I take a deep breath and explain, as I've had to for too long. "I don't know if she is dead or alive. She vanished. She left us one day without a word. I was twelve years old. My sister was seven. We never heard from her again."

"She disappeared?" He nods and I cannot escape the feeling that he already knows anything I might tell him. "I am sorry."

Tears well up in my eyes now. Not for my mother, but this time, for me. How can I explain to him that I believe I am disappearing, as well? That pretty soon I'll be gone.

Tommaso stares at me. "I will find the keys," he says.

65

HOW DOES A MOTHER DROP OUT of your life? Hide behind a cape in a magic show and, poof, there's a pony in her place. Only to reappear sitting next to you in the back row of a theater. A magician did that to me once when our father took us to Vegas, a year or so after she left, and I cried and cried. The magician looked hurt and surprised, certain he'd picked just the right girl to have the woman appear beside. "Is she all right?" the magician asked.

My father replied, "Does she seem all right?"

Later, back in our hotel, I asked my father, "Are there any women magicians?" and he hemmed and hawed. "That's an interesting question," he replied. Which is what he always said when he had no answer.

But have you ever seen a woman pull silk scarves out of her sleeve or turn a deck of cards into a white dove that flies away? The only woman I've ever seen in a magic show was one who was being sawed in two.

66

THAT AFTERNOON, I WANDER AIMLESSLY up and down the narrow *trulli*-lined streets. Geraniums are everywhere. My head is filled with questions—only a few of which meeting Tommaso has answered. Apparently, my mother was a woman of secrets and stories, but she had seemed happy to me. I felt assured by her love. While what I saw yesterday chilled me to the bone, it does not explain her departure. Wouldn't she want to hold on to us, to the life we lived? A gloom comes over me, not only because of what I have learned at the Red House but also because I fear I will never understand what happened to her. Or why.

I stop at a trattoria and order a salad and a cold local wine. Then I wander back to my hotel, where I find Tommaso in an armchair in the lobby, holding a chain of keys. He smiles grimly. "We can go now if you wish."

I hesitate. "So you found the guy?" I am not thrilled by this news. I don't have to go. I can walk away. Except I know I won't.

"Yes. He's my son, actually. He is the guardian."

"Is he the person who kept it from becoming a disco?"

Tommaso nods. "Yes, my oldest."

I wish the guardian were not his son, that he had not found the keys. I was hoping this visit would not come to be. Call it what you like. A rabbit hole, Pandora's box. I am not sure I need to know more. I'm already angry about all the things I did not know. Still, I have come this far, and it seems to be an inevitability, a rock rolling down a hill that I can do nothing to stop. I follow him to his car.

ONCE MORE, WE ARE DRIVING along the pitted road. I cannot help but think what my grandfather saw as he drove this road daily with the captain. Diseases of the eyes. Children shaken with malarial tremors. Soon, the Red House looms, and we make our turn onto the long driveway. It seems even longer than before. We pull up in the shade of the oak trees and Tommaso gets out. Without a word, he walks ahead of me, his gait slightly off on the uneven terrain. We scramble through the overgrown weeds. Grasses scrape against my leg. I envision my mother, heading out into these fields to gather grain and forage. Or to meet her young soldier. As we approach the Red House, I can see it's in disrepair, but it seems to sit firmly, a neglected monolith of memory. As we approach, I am struck by a strange sense of familiarity.

At the steel door, Tommaso fumbles with the keys. Finally, he finds the right one and slips it into the large padlock that bolts the door shut. Removing the lock, he kicks the heavy door, and I can imagine the strong young man he must have been. The door heaves. Dust rises, and the air smells of mold as we walk into a dark cavern. At first, it is pitch-black. I can see nothing. But in some ways, I don't need to.

I get a sense of things when I walk into a house. It is part of what I do as a stager. I close my eyes. I smell the air. Is it fresh or stale? What about dust? But what I really feel when I walk into a house or apartment isn't anything tangible. It's almost a strange, mystical power. I know what happened there. I know when a woman was betrayed, or a beloved died, when a couple fell apart, or when it was just time to move on. The houses where people have "moved on" are the saddest. You feel the tug of ghosts.

The sensations come to me in snippets. A woman finds a receipt for a motel in the trash. A child coughs in the night. The man drinks his grief. Someone lies on a sofa, staring at the ceiling. A boy packs to go to college while his mother pulls weeds in the garden. I feel the losses of those I've never known.

And now, suddenly, I am gripped with an almost crushing despair.

At first, I see nothing beyond this cavernous room. There is one window, barred. Dim afternoon light filters in. As my eyes adjust, I see that the room is empty except for an old rusting automobile. It has no tires. The chassis just sits against a wall, rusting on its axle. "This was the car the capo drove," Tommaso tells me. "He took your grandfather to the dental office in it every day."

"My grandfather?" I stare into the car. Its leather seats are shredded. My grandfather, who was never mentioned to me, rode in this vehicle every day that he was here. I walk around it. I run my fingers along its rusty fenders.

Tommaso stands behind me. He rocks on his heels as I take it in. Slowly, I move around the room. The walls have crumbled, and chunks of mortar are strewn across the floor. On one wall, a sheet of paper is pinned. I try to make out its faded writing. It's a list of names. Besides the names there are two dates, meticulously recorded. And beside the dates, a list of books. There was a library here. I glance down the sheet. Gilla Gremigni checked out *I Prommesi Sposi* on May 24, 1943, and returned it July 23. And Josef Malkin checked out *The Count of Monte Cristo*. I look at the date. December 21, 1942. But it was never returned.

Tommaso points to the entry for the book that was never returned. "Your grandfather checked out that book. He read it to his children every night."

Malkin. Was that my mother's maiden name? I never knew that. I'm not sure I ever knew what her family name had been. It was just another part of her buried past. I gasp, my hand over my heart. But why was the book never returned? Why would my grandfather keep a library book?

I shake my head. That is when I see the words, carved into the wall. The carving is crude and very old, but still, I can make it out. I touch it as if I am reading braille. Run my fingers through the carved words.

Non sarò qui per sempre.

This is what she wrote on the back of her paintings.

Now I know that she really was here.

THE

THIRD STORY

———

67

THE LAST BURST OF AUTUMN warmth is gone, and a chill has settled in. In the morning, they can see their breath. There is nothing to protect them from the wind, the cold, the rain that has begun sweeping through the upper floors of the Red House. It has become an obsession. Fathers stand at the window, staring out, wondering how they will keep their families warm. Mothers, tears in their eyes, serve up cups of watery broth. But nothing can compete with the chill that has entered their bones. Even the sparrows have stopped coming into the Red House. They have found warmer spots to roost.

At night, families huddle to get warm. Most of them are still wearing the clothes they arrived in. Summery cotton dresses, short-sleeved shirts. Though they complain bitterly, they have no blankets. Viola lies in bed, her teeth chattering despite her mother's encircling arms. She listens to her mother's breathy sleep, her brother's short gasps. Her father breathes heavily, never snoring, because he lies awake, trying to find a way to escape. On the rafters, a pair of doves tremble. They have yet to find another home. Home is all Josef can think of. He needs to find the way home. Rudy whimpers on his pallet. He is hungry. They all are.

Except for Viola. She devours whatever Tommaso brings her. She tries not to. She tries to save a morsel and give it to Rudy, but the minute Tommaso hands her the sack with cheese, bread, the leftovers his grandmother made, she can't help herself. She is a greedy child, and she curses herself. She eats whatever he provides. She listens to the grumbling of stomachs. Mothers grow thin as they give what little they have to their children. Fathers wring their hands. But Viola sleeps, her belly full.

From time to time, she slips Rudy a crust of bread, a rind of cheese. She shares a boiled egg. He cups it in his hand, as if he has never seen anything like it before. Viola puts her fingers to her lips. "Shush," she whispers. "It's our secret. If you tell, it will go away."

Rudy never tells. He remains loyal to his sister. He doesn't know where the food comes from or when it will. He never says no, but he also never asks. But mostly she doesn't share. In the fields, she gobbles down whatever Tommaso brings her. While the others grow thin, she keeps flesh on her bones. One day, one of the Lithuanian women pinches the fat of her arm and stares at her with disdain. Viola pulls away. She has avoided that woman ever since.

Rudy is such a small boy. Frail, like Viola was as a baby. She feels remorse every time she eats. When she does not bring him something, he looks at her like a cat waiting to be fed. She knows that she should share with the others, or at least give more to her brother, but she can't help herself. Hunger is the animal that lives inside her, one she cannot tame. It eats at her faster than she can consume. She can smell the soldiers cooking in the early morning and late into the evening. The others smell it, as well. The mothers plead as the soldiers turn away.

68

THE BLACK MADONNA LIVES IN the hills. She has a shrine on the highest peak, and from here she presides over the fields of wheat, the vineyards and olive trees. From the time the first shepherd heads into the hills in springtime until he returns with his flock in the fall, she watches over his sheep and goats. The Dark Mother, as she is also known, makes sure that the crops grow and the animals are not eaten by the predators that roam the hills. At night, the residents hear them howl. The sheepdogs wear collars studded with nails to protect them from the wolves, which go for the throat.

In the fall, as the harvest begins, the Black Madonna journeys back to the church where she lives during the winter months. As she makes her way down the hill, a huge procession follows, and the whole town comes out. Wheat is tossed into the air like rice thrown at a wedding. Afterward, the fireworks begin.

The morning before the procession, Captain Cassini makes the happy announcement that the residents of the Red House may stay up an hour later than usual to watch the fireworks. And they may be outside during the spectacle. That afternoon, Tommaso whispers to Viola, "Meet me in the grove of trees. At nine." In the evening, as it grows dark, the residents file outside. When the crowd grows thick, Viola slips away. She sneaks into the darkness, heading to the grove. Tommaso is waiting for her.

He reaches for her hands. "You're cold," he says. Tommaso puts down his coat and motions for her to lie down beside him. She shivers as he holds her close. He hands her a sack that contains a hunk of cheese and bread. She eats like an animal. It is difficult for Tommaso to watch.

Then they lie back in the grass, and he strokes her face, burying his lips in her hair.

"It's getting too cold to meet here." He points toward another grove across the field. "There's a shed over there," he tells her. "If I can, I will come in the afternoon, about four o'clock, after my shift. I'll wait for you."

As they curl in each other's arms, the sky bursts into fire. In the hills, a Roman candle explodes, Catherine wheels spin, Bengal lights burn. Golden sprinkles rain down. They watch, pressed against each other, their faces aglow. The sky seems illumined only for them. Then, just as quickly as it began, it is over.

Viola extricates herself from Tommaso's grasp. "I need to go. My mother will notice."

He kisses her on the cheek. "I will see you tomorrow. And all the days after that," he adds with a playful laugh.

She tickles him as she rises. "I'll be there."

She kisses his lips, his warm hands.

THEN SHE SLIPS OUT OF the grove and back into the dark, empty fields. As she heads toward the oak tree, someone waves at her. Viola hurries along, but Leila catches up. "So," she says, "you've been with your soldier."

Viola walks more swiftly. "I don't know what you're talking about." She worries that there are crumbs on her lips from the bread she devoured. She runs a hand over her mouth.

"Yes, you do," Leila says. She bursts into laughter, and Viola hurries away, leaving her standing in the field.

69

A MOTHER KNOWS. EVEN AS THE fireworks explode overhead, Anna knows that her daughter is not here. She can feel it. Viola has slipped away. Every branch blowing, every shadow passing over the fields leaves Anna wondering. Even as the residents stand, heads tilted back, pointing at the green and red and blue starbursts overhead, Anna scans the crowd. She gazes out toward the darkened fields. Perhaps she can catch a glimpse of her daughter darting across the fields. But Viola is nowhere to be found.

When they were living in Turin (because now they are living here, aren't they?), she always knew where Viola was. If she wasn't in the apartment, she was at school. If she wasn't at school, she was upstairs with her grandparents, or down the street at one of her friends' houses. The circle she traveled in was small, known, predictable. But the Red House is a convoluted maze of stairs, corridors, passageways to get lost in, dead ends, with soldiers smoking in the shadows. There are hidden spaces, and then there are the fields. Miles of fields, with little fencing. Only the guards to keep them from wandering away.

And somewhere out there, her daughter roams.

WHEN ANNA WAS PREGNANT with Viola, she knew it would be a girl. She felt differently than she had when she was pregnant with Michele. He was restless and wild in her womb and nothing about him has changed much since. But with Viola, a kind of peace came over her. She loved being pregnant. She luxuriated in it. She never felt sick. Just tired. Deliciously tired. She could sit for hours in her favorite chair in the parlor and just stare out at the sky, the trees, the street. It gave her an incredible sense of joy. She'd rub her belly, and she could almost feel the child in her womb touching her back. If Michele was her love child and Rudy her mistake, Viola was the one she planned for. The one she truly wanted.

Ever since Viola was born, Anna has felt a strange connection to this child. Whatever sickness Viola got, Anna got, too, and vice versa—though this never happened with Rudy or Michele. They look alike, with their lush dark hair and doelike eyes. Anna's own mother, when she first saw Viola, clasped her hand to her heart. "She's you, the spitting image." In pictures, Viola resembles a younger version of Anna.

Since they have come to the Red House, Anna has felt her daughter slipping away. She is almost a stranger to her. But what bothers Anna the most is that she knows her daughter isn't telling her the truth. A wall has gone up between them. Now, Anna watches her daughter like a hawk.

The fireworks have stopped, and when Anna turns, she finds Viola standing beside her. It is as if she appeared out of air. Anna starts. "You frightened me," she says. "Where did you go?"

Viola shrugs. "I was just walking."

Her mother looks at her askance. "Alone?"

"Yes." Viola nods. "I'm always alone."

70

JOSEF HAS OPENED A MAKESHIFT dental office in one of the empty cells of the Red House. After his day in town, residents line up. He checks for cavities. He listens to their complaints about toothaches. If need be, he will pull a tooth.

Then they head down to the mess hall, where they eat whatever the cooks have been able to concoct, given the limited ingredients.

Afterward, Anna takes Josef by the arm. Despite the chill in the night air, she convinces him to stroll in the fields. As they walk amid the stubble, he chats about the goings-on in the dental office, and his rides with Captain Cassini. "His songbirds. It's all he talks about." Josef shakes his head. "Canaries. The country is going to hell, and he's talking about canaries." There's a cold breeze. Steely gray clouds mark the horizon. It might be smoke.

"Poor man," Anna says, though she can tell that her husband is happy to be working again. "He must be lonely." Josef grimaces. He has little sympathy for the captain. Anna squeezes her husband's fingers. "I want to talk to you about Viola."

Josef smiles. "Viola is an angel," he says.

"Yes, but I think she is seeing someone. Perhaps one of the soldiers." Anna shakes her head. "Not one of the boys here."

Josef shrugs. "Even if this is true, they're just children. What harm can it do?" His heart is racing. He's never told Anna about the young soldier coming to his office. He's known for some time that Viola has been seeing him.

"We were just children once, too," Anna replies, blushing.

Josef shakes his head. "You know it's not like that. She's still a child."

Josef keeps walking, but Anna stops. "I don't know where she is. I don't know where she goes. She is hiding something from me. She's my daughter and I know her."

He strokes his wife's face and then loops his arm through hers. "I will keep an eye on her. We will talk to her if need be."

That night, Anna breathes in the smell of grass in Viola's hair, not the powdery child she once knew. Anna plucks a blade from her thick strands. "Where are you going?" she whispers into the night.

71

ONE EVENING, ABOUT SIX MONTHS after my mother goes missing, our father comes home with a shoe box, which he puts on the dining room table. He looks pleased, satisfied with himself, though the sadness is always there, and for a moment, I think the box contains a puppy. That he's finally broken down and gotten us a puppy. We'd been begging for one for years. Of course, it doesn't occur to me that he wouldn't put a puppy in an ordinary shoe box. Nor would he get us one now, when he can barely keep the three of us together. Still, Janine stands back, biting her knuckles, as I open the lid.

There's no furry animal inside. Instead, as I peer into the darkness of that box, all I see is my mother's face. It's as if I have dragonfly eyes; I find myself staring at dozens and dozens of replicas of that smile with her warm, red lips, her dark, curly hair, and that round face. Like a plump Snow White. And she was plump—pleasantly so, as our father would say. She struggled with her weight and never really liked to have her picture taken, but I remember when we took this snapshot. We'd rented bicycles for the day. It was a happy time, and we'd fished, and even managed to catch one that our father made us throw back. It was too small, and we weren't going to eat it. "Not a keeper," he said.

The truth is that this picture is exactly how I remember her. If I see an image of her in my mind, it is this smiling face. Her dark eyes dancing, as if she's just playing a great trick on you. But not at your expense. She never laughed if you dropped your ice-cream cone, or if your fishing line got caught in the tree, as mine did shortly before this picture was snapped. If that happened, she wouldn't hesitate. She'd give you her cone; she'd climb the tree to free your line.

No, my mother never laughed at you. She always laughed with you.

And now I look down at the face, hundreds and hundreds of times, a fun house, in buttons. Hundreds of buttons, with violet trim. In a circle along the top is written "Have You Seen This Woman?" and on the bottom, the phone number for the Cherryvale police department, Detective Hendricks's direct line, beneath our mother's face.

"What are we supposed to do with these?" I ask my father once I've recovered from the shock of seeing her, multiplied over and over again, staring up at me from the inside of a shoe box.

"We're going to wear them," our father says. "And we'll give them away. Someone must have seen her."

But I don't want to wear them. I don't want to be known as the girl whose mother disappeared. Why not have me wear a yellow star? That would mark me just as well, wouldn't it? I actually said this to him, not knowing, of course, what I know now.

When he made us wear these buttons to school or to a party, we'd take them off as soon as we were out of his sight. But he wore them. Not only did he wear them; he handed them out at parties, at bake sales, at the office. He wore them to parent-teacher conferences, until we became not only the family whose mother disappeared. We became the family who wore the purple buttons.

I despise those buttons. And I hate the box. But I rationalize that at least once it's empty, there will be no more, and this phase of our lives, almost as horrible, and certainly as humiliating as the last, will be done. Besides, we try to reason with our father: "If she'd really run away, wouldn't she have dyed her hair blond and begun wearing glasses?" "But what if she has amnesia?" he'd argue. "What if she's had some kind of accident? She could be in a nursing home, a morgue."

But when the buttons are done, this will be done. Except the box keeps replenishing itself. Like Mary Poppins's carpetbag or the brooms in "The Sorcerer's Apprentice," they kept coming, until it occurs to me that this will never stop. This will go on and on.

72

ONE OF THE TEACHERS CLEARS OFF a shelf in the makeshift classroom where lessons are given in the mornings. On the shelf, she arranges books she has collected from the residents. She provides a sheet of paper and pen. That night at dinner, she bangs on her tin dish and announces that there is to be a small lending library. People who have brought books with them may leave them here for others to read. On a sheet of paper, she writes down the names of all the books people put on the shelf. She draws columns, with a place to write name, date borrowed, and date returned. Soon the shelf is thick with books in Hungarian, Romanian, German, and Italian.

One morning before leaving for work, Josef stops in the classroom. He runs his fingers over the books. Some of the titles are familiar to him. He has read many to his children over the years. *Les Misérables, Don Quixote, Robinson Crusoe.* Josef loves reading out loud. He has the voice of a radio actor—deep, resonant. When they were back in Turin, he practiced the different voices before he read a book to his children. They were mesmerized, not only by the stories but by the way he portrayed them.

Now he is looking for something new.

He skips over several that he has already read. And several he cannot read because they are in languages he does not speak. *Quo Vadis,* though in Italian, seems too ponderous. Then his eye lands on a thick, well-worn volume—one he has never read. *The Count of Monte Cristo.* He has heard of Edmond Dantès's perilous escape, and the revenge he ekes out against those who have wronged him. He has heard it called one of the great adventure novels. It's a long book. Josef doesn't care. It will take him six months, he reasons, to read it through, and by then they will be heading home.

He picks up the pen and writes his name on the sheet of paper. He checks the book out. December 21, 1942.

THAT NIGHT, BACK IN THEIR ROOM, Josef opens the book. His children huddle around him. Rudy and Viola sit on the pallet beside their father, while the Romanian boys play marbles in the corner, but as soon as Josef starts reading, they stop. They wander over and sit at Josef's feet. Josef is not sure if the boys understand the Italian, but they seem to be listening. Even their parents appear to listen. The novel is almost twelve hundred pages long, and there are many chapters. Josef decides to read ten pages a night.

Somewhere in the distance, paratroopers drop from the sky. Artillery fire resounds. Bombs are being dropped on Naples. Cities are left in rubble. Meanwhile, Josef is reading. "On the 24th of February, 1815, the lookout at Notre-Dame de la Garde signalled the three-master, the *Pharaon,* coming from Smyrna, Trieste, and Naples. As usual, a pilot put off immediately . . ."

And so he begins.

73

RUDY WAKES UP SCREAMING. Josef clasps him in his arms, but he will not be comforted. The Romanian family wakes and Rivka looks over, scowling. Anna slips onto Josef's pallet, clasping her son. "It's just a dream," she tells him. "Nothing real." He whimpers in her arms. It happens night after night. Perhaps it is the hunger. Or the cold. Whatever the reason, he wakes shouting. Anna knows how frightening this is.

She, too, experienced night terrors as a child. She recalls her mother reminding her, almost laughing. Perhaps such things are funny in hindsight. But the monsters seemed real. They came out of the shadows. They perched above her bed. No amount of comforting could console her, either.

Anna holds him to her in the cold darkness. She can't help wondering. It seems as if we spend our whole lives overcoming the terrors of childhood, the monsters that hide under the bed, curl in the corners of our sleep, perhaps only in order to be brave enough to grow old and leave this world. All the courage we gain as children seems to be for this one eventuality—to face our own death. What a dark thought. Anna has no idea where it came from.

She shudders. How can she comfort her sobbing child? How can she reassure him that all will be well, when she knows that, in fact, everyone we love will leave us, or that one day we will leave them? Or perhaps his needs are simpler. Perhaps all he wants is his warm bed and a home-cooked meal.

But Rudy can't help himself. He keeps screaming. Viola sits up. "Shut up," she shouts. Startled, Rudy cowers. Her parents glare at her. "I can't sleep," she says. "I just want to sleep."

74

RISING EARLY, VIOLA CAN SEE her own breath. Outside, the swallows perform their intricate dance, weaving in and out of the dawn light. She slips out of the warmth of her mother's arms. Shivering, she tiptoes into the cold hallway. It's still dark out. She looks carefully up and down the corridor. Not even the soldiers are stirring. She makes her way to the stairs. She's had enough. Viola can't bear Rudy's nightly whimpering, his night terrors. His cries that wake her. He knows that she is eating.

Surely there is a granary, a storage room where the soldiers keep their provisions. All she wants is a potato. A handful of grain to make a mash. She thinks of all the wheat the peasants scattered when they brought the Black Madonna down from her shrine, back to the church in town. She wishes she'd thought to gather some of that wheat in her hands.

She walks through the dark and chilly corridors with only her thin sweater to protect her from the cold. She pushes on doors that are locked or won't open. She wends her way through the maze of hallways. She comes to a large double door, the arched kind you'd find in a barn. She never noticed it before. The door is ajar, and a light comes from inside.

Viola peers inside, but all she sees is the glaring light. Gently she nudges the door. Inside, a man stands on a ladder with paintbrush in hand. Looming above him, as her eyes adjust, a white angel soars, its wings on fire.

75

WHEN THE DOOR CREAKS BEHIND HIM, Angelo turns. He expects to see the captain, who has been coming almost daily to check on his work. The captain can appear at any time. He never says much, sulks around, and leaves as silently as he came. But instead, a girl emerges from the shadows, her hair lush and flowing. The morning light shines behind her like a halo. Even in her tattered sweater, he sees how beautiful she is. She must be one of his angels. Then she speaks and he knows that she is real.

"Excuse me," the girl mutters, backing away. "I was looking for food."

"Ah, well, if you find any, please let me know," the man answers in a thick accent as he steps down from his ladder. He motions for her to come closer. He has the face of a young man, but his hair is streaked with silver. His skin is pale, with dark circles beneath his eyes. It occurs to her that he's been painting all night. He studies Viola. If his son had lived, he would be about her age. Perhaps they would have been friends, and played together. They might have become lovers. Now she is just a reminder of all he has lost.

As he stares at her, Viola looks around. It is as if the walls are dancing. They are covered in sheep and cattle, donkeys and dogs. There are saints offering blessings, and angels soaring through billowing clouds, flying through the heavens. They seem to be moving, encircling the room. Viola shakes her head, as if waking from a dream. "Where am I?" she asks.

The man smiles but says nothing. He hands her a brush. Guiding her to the wall, he folds his fingers over hers and shows her what to do. He helps her make wide, even strokes. He catches the paint as it drips down the wall. She dips her brush into the blue pigment and then the white. She paints the wings of angels, the flight of birds. She captures the clouds.

76

THOUGH HIS GRANDMOTHER PUTS HER savory sauces, her fish stew, the pasta she makes from scratch in front of him, Tommaso can barely swallow. He sits in front of her, pushing around his food, the way he did as a child. It is as if something is caught in his throat. He finds excuses to fix things around her *trullo*. There's the faucet that leaks and plastering that must be done because moisture is seeping in. "Nonna," he says as she stares at his plate, the food getting cold, "look at that wall. It's crumbling." He gets up and rubs the wall to show her the dust—anything to avoid the food placed before him. "I will go and get some stucco."

"Fix it tomorrow," Sofia says. "What is wrong?"

"I cannot eat while they are starving," Tommaso says. "They eat a thin gruel in the morning. A dry piece of bread. There is no milk for the children, no meat for their stews. Once a week, they are given a piece of fatty meat, which some refuse to eat. They forage for mushrooms and potatoes. How can we eat all of this when these people have nothing?" He cannot bear seeing the ravenous faces around him every day at work.

"Then we must feed them."

THE NEXT MORNING, SOFIA RISES earlier than usual. She heads out on her errands. Her first stop is Giovanni, the knife-wielding butcher. The shop is not crowded. Only two people are ahead of her. Giovanni gives her his big grin. "I'll be right with you, signora," he says. The man ahead of her is married to a woman who is very particular about her cut of meat. Sofia settles down for a wait.

As she waits, she observes Giovanni. He is not a happy man. Behind his smile, there's a sadness. He knows that his clients pre-ferred his father. They don't say so, but it's clear they are always comparing the two. "Oh, your father sliced the mortadella so thin." "It was never tough when your father carved it." Sofia thinks about this as she waits her turn.

"And so, Signora Bassano, what can I get for you today?"

"I'd like the head of a goat, please." He looks at her askance. "And any scraps you can spare." Sofia hesitates. "But no pork." Giovanni looks at her again, nods, and disappears in the back. He returns with the severed head of a goat, which he wraps, along with some fatty scraps he usually tosses to the stray dogs in the alley at the end of the day.

As she reaches into her purse, he shakes his head. "No charge today, signora. My gift to you."

She gives him a crooked smile, then thanks him and continues on her way. At the bakery, she asks for day-old bread. At the veg-etable stand, she wants the vegetables the vendor will not be able to sell. He gives her a big bag of cabbage and tomatoes and onions.

Then Sofia makes her way home.

77

TOMMASO NO LONGER LOOKS FORWARD to the end of the day. He finds the trek to his grandmother's arduous. He prefers to remain at the Red House to be near Viola. She is all he thinks of. He is always looking for her, hoping to run into her. Tommaso dreams of Viola. Even though he wants her as much as he's ever wanted anything, he won't touch her—not in that way. But he envisions a life together. He has learned the secrets of his grandmother's sauces. He can make Sofia's eggplant Parmesan with mortadella as well as she. He goes to her house as much to cook with her as he does to spend time with her.

He grates her Parmesan and chops her eggplants so thin, you can see through them. He kneads the dough for the orecchiette. She allows him to shape the dough into the tiny cups of pasta Puglia is renowned for. He tends her tomato plants, picking them when they are just ripe enough for the sauce. In summer, he peels the tomatoes, removing the seeds deftly with his knife. He stands with her at the stove as she stirs the sauce. Onions, basil, and tomatoes, which cook slowly for hours. On her stove there is often a pot of Bolognese, cooking slowly, a rabbit or chicken stewing in its own juices in her oven.

One day he will open a restaurant. It will be small. Maybe twelve tables, and he will cook all the recipes he learned at his grandmother's side. Viola will be with him in the kitchen, cooking, their children running in and out. He envisions a future for himself, as if he has been walking in a thick forest and suddenly a path opens that he must take.

When he reaches his grandmother's, she hands him a sack. He looks inside and sees a goat staring back at him. She hands him another sack filled with bread and vegetables. There is also a hunk of old cheese. He looks at his grandmother, not sure of what to do. "Make soup," she tells him.

THAT NIGHT HE SLEEPS AT his grandmother's. His mother never notices if he's home or not. He sleeps on the sofa and leaves early. It is barely five in the morning, and the ride is cold, dark, and slow because his saddlebags are heavy, weighed down by the head of a goat.

He goes to the mess hall and takes a large cauldron. He turns on the stove and drops in the onions, celery, and carrots he chopped with his grandmother the night before. Once they are sautéed, he adds several quarts of water. As soon as it comes to a boil, he drops in the head of the goat.

78

I FOLLOW TOMMASO THROUGH A warren of cement rooms, through the mess hall with its long wooden tables and the iron cauldrons still stacked in a corner. As we walk, he tells me about the head of the goat. "It made good soup, Laura," he tells me. He pronounces it "Lara." He leads me up several flights, past bathrooms with rusted sinks and filthy latrines, the cells with their straw pallets. I stare into rooms with no windows, only bars. This is a prison, plain and simple, yet my mother lived here. In the empty rooms, sparrows roost and fly in and out, and I realize that no amount of staging can hide what once happened here.

Now we walk in silence.

At last, he pauses in front of one of the cells. "This was their room," he says. He stands back and lets me step inside. The room, not much bigger than my bathroom at home, is gray and crumbling. Dark mold blooms on the walls. The straw pallets, all four of them, are still here, pressed against those walls. No wonder Rudy coughed. I try to envision my mother and her family sleeping in this cell, sharing it with another family. The wind blowing in. The cold. My mother as a girl here, pressed up against her mother. I run my fingers along the wall the way the blind children did. A dusty chalk coats my fingertips.

When I turn, Tommaso still stands in the doorway. It is as if he has reached a barrier that he cannot cross. But somehow I have been able to walk through this portal. I walk past him and he leads me outside. We emerge out of darkness into sunshine. Its glaring light makes me wince, and I blink back tears. We traverse the fields that lie fallow, moving toward a grove of trees. I follow him to a broken-down shed, its roof long ago collapsed. I peer in through a window. There is a cot, covered in filthy linens from decades ago. Again, Tommaso is silent. He shoves the door in slightly. It falls off its hinges. He tests the floor. Then he steps back and motions for me to enter. Inside there's the cot, a table, chairs, and a small stove. The room is coated in dust. Tommaso follows behind me. He heaves a heavy sigh.

"I haven't been here in a long time." He runs his hand over the cold stove. "It seems as if no one else has, either." He walks around the small space, then goes over to the bed and sits down. "This is where we came. Together."

I join him at the edge of the filthy cot. It is decades since my mother met him here. We sit side by side, as if we are waiting for someone to walk in the door.

79

VIOLA DARTS ACROSS THE FIELDS. The weather has turned cooler, and she wears only a thin cotton sweater around her shoulders. Her long, dark hair flies behind her in the wind, like a horse's mane. Her heart pounds in her chest and she can barely catch her breath, but she runs faster. The ground is hard, almost frozen, and her feet are in sandals—the shoes she wore here—but she doesn't care. She finds the cold bracing. She has never felt more alive. That morning, Viola tore through her lessons and raced upstairs, where she splashed water on her face. She made her way stealthily down the back stairs of the Red House. She came to the door that opened to the fields. It was unlocked and she slipped out, past the giant oak, heading toward the fields. And now she is running. Not running away, but running toward.

At the edge of the field, on the crest of a small hill, stands an old toolshed, ramshackle and long since unused. The windows are covered in newspaper, and the door hangs by only one hinge. But this is where Tommaso said to meet him. She peers inside. She can barely make out a small stove, a mattress with a clean quilt on it, and a table. On the table are some oranges. But no sign of Tommaso. Viola doesn't want to wait inside. Instead, she flings herself to the ground at the top of the hill.

The Red House is behind her. All she can see is the great expanse of fields, where wheat has been cut down to the stubble. Fields lying fallow, but once spring comes, they will be alive with olives and lemons and grapes. For now, it is a brown, grim landscape. There is a pink tinge to the clouds, and no breeze blows. Viola closes her eyes. If it were not for the Red House, this could be a farm anywhere. And she could be waiting to see her boyfriend, just like any other girl.

The late afternoon, just before dark, is the best time of day for them to meet, when the daytime guards head home, and before the new guards have taken over their posts for the night. But he is late. A million thoughts race through Viola's head. He has been teasing her all along, or this is a trap that she has fallen into. But would someone leave a clean quilt and oranges on the table if they were setting a trap?

She hears a whistle and sees him coming across the fields. He's grinning, his blue eyes sparkling, and as he draws near, he holds out his arms. "There you are," he says. "Why are you waiting outside?" He grabs her hands. "You're chilled."

Viola isn't even aware that she's cold. She feels warm, flushed. "I wasn't sure if you would come."

He laughs again. "If I say I will, I will. You can believe me."

Viola laughs, too, but her laughter is more nervous. Can she believe him? Can she believe anyone now? "I just wasn't sure," she says again.

He wraps an arm around her waist. "Come. Let's go inside."

INSIDE THE SHED, IT IS dark and musty, and it takes Viola a few minutes to see. There's a table and an old cot. Some old tools lie in a corner. There's a small potbelly stove that is cold, as is the shed, but it is not as cold as outside. It has windows, a door—luxuries Viola can barely recall. "Thank you," she says.

Tommaso folds her in his arms. He breathes in her hair, kisses her cheek. For a time they stand like this. They are two young people who do not know what else to do. When Tommaso leads her to the cot, she hesitates. "Just sit with me for a while," he says.

She perches at the edge of the bed. Though it smells musty, the cot is soft as a sweet memory. Tommaso runs his hands up and down her back. He cups her face in his hands. They lie down, and he buries his face in her hair, against her breasts.

She sits up abruptly, remembering where she is. "I should get back," she says. "My mother will notice." He kisses her once more. Then Viola pulls herself away.

80

Dear Michele,

I am wondering how you are. I think of you all the time, as does your father. We are doing well here. Your father has been allowed to work in town as a dentist and he is very pleased about this. He seems more like his old self than he has in years. I am working in the tailor shop. It is not the most interesting occupation, but it keeps me busy, sewing and repairing uniforms for the soldiers who watch over us here.

The weather has turned colder, even here in the south. I had no idea. I assumed it would stay warm. I imagine it is cold at home, as well. But we are making do. The food is not what we are used to, but the children are well.

I will keep this short because I do not know if these letters are reaching you, or if you are writing back. I would love some word—even a postcard—about you and your grandparents. How are they faring? I hope you have time to check on them and have a meal with them from time to time. And Viola keeps asking for her cat. I hope you are stopping in to feed him. Any word would mean the world.

I pray that this reaches you and that I will hear from you before long.

As always, your loving mother.

81

WHEN TOMMASO ARRIVES AT HIS grandmother's, Sofia scolds him. "Ah, you're late, as always." She waves her spoon at him.

"It's good to see you, too, Nonna." He kisses her three times on the cheek.

She hands him a knife. "Get to work," she says. He has no idea whom they are cooking for. All this chopping and slicing. All he can think of is Viola as he slices an onion paper-thin. Then he starts on the potatoes. She will bake them with the onions and cheese. It is one of his favorite dishes. Today he has little appetite. He tries to imagine the restaurant he will open and Viola greeting their guests, their children running at her feet. He smiles as the knife slices his finger. Sofia sees the blood gush before he does.

"Oh no," she says. Quickly, she hands him a cloth. "Go into the bathroom. Wash. Are you all right?"

"I'm fine," he says, holding up his finger and pressing the cloth to staunch the bleeding. He glances at his finger. Just a knick, but fingers bleed, and he has gotten blood on his shirt.

"Take that off," she says. "Go clean up and get out of that dirty uniform." She puts a clean shirt for him and his uniform in the bathroom, but first she inspects his finger. "Yes," she declares, "just a little cut. But so much blood."

In the bathroom, he runs his hand under the water. The bleeding is already subsiding.

Gingerly, he removes his stained shirt and leaves it on the edge of the tub, where his grandmother will soak it. Then he removes his dirty uniform, as well. Standing in his underwear, he throws cold water on his face. He washes his hands again. The blood still flows, but it is easing. He keeps the rag wrapped around it as he puts on his clean trousers.

The tortoiseshell hair clasp Sofia wears to pin up her thick silver hair sits at the edge of the sink. He looks at it and then picks up the clasp, cradling it. He has a flash of Viola, her lush dark hair tumbling across her face. He hesitates, then slips the clasp into the pocket of his uniform.

When he comes out of the bathroom, he holds up his hand. "Look, Nonna. All better."

But at dinner, he barely eats. "Are you unwell?" Sofia asks.

"I'm just tired," he replies.

"Maybe it's that cut. It's unlike you. Maybe it made you ill."

He nods. "I'm just very tired," he says.

"Well, you should go home and get some rest." She clears the table. Then she hands him the sack of food scraps and vegetables she collected that day—things he will drop into the soup at the Red House. She shoos him out the door.

IN THE MORNING, SOFIA IS preoccupied. Her sleep has been restless. She's worried about Tommaso. Perhaps his work is more difficult than he tells her. He seems distracted. Not his usual self. She's thinking about him as she gets ready to set out on her errands, collecting scraps from the butcher, stale bread from the baker. She stumbles into the bathroom, flipping on the light. She washes her face, cleans her teeth, and then brushes her long silver hair. When she is ready to put it up, she reaches for her tortoiseshell clasp, but it is not on the edge of the sink, where she always leaves it.

Stooping down, she looks on the floor, behind the sink, the toilet. It's not on the floor. "Oh, Carlo," she mutters. "I'm losing you one piece at a time." She looks around her *trullo,* under her bed, in the kitchen. But the hair clasp is nowhere to be found. "I'm so forgetful," she says again to her dead husband. "If you were here, you'd know where I left it."

She heads out, her silver hair flowing behind her.

82

YOU CAN ALWAYS TELL THE DAUGHTERS who don't have mothers. Their shirts aren't pressed; their hair is a tangled mess. A rat's nest, my mother would say. You can tell the girls whose fathers don't know what to do. With boys, it's different. They're half feral. Their socks never match. Their jeans have holes. Our father tried, but he was useless. When he combed Janine's hair, she complained of too many flyaway strands. When he used oil to tame it, she cried, "I can't go to school looking like this," and flung herself onto her bed.

I presented a different set of problems. He could not get a brush through my tangles. At one point he threatened, as my mother had from time to time, to have me shorn. We hired a housekeeper, a woman named Evelyn, whom my father found through an agency after it was more or less apparent that our mother wasn't coming home and he couldn't manage alone. I'm not sure what he told Evelyn about our mother, but she never asked or mentioned her.

She arrived on Monday mornings from wherever she lived— somewhere in the Bronx—and she stayed until Friday afternoon, when we got back from school. Fridays were memorable because Evelyn was always antsy, looking at the clock. She had to make the 4:17 bus. Evelyn cooked and cleaned for us. She made casseroles, which she put in the freezer for the weekends. She was waiting at the bus when we got home from school.

But she wasn't a warm, fuzzy person. She had a job to do and she did it. There was the whole matter of our periods. My father was helpless in that regard, and Evelyn not much better. She assumed that somehow we'd know what to do. Perhaps she couldn't grasp that no one had ever told us. When I started to bleed, she handed me a box of sanitary napkins and a booklet. That was how I learned I was a woman.

It didn't occur to me until I was older that Evelyn probably had children waiting for her at home. Still, I liked her. She was consistent. She was always there. But she had an uphill battle with us, and as soon as Janine entered high school, she left. She came for a visit once, but then we never saw her again. After that, we were more or less on our own.

83

THERE ARE NO MIRRORS AT the Red House. No way to see how your hair looks in the morning, if there is a blemish on your face. No way to check if you have bags under your eyes, if your cheeks are gaunt. No windows where you can walk by and catch your reflection. No silver platters like the ones they have at home. Here, you can only see yourself through the eyes of others. A concerned glance, a look away. Unless someone tells you that you look tired or your hair is turning gray, there is no way to know.

Still, Anna tries to see herself in the bottom of the tin plates they wash after their meager meals. She polishes the plates, but no matter what, they are too dull. All she can make out are dark ghostlike shapes and shadows. For Anna, this is especially disconcerting. She has lived much of her life in front of mirrors. Her parents' dining room was walled with them in a way that made the room look much bigger than it already was. She spent her meals glancing at herself, making quick adjustments to her dress, her hair. She would look over the shoulder of whoever sat across from her—it could be her brother, a family friend, or a prominent associate of her father's—to move a strand of hair that was out of place. Often, her mother teased her. "Anna," she'd say, "remember what happened to Narcissus. You're going to fall in and drown if you aren't careful."

When she became a dressmaker, she understood that she was not alone in this regard. The women whose dresses she made were endlessly assessing themselves. "Does this look good?" "Do I look fat?" "Does it make me look younger?" Anna understood that most women loved praise, but what good was praise if you couldn't see for yourself? How could you even know you existed if you did not see yourself reflected back? Early in her days as a couturier, Anna had mirrors installed on all the walls. She wanted her clients to be able to see themselves from every angle. To admire the sleek back of an elegant navy blue wool suit. To see the neat fit of the bodice.

Anna always loved fashion. Even as a young girl, she combed magazines for pictures of clothing that appealed to her. Sometimes she asked her mother to have an item made for her, and her mother would drag her to the tailor, who would fashion for Anna exactly the dress she desired. Once the tailor made a silk dress in a floral pattern that was not the one Anna had picked out. She refused to wear it, and eventually gave the dress away. It was not long before Anna began making and designing dresses of her own. She had her parents buy her a dress form that was close to her size, and on it she pinned the dresses and coats and suits that would become her wardrobe. She grew obsessed with hemlines, snug fits, neutral tones. Black, grays, soft beige. No red, no turquoise, no yellow. Those bright colors were for peasants. Not for her.

She didn't need a job, but she wanted to work, and she'd loved it until the Racial Laws were passed and she lost her clients. Then she began inflicting her obsession on her daughter. Anything Viola wore had to pass inspection. A hem had to be just so, the back smooth. Yet when it came to the small, practical tasks—a button that needed sewing, a sock to darn—Anna would not even bother to thread a needle. It was high fashion that interested her. Classic patterns and simple accessories. Patent-leather pumps, a strand of pearls, a thin veil on a hat—one that would just barely conceal a woman's face.

Now, at the Red House, Anna finds herself disappearing. What does her beauty matter if she cannot see her own face? How can she believe Josef when he tells her that she is as beautiful as the day he met her? He will not tell her if her hair is streaked with gray, though she has been discovering gray strands in the shower. He won't tell her if her eyes are sunken and red. He just says, "You are always beautiful to me." It is never enough. She tries to find her reflection in Josef's eyes. But she is so tiny. It is impossible.

84

MY MOTHER SITS AT HER vanity table, putting on lipstick. I don't knock because it's a bathroom we all share—even my father, though he has a half bath off the kitchen where he shaves and reads the newspaper on the toilet. She never seems to mind when I burst in. But she doesn't move. It's as if she's in a trance. She's just staring into space. I go to run the bath, and she snaps out of it. She brushes her hair furiously.

I slip into the hot water and watch as she twists her hair around her fist like a tightrope and fastens it with her hair clasp. I expect her to sit by the side of the tub and brush my hair, as she often does. Instead, she gets up to leave. She turns and looks at me. "You should knock next time," she says.

IN MY TEENAGE YEARS I have bad skin. I pick at it. I try to cover the damage with oily makeup, which, according to my grandmother, only makes me look worse. My father takes me to a skin doctor, Dr. Lazar. He's a kind, gentle man and he looks at my skin as if he's reading a sacred text. I feel no judgment. Only Dr. Lazar, searching for the right words.

Finally he says to me, "Don't look too closely in the mirror. You'll only see the flaws."

85

VIOLA COLLECTS THE TINIEST of things. In the fields, she finds a dull coin, the blue eggshell of a bird long ago fledged, a gold stud that no longer has its mate. Back in Turin, she did the same. Like a crow, she grabbed anything shiny. She kept them in little boxes. Sea glass from their summers by the shore, bits of broken ceramic, a butterfly's wing. She guarded them all, her treasures. She has a new collection: a yellow feather, a pinecone, a mysterious black stone.

When she and Tommaso meet in the shed, he brings her something. But nothing like her little treasures, which she tucks in a corner of their cubby. What he brings, she devours. He brings her an apple or an orange, and one afternoon a piece of chicken. The aroma makes her weep. She thinks of her grandparents, the Friday-night dinners at their table. Viola swears she will save the chicken for Rudy, but she cannot resist its savory smell. She tears the flesh from the bone. The chicken is still warm, and the juice slides down her hand. She has never tasted anything this good before.

Tommaso says nothing as she licks her fingers. He has never seen anyone eat in this way. Like an animal. He watches her with a tender fascination. He digs deeper into his satchel. "Close your eyes," he tells her. "I have a surprise for you."

Hesitantly, Viola shuts her eyes as his fingers fondle her hair, twisting it. She feels the clasp. She opens her eyes. Reaching back, she touches it, then takes it into her hands. It is tortoiseshell, polished, translucent. She holds it up to the light. "It's the most beautiful thing I've ever seen." She fastens it in her hair.

With an index finger, he raises her chin to his. His lips are moist and salty. She licks them with her tongue to taste him. He cradles her face. His touch is both gentle and harsh. His hands rough and smooth. She grasps his arms as if she will fall. His muscles are taut. She wonders if he couldn't just carry her away. They kiss for so long, Viola thinks she will faint.

THAT EVENING AS SHE IS WASHING in the rusty sink, Leila comes in. "So are you enjoying yourself?" Leila asks, barely able to hide her amusement. "I've seen you," she says. Viola feels a shiver go through her.

"Seen me?"

Leila winks. "You know. In the fields. With the soldier."

Viola shrugs. "I don't know what you're talking about." Leila tosses her head back, laughing her high-pitched laugh.

Viola suddenly fears her mother's rage. "Don't tell a soul. Promise?"

Leila puts her finger over her lips. "Your secret is safe with me." Then she laughs again.

86

AS TOMMASO APPROACHES HIS GRANDMOTHER'S house, he doesn't remember how he got here. It's as if he's walking in his sleep. He can't get Viola out of his mind. She's all he can think about in the morning when he rises, and at night when he slips between the sheets. He wishes he had someone he could talk to about her. The father he never knew, the brother who never has time. Tommaso has never been in love before, but he trembles when he sees Viola. He recalls the look in her eye when he first saw her. As he helped each of the Jews down from the buses, it was her eyes that caught his. For an instant she returned his gaze, and that was enough.

Through the window, he sees his grandmother at the stove, her silver hair tied up with pins. He can smell his favorite Genovese sauce. It has been cooking all day. His mouth waters at the thought of it, yet he will eat only a small amount—as little as he is able. And then his grandmother will wrap it up into a parcel he will carry to Viola the next day.

"Ah, at last, there you are," she says without looking up. "Tommaso, you haven't seen my hair clasp, have you?"

"No, Nonna." Tommaso shakes his head. It is odd that she doesn't look at him. Perhaps she suspects something. "I'm sure you left it somewhere."

"I've looked everywhere," she tells him.

Tommaso shrugs. "Look again." Then he adds, cruelly, "You must be getting forgetful."

87

THE ROOM WHERE ANNA SEWS uniforms is dark and dank. She can barely see what she is doing. Fortunately, it is not complicated work. Mainly buttons and tears. She never got the dress form she requested. She cannot make new uniforms, though she can recut the ones she is given to fit other soldiers. Some of the uniforms are pierced by bullet holes. Some are splattered with blood. She does what she can to conceal these flaws.

Anna looks at her hands. Her nails, once carefully shaped and lacquered, are broken. She picks at the dirt beneath them. Her work is tedious and solitary. She comes in each morning to a pile of uniforms waiting to be mended. No one ever brings more or picks them up while she is here. She is just supposed to sew.

It makes her sleepy, this tedious work, and lonely, too. She worries about her parents. Even though she writes to them dutifully once a week, she never hears back. She does not know if they are well. She has no idea if the letters reach them. She assumes that they are fearful for her, too. She worries about Michele, and wonders if he remained at home, or with his antifascist friends, who will only bring trouble. Perhaps he is in prison. And poor Rudy, with his cough and his sweaty brow. She worries night and day over that child, even as Josef stays up, listening to the boy's heart and holding his feverish body against his own.

And then, of course, there is Viola. Her precious daughter. Anna always wanted a daughter, and for the first ten years of her life, Viola was the child she'd dreamed of. So loving and obedient, always ready to help her set the table or to assist at the shop. But that stopped a few years ago. Viola began to have friends, and she wanted less to do with her mother. Anna did not resent it.

But now, in this place, Viola disappears and Anna is certain she's spending time with that soldier. What can she do about it? She can't punish her daughter. She can't keep her home. But she will warn her. The soldier will only hurt her. He's not to be trusted.

She turns back to her sewing.

THAT NIGHT, WHEN THEY ARE in their room and everyone else is asleep, Anna whispers to Viola. "He will leave you," she says. "The minute something happens, he'll be gone."

Viola purses her lips. "I don't know what you are talking about."

"Do you think I don't see you? You think I don't know?"

"Well, whatever you think you know, it's not like that. He is decent. I trust him."

Anna laughs. "You don't know what trust is. You are too young."

Viola gets off their pallet and goes to the window. "I am not that young, Mama."

"I'm still your mother, and I am warning you: Don't get carried away."

Anna rolls over and tries to sleep. Viola stands at the window. The breeze chills her, but she doesn't go back to bed.

88

"LET'S GO OVER THIS AGAIN," Detective Hendricks says. His partner, a big Irish guy named Duffy, pretends he is my mother. He opens the door with his key. Janine and I watch as my father narrates the disappearance as if it were a story.

It's odd, watching our father try to tell a story. He prefers facts. Porcupines have over thirty thousand quills. It's difficult to relocate bears because their inner compass has already determined where home is. Trees can die of grief. Our mother wasn't like this. She was good at telling stories. She didn't need to read them from a book. She made them up, like the one about a wolf cub who befriended a child.

We acted them out with her, along with our regular fairy tales. I'd be the wolf and Janine was a little girl who found its lair. But Cinderella was our favorite. I loved the way the mice and the pumpkin and even Cinderella transformed themselves into footmen and a carriage and a princess. I was usually Cinderella, because I was the older one, and Janine liked being one of the mice. I was nervous when the clock struck midnight. "Tick-tock," our mother would say.

Tick-tock, pretending to be the clock.

I would have to rush out of the palace and lose my glass slipper. Would we turn back into our real selves again? Would the prince find me and cherish me? He always did. Was this my mother's story? Had she morphed and found herself at the center of a story different from the one I knew? Usually, our mother had Cinderella declare her independence and insist on having a career. We laughed at that version. It was so silly.

"She'd take off her coat," my father says. "She'd hang it on that hook."

He points to the hook on the wall. Duffy pretends to hang up his coat. But my eyes are on Detective Hendricks. I observe his icy blue eyes, his sturdy back. Nothing misses his hawklike gaze. Then Duffy goes through the motions of sipping juice, making an invisible sandwich, which he proceeds to take a bite out of. He hears a silent knock. He looks up, goes to the door. He looks through the peephole. He lets someone in. Not a stranger, Hendricks reasons. Someone she recognizes. She departs with that person, and leaves everything else behind. Her wallet, her keys, us. Perhaps she was convinced that something was wrong. An emergency. There's been an accident. Nothing terrible. Nothing too serious. She expects to be back soon.

Or perhaps none of it's true. Perhaps she just left of her own volition.

"All right," Detective Hendricks says, "let's go through this one more time." We are actors trapped in an endless play. And so we begin again.

89

I WAS RAISED IN A HOUSE of hooks. There were hooks to hang your towels, which were assigned to us by color. Mine were blue; Janine's were orange, a color she despised. Hooks to hang your jackets and rain gear, your pajamas and your robe. Hooks for pots and pans, for soup ladles and spatulas. Everything in our house had to be put away in its place or hung on its hook. Though my father was a military man and valued order, it was our mother who insisted on all the hooks.

She came to it gradually. At first we thought it was charming, her need to hang all our belongings up. Only as we grew older, after she was gone, did it seem to reflect a more sinister side. There were picture hooks on the wall leading up to our bedrooms. "The gallery," she called it. Pictures of us as we ascended the ladder of time, being born, aging, and then freezing just a few steps from the top. At the bottom, my parents' wedding in Naples, my mother walking barefoot on the shore, tossing her head back and laughing, the waves lapping the hem of her wedding dress, my father, trailing behind her, also barefoot, his pants cuffs rolled up. He is tossing rose petals into the air.

My mother cradling me in our apartment in Brindisi shortly after I was born. Pictures of us on the shore, then the four of us shortly after Janine was born. After that, we moved to New Jersey. Here we are on a fishing trip somewhere up north, on a hike in the Catskills. It was Janine who pointed out that our mother's bright smile fades as she climbs the wall, but I didn't see it. "Look how happy she was before she came here," Janine liked to say. It is true that she missed the place where witches made new broomsticks on a June night and the inhabitants collected green walnuts to make a potent brew. But I never thought of her as unhappy.

Slowly, our mother disappeared from the wall. "She was taking the pictures," I argued, but Janine said that wasn't so. "She wasn't even there." Janine claimed she didn't really go to school plays or camp weekends. "You're remembering her wrong." Whatever the truth, the photos stopped abruptly near the top of the stairs, as did the marks on the kitchen wall that indicated how much we'd grown each year. Yet she'd already hammered the hooks into the wall. It was odd to climb those stairs and see the empty hooks—a constant reminder of what our lives had become.

90

IN THE MORNING AFTER HER CLASSES, Viola rushes down the stairs and along the cold, dingy corridors until she comes to the large double doors. She pushes to see if they are open, and when they are, she goes inside. Angelo is on his ladder, brush in hand. On the wall he has sketched angels and saints, donkeys and dogs, clouds and the sky. His brush drips blue paint. He is working on heaven. "Ah, you are here," he says in his rudimentary Italian, a soft smile on his lips. "I wondered when you would show up."

"I wasn't sure if you wanted my help," she says shyly.

"Oh, but I do. I need your help."

She smiles. "Good."

"I don't want to take you away from your friends or your studies."

Viola shakes her head. "I prefer to be here."

He points to the green pigment. There's a dragon that needs tending. "Dip your brush in there." The dragon has an arched neck, short legs, and a fiery mouth. In front of it, Angelo has drawn a woman with long, dark hair who holds up her hand, taming the beast.

Viola knows little about Angelo. They barely speak the same language, though she knows he is Hungarian. He wears a wedding ring, but she has not seen him with a wife. His face is riddled with wrinkles, but she does not think he is that old. She cannot know that long ago, in some previous life, Angelo was an expert forger. There was little he could not copy or duplicate. Passports, paintings, even money, though he found counterfeiting too time-consuming. If a musician can have perfect pitch, then Angelo has perfect sight. He went by various aliases, posing at one time as the famed, but nonexistent, Hungarian composer Riccardo Durgno.

As the phony composer, he sold musical scores that he attributed to Mozart for a significant sum, and he would have gotten away with it had not some other, legitimate composer found numerous copying errors when he tried to lead an orchestra using one of Angelo's scores. He might have languished in prison had the fascists not released him, finding him useful to their cause. For a time, he was tasked with forging Italian identity cards for the Nazis. Eventually, Angelo crafted his own identity cards, and sneaked into Italy himself. He became an itinerant restorer of churches until some petty bureaucrat discovered that he was Jewish, stamped his passport "ALIEN," and he ended up here.

Together, they work on the dragon, and while it is drying, Angelo guides Viola to another place on the wall where she is to paint. He has already etched the drawing into the cement. A tree of life. It is a large pine with many branches, each hung with a different fruit. Viola paints an apple and grapes. She dips into the blue pigment and mixes it with some white. Even when the paint drips, Angelo does not correct her. Even if it is not perfect, he doesn't seem to mind. He watches as she paints a bluebird. While the paint is drying, he hands her a knife so that she can carve the mosaics where he has drawn the lines.

"Why do we carve up the paintings?" she asks.

"In my country, this would be a mosaic," he explains. "Here, we can only pretend."

91

VIOLA OBSERVES EVERY LEAF AND flower, the shape of every cloud. No detail is lost on her, as if a curtain has been opened. The dying vines, the shafts of wheat have all been made visible. Any mood that travels across her mother's face, the despair in her father's eyes. In Tommaso, she perceives a deep longing, deeper than any she has ever known. In Angelo's face as he paints his chapel, she envisions a glow. It seems to engulf him. She cannot explain it. She only finds satisfaction if she paints it.

In the morning the swallows dart, and they become brush-strokes. The clouds on the horizon are billows of white and gray pigment. In the clouds, dragons, castles, princesses reside. Everything takes shape. She draws. In the notebook she has been given for her lessons, she sketches her hand, a soldier's face, the oaks, their trunks entwined, that soar outside the window. She is about to blossom like a flower. She feels it in her bones. She is outgrowing her skin. She is a butterfly emerging from its cocoon. She's about to pop open, and another person will appear.

It is as if she has been in shadows. Now she has kissed a boy. She has painted an angel. And nothing will ever be the same.

92

IT WAS UNDERSTOOD IN OUR FAMILY. Do not touch our mother's paints or brushes. *Verboten,* my mother used to say, for some reason using the German word. Forbidden. Yet somehow, that room behind the laundry where she painted was the only room I wanted to explore. It was as if, among the scents of oils and turpentine, I could breathe my mother in.

One day, when she's out, I go into her little room. I'm not very old. Maybe nine or ten. But I am jealous of whatever fascination this room holds for her. I dip two of her brushes into the paint that lies thick on her palette. I rub the paint onto a blank sheet of canvas. I do it again and again, adding red and blue, crushing the brushes into the canvas.

Later that evening, just after dinner, my mother comes upstairs. In each hand, she holds one of her precious sable brushes, now destroyed. "Laura," she asks me, her voice firm, "did you go down to my studio? Did you do this?" Of course I deny it. I blame it on my sister. It's easy, because she's five years younger. Easy for her to take the fall. But as she continues interrogating us, it becomes more and more apparent that my story is falling apart as Janine holds true to hers. She did not touch the brushes.

I'm sent to my room. Straight to bed. I'm crying into my pillow when my mother comes in. Then she tells me, "I don't mind that you used my brushes as much as I mind that you lied to me." She puts her hands tightly around my arms. "Promise me, Laura. Promise me that you'll never lie to me again." I sob as she holds me, repeating that it was the lying, not the brushes, that mattered to her.

As far as I can recall, I never lied to her again.

93

"THE LAST PERSON TO SEE HER is the first person we suspect." That's one of the basic tenets of police work. But that would be me. I'm the one whose hair she tucked behind my ear. I'm the one she last kissed good-bye. I suppose one could include Janine, though our mother slipped away before the play was done. Or Mrs. Grunska, the head librarian. Mrs. Grunska is a white-haired widow who always has a pencil tucked behind her ear and sits in a rocking chair, reading to six-year-olds during story hour. I doubt that Mrs. Grunska could be a suspect for anything—not even stealing a cookie from the bake sale.

I have an alibi, but I'm in seventh grade.

It's my father they focus on. "We just have to rule him out," Detective Hendricks would say. They ask him an endless barrage of questions. "How did you and your wife get along?" "Any bumps in the road?" "How was your intimate life?" They come over so often that my father decides he needs a lawyer. "Just in case," he tells us. In case they press charges. It's standard operating procedure. By the time I'm thirteen, I'm fluent in the language of law enforcement: perps, vics, the ME.

I never once suspect my father. I'd never seen them fight. There had never been a harsh word, at least not one that I ever heard. At the movies, they held hands. In the evenings after dinner, we'd find them cuddled together on the couch, watching TV. I don't think they ever slept a night apart.

Now, at night, my father cries. Deep, guttural, almost inhuman sobs. I hear him through the walls. Years later, at a zoo, a peacock that lost its mate shrieks in this way and flings itself against a glass door. It will make me think of my father.

While I never suspect my father, I'm pretty sure Detective Hendricks does. There are times when he'll glance over at Duffy or heave a loaded sigh, and I think that he's going to call child services and have them take us away. Every few months, a lady in a pantsuit and clipboard rings the bell. She looks at our rooms, checks the pantry, and makes sure we don't have any bruises. Her visits infuriate my father, but he says nothing.

While I never suspect him, there are times at the mall, or when he's dropping us off at school, often walking us right up to the door, because *one never knows, one can never be too careful,* I feel eyes on us. I have no idea how a person can sense that, but apparently there's some scientific evidence that attests to the fact that we do have eyes in the back of our heads. We know sometimes when someone is staring at us, even if we can't see who it is. There's always a parent or teacher in the produce aisle, staring at us. It seems as if you can accuse someone, indict and convict a person with just a look. It's an expression my father used sometimes: "If looks could kill . . ." I didn't understand it when I was young, but I understand it now.

Some nights, he doesn't even bother going to bed. It's clear in the morning from his ashen face and the dark pockets beneath his eyes that he's barely slept. I trot off to bed as he combs through records. Their bank statements and credit cards. Looking for a hint of where she's gone. Even of her own free will. But this—this void, this emptiness—it is impossible. Janine thinks that she was taken by aliens.

At night I sit staring at the TV, waiting for the door to open, for her to walk in with that singsongy voice of hers. "Laura, it's Mommy. I'm home." We don't understand any of it. We keep asking our father when she's coming home. Why is it taking so long? As if this little charade, this game of hide-and-seek, will be over soon.

It's difficult for me to remember. I try, but memories slip away. I'm no longer sure what I've made up. Sometimes I recall her one way, sometimes another. My father tends to idealize her. ("She was perfect," he says in his grief. "Perfect in every way.") I remember her that way, as well. But not Janine. It's as if we didn't have the same mother at all.

94

STEAM RISES FROM THE CAULDRON as Tommaso stirs the pot. He tastes the sauce. The balance of garlic and basil is good. The tomatoes are cooking down nicely. He drops in a few more basil leaves and lowers the flame. He will let it simmer another hour or so. In a pan he sautés chicken cutlets. Tommaso has become chief cook for the barracks. The soldiers realized he was better at cooking than anything else. As a guard, he engaged too much with the prisoners, slipping them contraband such as soap and towels. Captain Cassini wasn't pleased.

But he is good at this. He cooks for the other guards in their makeshift kitchen in the barracks. He prepares their evening meal except for the pasta, which they make themselves. When he is done, he tidies up. He makes sure the lids are tight on the pots. He swabs the stove. Then he slips into the prisoners' mess hall. It is the late afternoon and everyone is out in the fields and the guards are changing their shifts. In the mess hall, large soup kettles sit on the stove. Into these he drops the meat scraps from Giovanni, the butcher, and overripe tomatoes from his grandmother. He has bread that the bakers were going to throw away. He has carted these in his saddlebags. Tommaso stirs the pots and covers them again. Then he goes downstairs to leave.

As he makes his way to his bicycle, he sees the women in the fields. Today he is late, and must get to his grandmother's before dark. Viola will understand. It happens from time to time. She's stooped over, foraging, but she looks up and gazes around her. "You know I'm here, don't you?" he whispers in her direction. "I'm watching out for you."

AS HE HEADS UP HIS grandmother's walk, Tommaso carries a sack of fresh bread and wine he picked up on the way. His grandfather always brought something home to her, and he's happy to do the same. Tommaso contemplates what his life would have been like if his father had lived. How different would he have been? He runs the same thoughts through his head day after day, and they always bring him back to where he started. Perhaps he should have gone to trade school or studied law. Instead, he wears a soldier's uniform, and his future is a foggy road he has yet to travel.

Tommaso has never had a mission, a purpose to his life. But now he feels as if he does. He wants to help Viola and her family. He wants to save them. As his grandmother is preparing orecchiette with cheese and tomato sauce, Tommaso tells her he is worried that the Red House is just a holding pen. Soon they will be moved. Who knows what will happen to them?

Sofia Bassano pauses as she stirs the sauce; then she looks at her grandson, perplexed. "Why?" she asks. "Why would anyone send them away?"

95

THE SHED IS WARM, ALMOST HOT. The heat stuns her. She has been cold for so long. Tommaso came earlier and stoked wood in the small stove, and though the fire has since gone out, it has kept the place cozy. He tosses two more pieces of wood into the stove and puts on a pot for coffee. "You need to warm yourself," he says.

He reaches for a sack on the table. "And this," he says, "is for your soup tonight. It's from my grandmother." He opens up the sack. It is filled with mushrooms. Tears come to her eyes. "It's not much," he says, "but I will bring more every day."

He rubs her hands with his. In a few moments, the water boils and he pours coffee. He has brought cheese sandwiches for them. Viola devours her sandwich and the coffee. Then he guides her toward the bed. Viola hesitates. Tommaso wraps his arms around her. "I will never hurt you," he says, a promise that will prove empty. But Viola is young and naïve; she believes what he says. Like Tommaso, she has never been in love before. This world feels new, fresh, as if no one has ever lived in it before her.

Tommaso has gone to some trouble. He has swept and brought wood. He has put a clean quilt on the bed, and clean linens underneath. And he brought her oranges. They sip their coffee. "Do you know anything?" she asks him. "How long will they keep us here?"

"I don't know." He shakes his head. "But I don't think you'll be here long. The Germans cannot control Italy forever. This war will end, and you will go home."

She looks away. "I'm not sure I even want to go. . . ." He cradles her, kissing her forehead, her cheeks. "But we have heard of people being sent north. . . ."

"I don't know about people being sent away. But I know you will be safe here."

Viola trembles. "How can you know for sure?" She shakes her head. She wants to stay in this shed with this man forever. She wants to stop time. "Please, let's not talk about this. I'm sorry I asked."

Tommaso takes the cup of coffee from her hand. He pulls her close and kisses her. His tongue probes. Viola finds herself falling into that kiss and his arms as if she were tumbling down a bottomless well. Gently, he unsnaps the clip and her hair tumbles into his hands. He caresses her thick locks, breathes her in. After a while, they must leave. "Tomorrow?" he asks, kissing her one more time.

"Tomorrow." She reaches up to kiss him back.

As she is leaving, Viola digs her fingernails into the ground. The earth is hard and cold, but still she scrapes at it. When the grit embeds itself under her nails, she takes the sack of mushrooms and carries it home.

WHEN VIOLA RETURNS TO THE Red House, she dashes up the stairs. It seems as if she's always running. She is expected in the kitchen, where she helps the other women with dinner. On her way, she spies her father, returning with Captain Cassini. She runs faster and slips into the mess hall, where the women are peeling potatoes. It is her mother's turn to make the stew. As Viola races in, Anna looks up at her, pursing her lips.

"Where have you been?"

"In the fields. I went out walking."

Anna glares at her. "In this cold?"

"I can't just sit inside all day." Viola raises her voice in a way that surprises her mother. "I need fresh air. I need to walk." She shows her mother her filthy hands. Then she opens the sack. Anna peers inside. There is a rich, earthy smell. She reaches in and fondles the mushrooms. Anna looks at Viola's filthy hands. "You foraged for these?"

Viola nods. "I did."

Viola has never lied to her mother before. Not about anything big. A gelato she'd had with friends after school, homework she'd said she'd finished. Later she would confess, because she always felt Anna could see right through her. There was something about her mother's stern gaze—not the loving motherly one, but the one she used when she had an inkling of doubt about what her daughter was saying.

Now she is surprised at how easily lies slip off her tongue. How she learns to build one upon the other, memorizing them like conjugations of a language she is determined to learn. At first, she thought that they would slip out of her body into her mother's, like some parasite. But she has settled easily into falsehoods. They have become second nature. If anyone had told her that she'd become a liar, she would have doubted that person, but it is easier than she imagined.

That evening as they sit down at their long tables, one woman weeps. There are mushrooms in the stew.

96

VIOLA LISTENS TO THE WIND. Though she shivers, she doesn't mind the cold. Perhaps her body is warming itself from the inside out. She thinks of all the startling changes that have happened to her over the past few years. She was forced to leave the school and friends she had known and loved all her life, only to learn that they were not really her friends in the first place. As soon as she was forced out of school, they forgot about her. She left behind the safety and comfort of her home, her grandparents, who wept and clutched at her as they left, and came to this place of hunger and hardship.

Yet now, in this cold prison, she has found a mentor who is teaching her how to paint and a young soldier who is teaching her how to love. Before coming to the Red House, she was a silly school-girl, concerned with her looks, her clothing, with notes passed in class and secrets whispered in hallways. She was crushed when her friends forgot about her. Now she barely recalls their names. Their faces have blurred. All she thinks of is being in Tommaso's arms. And standing on the scaffolding, holding a paintbrush or putty knife in her hand as Angelo guides her.

In a matter of months, she has gone from foolish girl to a much wiser one. She runs her hands over her hips, her thighs, her breasts, which have blossomed. She is thin—they are all thin and hungry here—yet her body is fuller, more complete. It is a body men will yearn for. She is admired by an artist, loved by a soldier. She has left childhood behind. As if, in entering the Red House, she passed through a portal from which there is no turning back. Beside her on his pallet, Rudy coughs.

The winds that blow across the fields keep him shivering and awake. Winter is creeping in. As Rudy rests, his breathing heavy, Viola glances toward the open window frame. It has begun to snow.

97

IN THE MORNING EVERYTHING DISAPPEARS. The fields, the trees, even the Red House. The snow came silently in the night, sneaking up on them—not like rain. The dusting of snow looks ghostly. In the morning light, Viola shivers. She is so cold, she thinks her teeth will crack. The fuzz on her arms and legs stands up. Even her mother's touch is freezing. She pulls away and crawls off the pallet. In the morning, she is as tired as she was the night before. There is no rest here for her, or for anyone. She sees it in her parents' eyes, in their hollow stare of disbelief.

There is nowhere they can go, nothing they can do to get warm. One of the older residents—someone's grandfather—has gotten ill and has to be taken away. Others are weak. There is no hot water to bathe in, no heat except the stove where they warm their meals. Just weeks ago, Viola was at home with her cat. She played the piano and took drawing lessons. Whenever she wanted, she could race upstairs and see her grandparents. Now all of that is gone.

When they were told they were leaving, Viola had gone through her things. She had worn a favorite summer dress and a light sweater. She didn't bother packing her wool dress, her winter coat. They were going to the south, after all, and besides, how long would they be there?

When she asked if she could take her cat, her mother laughed. "Your cat will be waiting for you when we come home."

98

IN THE EVENING, VIOLA SLIPS into the chapel. She has gotten into the habit of going there at dusk or after dinner, when Angelo will not be working. She likes to stand alone, beneath the angels and the beasts, the dragons and the saints. When she is painting, she never stands back to see what they are doing, but when she stands alone in the cold, dank room, she feels awed. They make her feel safe, as if they are looking right at her, as if their only purpose is to protect her.

Viola has never been religious. Temple was not a part of their lives. But there is something about this chapel and the paintings on these walls that make her believe, as if they are speaking to her. She gazes at the fiery dragon she painted, its burning eyes, its menacing look, and at the woman who stands before it, her hand raised, as if she could tame the beast.

Viola has never considered death before. Why would she? No one she loves has died. And all of them—her grandparents, her parents, Rudy, and now Tommaso, and, yes, even Angelo—they love her back. But suddenly, in this room, she thinks about her sins. She thinks about the old man who was taken away. She has lied to her parents. She has eaten while others are starving. She has not shared her food. And her thoughts are impure. Perhaps she should become a Catholic and go to confession. Tell a priest all she has done. She tries to make the sign of the cross, as she has seen her friends do. She understands, standing in the chapel she is helping Angelo paint, the promise of Paradise.

And what would heaven be like? It would be filled with cats. On walls and thrones and beds. Everywhere. She smiles at this thought, thinking that Angelo should add cats to his vision of heaven, when she hears the door creak behind her. Turning, she expects to see

Angelo, but it is her father who stands in the doorway. "I was wondering where you disappear to." He gazes around in the dim light. "You come here."

"Yes, mostly I come here."

"What is this place?" Josef steps in and pauses, looking up at the murals.

Viola shrinks, afraid that he will be angry with her. "A chapel. Angelo invited me to help him."

"Ah, the Hungarian painter. You have been helping the artist?"

Viola nods. "He has been teaching me. I like to paint."

Her father steps farther into the room, putting on his spectacles now. "And what have you painted here?"

She points with pride to the dragon. "I painted his tail."

Her father smiles. "He frightens me."

Then she points to a woman. "She's taming him."

"Women can be very strong." He strokes her hair. "Sometimes stronger than men." He drapes his arm around her shoulder and together they look at the murals.

She shows him the clouds she helped with, and an angel.

"Ah, you painted an angel." He smiles—proudly, Viola thinks. "You know, they say that when a child is born, it possesses all the knowledge of the world. It knows everything, but then an angel touches the child right above the lip, shushing it, and erases all the knowledge." He taps Viola in the dent between the lip and the nose. "That dent," he tells her, "the philtrum, is where the angel touched you."

Viola runs her finger along the dent.

"Come, Pigeon," he says, taking her by the hand. "It's time for bed."

99

THE SOLDIERS CHATTER AMONG THEMSELVES and the residents overhear. Rumors float around the Red House. This is not their final stopping point. It is just a way station. They are to be sent somewhere else. Shipped to the north. The inhabitants whisper among themselves. There are stories of houses with Jews living inside being boarded up and set on fire. Businesses destroyed and shopkeepers dragged into the streets, never to be seen again. There is talk of trains full of Jews. The kind used to ship animals to slaughterhouses. No one knows where these trains are going.

Of course, they don't believe these stories. How could they? These are folktales, meant as warnings to instill fear. No one, not even Josef—a man given to scientific inquiry and a belief that where there is smoke there is fire—would believe these *bubbameisters,* these old wives' tales. They push them out of their minds like cobwebs. They are just rumors. This is what Josef tells Anna. But she is terrified for her parents, to whom she writes diligently, without response. And Michele. Do the letters even reach them? Why don't they write back?

There is talk of deporting the Italian Jews, as well. Not only those in the north but those who have been sent south, too. Mussolini's biggest obsession is for cars and roads. And now that he has built all those roads, it is clear he wants them traveled. Half the Jews think that this gossip is rubbish. They have been brought to the Red House—even if they are living under hardships—for their own protection. But others take a more sinister view. This is a way station. A stop along the way, as more and more Jews are gathered together before they are shipped away.

Josef does not believe this.

But Anna does.

100

CAPTAIN CASSINI'S WIFE HAS THREATENED to leave him. "It's me or those birds," he tells Josef. "It's her sense of humor," the captain says. "She can be funny that way." As he drives Josef to the dental office in the morning, the captain ruminates about his trouble. "I love my birds and . . ." He hesitates. "I love my wife. I can't just let them go. They can't live on their own."

Josef recalls his father's dovecot. How all the pigeons huddled together, how he'd muck out their little cages and give them fresh seed and water. They'd perch on his finger and stare at him with their red beady eyes.

"Isn't there somewhere else you could house them?" Josef has grown weary of the captain's endless chatter about his birds. There is something unnatural about it. It disturbs Josef that the captain worries about birds but doesn't seem to notice the people under his care who are hungry and cold.

The captain slaps his hands on the wheel, startling Josef. "I don't know why it didn't occur to me." He grins as they bounce along the pitted road. "I will have an aviary built at the Red House. It is the only way to keep the peace at home." The captain plans his aviary. He wants it painted bright yellow. With floral designs. It will brighten up the mess hall. "Don't you think the residents would like it?" Captain Cassini asks Josef. He can hardly contain his excitement.

Josef holds his instruments, which he still carries back and forth, in his lap. "Yes, I'm sure they will."

THAT EVENING, WHEN THEY RETURN from town, the captain approaches Angelo. Given that Angelo is designing a chapel, the captain assumes he can build a birdcage. The captain explains that he needs him to build an aviary. Angelo looks at him askance. "To house six songbirds. We will keep it here in the mess hall. I think the residents will enjoy the distraction."

Angelo nods. "They might."

The captain pulls out a piece of paper and a pen and begins to scribble. "This is what it should be like. There must be a section for the females. The males must be kept in a separate area, or they will not sing. We must build breeding boxes for when we are ready for them to mate."

"And obviously you know which are the males and which are the females."

The captain chuckles. "Well, sometimes the only way to know is if the canaries get into a battle to the death. The males will do that, not the females."

"There are other ways," Josef says, standing back. "You can tell a female if she lays an egg."

The captain laughs. "Thank you for stating the obvious."

"Or," Josef ruminates, "you can sex them."

Captain Cassini looks at him askance. "Do you know how to do that?"

Josef shrugs. "I know how to do it with pigeons. Canaries can't be that different."

Captain Cassini nods. "All right, the dottore here will be your consultant. I want two breeding boxes, two separate enclosures for the males, and larger areas for the females."

Angelo looks at the captain skeptically, but he has a vision. He wants the aviary to be large, so that the birds to have room to fly. It will have tiny portals and various feeding stations. "And perches," the captain says. "Of different heights. And private platforms for building their nests."

Angelo takes this all in. "I will need thick wire. And a soldering iron. A hammer, wire cutter, dowels." He rattles off a long list. The next morning, a delivery arrives.

ANGELO STOPS WORKING ON THE CHAPEL. He turns his attention to the birdhouse. He spends hours measuring, drawing, designing small perches, toys and platforms on which they can build their nests. Viola wakes to the sound of his hammering. When Viola can't find him in the chapel, she follows the noise to a room off the mess hall.

The slats have gone up. The frame is taking shape. Viola marvels at the intricacy, the platforms for their nests, the small wood carvings of butterflies and insects that hang inside for the birds to peck at.

Before Angelo can ask, Viola starts to measure the slats. She prepares the fine wire mesh. The mesh is sturdy, with tiny openings so that the birds cannot catch a claw or a wing. She stretches it out on the ground, holding it taut as Angelo cuts.

"You are a very good assistant," he tells her, ruffling her hair. He chuckles to himself. "Here I am, the great artist of murals and frescoes, building cages for birds." When he is done with the frame, he begins to carve little perches out of wood. He creates feeding stations. He fashions tiny tables with centers scooped out for birdseed. He makes a birdbath out of clay. It is a dollhouse for birds. He paints it yellow, as the captain requested.

While Viola is helping with the frame, Angelo begins carving flowers and paints them bright colors—red and blue and green. These he strings from the perches and the ceiling bars.

When it is done, he steps back, admiring what he has made. He turns to Viola. "We have made a cage within a cage within another cage," he says grimly. "Like Russian dolls."

101

WE LIKE TO TAKE ROAD TRIPS. That is, my mother likes them, and we all go along.

My father gave up on planning our travel. He's always losing deposits. She'll change her mind a dozen times—canceling one reservation, then making another. She thinks she wants to go to Florida but then decides that we should see New Orleans. Once, we drove all the way to Memphis, where we stayed in the hotel with ducks. Another time, we went out west, to the Grand Canyon and Monument Valley. What my mother loves about road trips is that if you see something you like, something interesting, you can just stop. You can stay as long as you want. You don't have to be anywhere. If you want, you never have to leave.

"Open-ended time" is what she calls it. Open-ended. Story of my life.

That's how we wound up at the Corn Palace. We stayed and stayed, and once we got on the road again, it was too late to find a hotel or even a place to eat. This is why she always throws pillows into the car and stocks a cooler with sandwiches and drinks. A jar of peanut butter, crackers in Tupperware so that they won't go stale, bananas, some ham and cheese sandwiches. Once or twice, we had to sleep in the car, but that was part of the fun. It was an adventure, she said. She seems to like that. She loves surprise parties, detours, unexpected guests, unplanned stops. Serendipity. We can be in the car, our teeth chattering, hunger growling in our stomachs, and she'll look at all of us and say, "Isn't this fun?"

But her favorite place is always the Pine Barrens. It isn't that far from home, and she loves to get lost on its roads, driving through its pristine forests. She says it reminds her of home, though we have no idea why. We're not even sure what she means by "home."

Once, we drove up to a large meadow where there was a young bear trailing after its mother. But every time the bear got close, its mother roared and chased her cub away. The cub ran off, but soon it was following her again. It looked like one of those silly, repetitive games mothers play with their children—like peek-a-boo. The cub approached and its mother chased it away. Except the young bear was howling and its mother roaring. "That's called bear emancipation," our mother said.

"Bear emancipation?" I asked.

She'd read about it somewhere. The cub had reached the age of maturity, and its mother was ready to mate again. So she sent it away. Often the cub doesn't want to leave and fend for itself, so the mother will chase it again and again, threatening her cub until it leaves her. We watched, mesmerized, as the cub kept trying to catch up to its mother and she roared until it skulked back.

Over and over the cub tried to catch up, and each time it was rebuffed, until finally the cub sat on its haunches, emitting a loud groan, as the mother, who never looked back, wandered off into the distance. We sat in stunned silence. I glanced at my own ashen-faced mother.

Tears streamed down her face, but she said nothing. She wiped them away and drove on.

102

MY DENTIST TOLD ME THAT scientists once thought that we inherited tooth decay and gum disease from our mothers, the way we inherit color blindness, baldness, and hemophilia. There seemed to be a direct line between mother and child. But there is a new theory. A baby's mouth at birth is pristine, devoid of bacteria. It is pure until it is kissed. And, in most cases, it is the mother who does the kissing.

I think about this as I wander through the town. My grandfather was a dentist. And my mother kissed me, once upon a time.

103

SHE CALLS. I'M SURE IT'S SHE. I'm about sixteen, and she's been missing for four years. I'm going to summer school for math and touch typing. I flunked math and I need to learn how to type, my father insists. "So you'll be able to get a job." It's hot, and no one else is home. On the second ring, I pick up. A woman's voice says, "Laura, is that you?"

"Mom?" I cry. "Mom?"

"How are you?" she asks. "It's been so long. You have no idea how much I've missed you." Her voice is surprisingly calm, almost robotic. She asks me about school, about how Dad is doing. She asks about Janine. And the dog. She knows about Moxie. How could she know this? I beg her to come home, and she says she will. She'll be home soon. "I'm not that far away," she says. And the phone goes dead.

I stand there holding the receiver. Was it a waking dream? I can't believe it wasn't real. She called me. I am sure of it. For days I walk through the house, numb. Janine thinks it's one of my "moods." My father thinks it's some strange female issue he can't begin to understand. But I know differently. At night I puzzle that call. Some prank. Am I losing my mind?

Though it's been years since I've spoken to him, it's impossible for me not to call him now. He's the only one who'll understand. The only one who'd believe I'm not mad. I still have his card. I've kept it all these years, in my sock drawer.

He answers on the first ring. "This is Detective Hendricks."

"She called me," I say.

He's silent. He doesn't even ask who this is. "Are you sure?"

"It was her voice."

"I'll be over," he tells me.

The first thing I notice is that he's aged, but in a good way—his features seem more solid, his eyes, if anything, more blue. And he isn't wearing his wedding ring. I point to his finger. "You're not married anymore?"

"Ah," he says, "now you're the detective?"

He looks me up and down. I'm in shorts and a red halter top. He can see that I've changed. I'm not the little girl I was when we met. This is the Gigi moment, I guess, a musical my mother loved. When suddenly you're not a little girl anymore. He can't help himself. His eyes go to my breasts.

Then he tells me that he's seen a lot of scams in his day. Forgery, counterfeiting, all kinds of cheating, but you really can't disguise a voice.

Still, he doesn't rule it out. "It might just be a crank, but if she calls again, ask her questions only she can answer." What was the name of the parakeet that escaped? (Petie.) What was the costume you made for me the day you disappeared? (Turtle.) What was the name of our first puppy? (We never had one.) "And listen to the sounds. Is she on a road? Do you hear background noises?" At the door, he turns to me once more. "Let me know if you remember anything else."

I start to cry. I haven't broken down in so long, but now I'm crying and I can't stop. "Laura," he says, "I'm so sorry." He wraps his arm around me, holds me to his chest. I put my arms around his neck. He smells of aftershave. His skin is smooth. I nestle deeper into his shoulder, my mouth on his neck. I haven't wanted boys my own age. I haven't been with any of them. I don't even know if I'm capable of whatever it is the girls say they long for in darkened rooms and the back seats of cars. But now I know. I want him.

And he wants me. He presses his face into my hair, kissing my head as I wrap my arms tightly around his neck. I'm kissing his neck, his face, reaching for his lips, but he pulls away. "Laura, this is a bad idea." Gently, he extricates himself. "I'm going to leave now." I beg him to stay, but he refuses. This time.

104

THE CANARIES HAVE ARRIVED. There are six of them. Captain Cassini brings them in a small carrier. Slowly, he releases them one at a time, while Angelo and Josef look on. The captain hands each canary ceremoniously to Josef, who tilts them over, spreads their legs, and separates the feathers to expose their soft underbellies. Once he declares if the bird is a male or a female, the females are placed on the little perches Angelo has built, and the males are given their own enclosures. The birds are so bright that Viola, who is standing beside her father, feels as if she is looking into the sun during an eclipse.

At first, the birds seem tentative in their new home. They stand in the corners, testing the bars. They pluck at the hanging wooden plants and caterpillars that Angelo carved. Soon they grow more comfortable. They flutter around. Some dip into the birdbath and ruffle their feathers. They eat heartily from the birdseed in the small feeding stations.

The residents file by and stare at the structure. Some cannot believe their eyes. Captain Cassini smiles like a proud parent as the birds flutter around their new home. "Step back," he says to the residents. Somewhat cowed, they obey. When they do, the birds start to sing. One of them plunges into the bath. It grips the edge of the small clay dish, dipping its beak into the water and splashing water on its wings. Another bird munches on a sunflower seed. There is a wool blanket folded beside the cage, and Captain Cassini instructs the residents that at night they must cover the birds. "Otherwise, it will be too cold for them."

One man mutters something in his own language. Later, Josef tells his family that the man was speaking Romanian. He said, "What about how cold it is for us?"

Still the residents stare at the birds in awe. Rudy smiles as he reaches a finger inside and strokes the soft feathers. The birds are friendly. They start to sing.

105

IT'S A COLD, WINTRY AFTERNOON as Viola races across the fields. Her birthday was last week but passes with little fanfare. But now she is a teenager. She shivers even as she runs. She still wears the summer dress and threadbare sweater she brought with her when they arrived in the early fall. A light snow has fallen, and her shoes leave tracks. Her toes are freezing, but she hardly registers the cold. Tommaso will be waiting for her, and in his arms she will be warm. She runs with a sense of purpose. Now everything she does has a sense of necessity. Her father would say that she has lost the sparkle in her eyes.

As she runs, Viola takes in the world around her. The endless

fields that lie fallow. In a few months, they will spring back to life
with grapes and olives and wheat. In the distance, she sees houses,
the hint of a village. The sky is big and the clouds immense. One
day, perhaps, she will paint all of it. Viola longs for her place in a
larger world. For now, this will have to do.

And there he is, in their warm shed. Tommaso has stoked the
fire. He waits for her, and when she reaches him, he pulls her to him
toward their cot. He has a thermos of hot, sweetened tea, which
he pours, and it warms her as they perch on the edge of the bed.
She cradles the cup in her hands. It is so hot that it almost burns,
but Viola doesn't care. Warmth has become unfamiliar. Tommaso
is wearing a wool overcoat, and she presses against it. Everything
about him scratches her skin. His coat, his beard, even the calluses
of his hands. She trembles at his touch.

They kiss. He kisses her hair, her neck, her hands. He slides his
hands under her dress. He is so warm, so gentle. "I brought you
something," he says. He smiles and his eyes twinkle. At first she
thinks it might be a gift for her birthday, though she did not tell
him because she has never shared with him her age. Besides, every
time they meet, he brings her an offering. Usually, it's the rem-
nants of the meal he shared the night before with his grandmother,
but today he reaches into his satchel and pulls out a gray sweater.
It's too big for her, and moth-eaten, but warm and soft. "From my
grandmother," he says. "She was going to throw it out."

Normally such an offering would appall Viola, as it would her
mother. Hand-me-downs would be given to their servants, or the
poor who beg on the streets. Anna would never think of allowing her daughter to wear anything used. In fact, Anna was always
cleaning out her closets, getting rid of things—often clothing or
shoes she had worn only once or twice.

"I can't take this," she says, thrusting it back at him. How will
she explain it to Anna? But the sweater is warm, and she is very
cold. Tommaso clasps her hands in his.

"You're freezing. Please take it. Tell her you found it in the fields."

When Viola returns, wearing the gray sweater, her mother looks at her, pursing her lips. Viola expects a scolding, but Anna never says a word.

106

TOMMASO RISES FROM THE BED. "This is where I loved her," he says, more to himself than to me. I find myself cringing at his words, as if this were something I was never meant to hear—which I suppose I wasn't. Taking my elbow, he leads me back out into the fields. The sun is blazing, and we both blink. Then he snaps his fingers, as if suddenly remembering something.

Once more, I follow him through the fields and tall weeds that line the perimeter of the forgotten Red House. He pushes through the heavy doors, and we move down another miserable corridor to another set of stairs. "Watch your step," Tommaso says. Stones lie in piles, as if an earthquake shook this place. In the darkness, Tommaso pulls a flashlight out of his pocket. I follow the stream of light. We walk until we come to a pair of double doors, bolted shut. Once more, Tommaso takes out his keys, fumbling with the lock.

107

AS ANGELO PAINTS IN THE CHAPEL, the angels talk to him. He is troubled, and they offer advice. He explains that a living angel has come to him. That she appears at his side and wants to paint with him. "I believe it is my son," he tells the angels in his head. "I believe he has come back to me." Never mind that his visitor is a girl. He is sure that his baby has been returned to him.

With difficulty, Angelo waits for Viola to show up. He cannot go looking for her. And he never knows when the door will creak and she will appear, bathed in light, ready to take brush in hand. In the months that they have been here, he has watched her change. She was a young girl when she arrived, but she has grown older, taller.

If he closes his eyes and prays, will she appear? Can he summon her at will? If she is truly one of his angels, then he should be able to conjure her. When he was a boy, waiting for a bus with his mother, she would tell him to close his eyes and will the bus to come. When he opened them, the bus would be miraculously there.

Of course, he realized when he was grown that his mother had already seen the bus, that she knew it would be arriving at any moment. But for years he'd believed. Now the door creaks, and there she is. His living angel, shining in the light. He has willed her here.

He descends his ladder. He goes to her, clasping her hands. Before she can speak, he pulls her to him, crushing her against his chest.

108

THEY WALK TO THE TREES. It is far enough away from the Red House that no one can see her. Once they are in the grove, Tommaso takes Viola's hand. His hands are rough but gentle. She loves to run her fingers over them. Her hands are freezing and she trembles. As they walk, they make small talk. He asks about her parents, and she inquires politely about his grandmother, whom she's never met. Then she says, "I'm worried about Angelo."

Tommaso looks at her blankly.

"The artist who is painting the chapel. He seems strange to me."

Tommaso nods, taking this in. "Artists can be strange." He hesitates, then adds, "Or at least that's what I've heard."

Somehow this assuages Viola's concern. It makes sense. He is moody. They slip inside the shed, where it is warmer, and sit on the edge of the bed. He has brought her an orange and some cheese, which she eats right away. Then, reaching up, Tommaso takes the clasp from her hair. He tries to push strange associations with his grandmother out of his head. Carefully, he places the stolen clasp on the table, where it seems to chastise him.

Her hair tumbles over her shoulder. Viola rarely wears the clasp, hiding it from her mother, but on days when she knows she will see Tommaso, she slips it into the pocket of her sweater. They sit together on the cot, and he kisses her, hands reaching toward her breasts.

She feels the urgency of his mouth, and his hardness as he presses against her. She feels a moist sensation between her legs as she presses back. A ripple begins to go through her—a feeling she's only experienced once before, when she stood on top of a high building, looking down. A tingling that expands, spreading down her thighs, until she thinks she will cry out.

THAT NIGHT, AS SHE LIES beside her mother, Viola wants to make that sensation happen again. She knows it is a secret. Her mother warned Viola about menstruation, and once, awkwardly, how babies are born, but her mother said nothing about this pleasure. Viola is sure this is not something to be shared.

She listens as Anna's breathing grows heavy; then she reaches between her legs, searching until she finds the spot and moves, ever so gently, so as not to disturb her mother, until that terrible pleasure sweeps through her again.

THEY ARE SO COLD. The night air blows in through the windowless frames. There are no covers. No way to get warm. The chill gets into their bones even as they huddle next to one another. During the day, it's not much better. There is nowhere to go to escape this cold. After meals, the children stand around the cauldrons, trying to warm themselves, but when they walk away, they are just as cold as they were before.

Somewhere down the corridors, the canaries sing until they are covered. Then they grow silent and sleep.

109

JOSEF SITS IN THE MESS HALL, listening carefully. The latest rumors have everyone on edge. There is talk of deportations. Work camps. Trains, not like the ones they came on, but cattle cars. In the evenings after their meal, the men sit around the mess hall tables. Some who have secured tobacco smoke. Others just sit, sipping their water, longing for wine. Viola overhears some of their chatter. They are worried. Jews are being shoved into ghettos in Warsaw and Krakow. Or they are being rounded up and sent away. But to where? No one seems to know.

The chatter around the table is in different languages. Somebody has heard a soldier say that Jews are being taken to open pits, stripped naked, and shot. Men, women, and children. Thousands have been tossed into mass graves, some still alive, then buried. Their belongings are sorted in town squares and sold or given to the soldiers.

Josef shakes his head. This cannot be. "It is one thing," he argues, "to confine or deport us, but to kill us? Because we are Jews?"

"You have no idea what they are capable of," a Lithuanian man replies. "We will all be sent to the north soon."

Angelo sits at the table, as well. He listens but doesn't say a word.

WHEN VIOLA GOES TO THE CHAPEL, Angelo is on the ladder. He does not look at her or say a word. "What should I do today?" she asks him. But he does not reply. "Are you angry with me?" Still he does not respond.

She looks at the mural. There is a winged horse rising from a corner. It has only been faintly sketched, as if Angelo is not sure. As she picks up a brush to paint it white, Angelo snaps at her. "Paint it black," he says.

"Are you all right?" Viola asks.

Angelo says nothing more. He is finishing the details on an angel that hovers near the ceiling. When he steps away on the scaffolding, Viola can see that he has given the angel her face.

110

ONCE I START CALLING Detective Hendricks, I can't stop. I call him in the morning, at work. I call him late at night. He's given me his card and I keep it in my wallet, next to my driver's license and student ID. I call him if I think I see her. I call him if she comes to me in a dream. After a while I don't even look for excuses. I phone him with whatever pops into my head. I beg him. I plead. I have to see him.

Other boys want me. I have an allure. A backstory, if you will. I'm always the girl whose mother disappeared. I'm interesting and I have the body to prove it. I can have any boy I want, but I want my mother's detective. I'm eighteen and he's just past thirty. It's legal. It doesn't even feel strange that he is a man, a grown man, and I am still a girl. We begin to meet. At his office. In his car. I don't care. After school, I walk to a corner and wait until he pulls up—never in his police car. Always an unmarked car, and we drive somewhere. At first, he resists. "I just want to be there for you, Laura," he tells me. "I want to be your friend."

I laugh. It's a strange, grown-up laugh. I rustle his thick dark hair. I tease him. "I want to be your friend, too." But of course I don't want his friendship. What I want is more. Much more. In the car, my hand goes to his thigh. And soon his reaches under my blouse. When I know I'm going to see him, I wear a skirt.

In the car, it's awkward. We fumble for each other across the gearshift. He tugs down my panties and I feel his finger probing. We do, as we used to say in high school, "everything but." One afternoon, Detective Hendricks tells me to get in the car. "Let's go somewhere else." He drives along the highway until we come to a motel. Even I know it's tacky. The clerk barely looks up when we go in. "This is my daughter," he says to the clerk. "We need separate beds." I've been waiting for this. Waiting for him. I've been saving myself for my mother's detective all along.

"Daughter," I whisper, punching him in the ribs.

The room is as I imagined. A scratchy bedspread, stained carpet. A picture of a dog running on a beach. He takes a shower and comes out with just a towel around his waist. I take a shower, too, and do the same, as if I'm an old hand at this. For a few moments we lie, damp, on the clean white sheets (the only thing in the room that actually seems clean). Then he leans over to me. He kisses me. He holds me.

His tongue slides over my body. I don't feel like a child, and he hardly seems like a man, nearly old enough to be my father, yet not my father.

When he moves inside of me, he's gentle. He doesn't force himself. Not at first.

When it's over, there's hardly any blood.

111

IN THE AFTERNOONS SHE DOESN'T meet Tommaso, Viola goes to the chapel to help Angelo. She can find him at almost any time of the day, his hands dripping with the paint from angel's wings, devil's horns. He must have permission to work into the night. The images have grown stranger. Wild mythological beasts with long nails dripping blood, a ghostlike child with dark birds flying from a wound in its neck. Viola stands below, staring. "Are you all right?" Angelo gazes at Viola, but he doesn't appear to see her. He has a distant look in his eyes.

Without coming down from the ladder, he speaks to her. "I received a message from my brother today."

"A message?" Though the occasional postcards arrive, Viola has no idea how a message could get through. Almost no letters have been received.

"He tells me that they are all being transported to Poland."

"Your brother?" Viola is confused. Could he have really received such a letter? She stands at the base of the ladder. "Who is being transported?"

Angelo shrugs. "Everyone," he replies. Then he shakes his head, not pausing from his painting. "Soon we will all be sent away."

112

AT NIGHT ON HIS PALLET, Josef longs to touch his wife. He craves the comfort of her skin, the softness of her flesh. He has memories of her holding him, warming his very bones. Instead, he feels her drifting away, both her body and his memory of it. It was like this with his parents in Romania, when he left to study in Turin. He lost them in pieces—his mother's laughter, his father's gruff voice, then their faces. They grew smaller and smaller in his memory.

Anna is slipping away, as well. She is not the jovial, buxom woman she was before they were sent here. She has grown mechanical in her movements. She is so thin, and her skin has an ashen undertone. Her voice has lost its playful lilt and has settled into a monotone, even with her children. At times in their marriage, Anna had seemed to drift off, slipping into one of her "moods," as her own mother called them. But never had it lasted more than a day, and Josef could always bring her back with a bouquet of flowers, an embrace, a loving gesture.

That night, he rises from his pallet, touches Viola gently on the arm, and asks her, "Would you mind sharing the pallet with your brother tonight?"

Sleepy and uncertain, she hesitates. Then she rolls away from her mother and slips beside her brother. In the darkness, for the first time in months, Josef lies down beside his wife. As he reaches for Anna, she shudders. "What is it?" she gasps. "What's wrong?"

"Nothing," he says. "Shush." He puts his finger on her lips and he gathers her into his arms.

LATER, JOSEF WAKES, HIS HEART racing. A dream woke him, but what was it? He lies there, trying to remember. Something he saw. Large and looming. A black figure. Was it a shadow, an animal? It was in a familiar place. Their apartment in Turin or on a train platform, waving good-bye? Is someone leaving him? Or is he the one who is leaving? He tries to recall, but the dream slips away.

113

DETECTIVE HENDRICKS TALKS TO ME about crime scenes. Perhaps he's trying to scare me away. I'll arrive at his apartment— often on my bike and unannounced—and as we sit on his couch, sipping Cokes, he tells me how he walks into houses with bloodied footprints, houses where whole families have been tied up and shot execution-style ("even the kids," he adds, as if this were some kind of a bonus). There was a teenage boy who'd hung himself in his closet, and Detective Hendricks had to cut him down. A father who'd jumped off a bridge. Women, he tells me, are rarely jumpers or shooters. They don't like to leave a mess. I take big sips of Coke as he tells me. He's been promoted to homicide detective. My mother technically remains a missing person, but he sticks with our case even as it grows colder and colder.

I'm not sure why he tells me these things, and over the years I've wondered if half of them were even true. "I've seen everything," he told me once. When I was thirteen, he was twenty-seven. When I came of age, he was thirty-two. (He waited for me.) He was patient. I was less so. Talking about crimes seemed to puff him up. Perhaps it made him feel more like a man. It was only later—much later—that I came to see that all this talk of blood and death and mayhem turned me on.

When we began having sex, I couldn't come. I wasn't entirely sure what was expected of me. Though I enjoyed myself, not much happened—not with his finger, his tongue, or his penis, though his tongue was the most effective. He told me to relax, but I didn't know how. My mind was always darting around. Then I began to tell myself stories. Not nice stories. My stories, as far as sex went, took a dark turn. My mind wandered into bloodstained houses. As I watched these horrors unfold, I'd come.

After that, sex wasn't about what I felt. It was about telling myself a story. Over the years, I've tried through meditation and mindfulness and various other Zen practices to stay in the moment, or at least find less cruel narratives, but in the end, my ability to reach a climax boils down to a story, a narrative, the kind I'd never share with a soul.

114

RUDY'S COUGH HAS SETTLED DEEP in his lungs. At first, it was only in the night, and seemed more like a slight shortness of breath. But then it morphed into a constant wheeze. At night, Josef stays awake, listening to his son's breath, trying to decide if it is the air, or perhaps mold on the pallet, or something more. He can hardly sleep. Listening becomes his vigil.

But Viola grows annoyed. Rudy keeps her up. In the mornings, she is tired and cranky. At night, she tries to get as far away from him as she is able in their cramped room. Everyone else seems able to sleep, but not Viola. One night in her frustration she gives Rudy a kick and he shouts out. "Why did you do that?" he cries.

"Because I can't sleep with you breathing like that."

"Viola," her father snaps, "leave your brother alone. He's ill."

Furious, Viola slips out of bed and pads down the hallway to the bathroom. But when no one stops her, she keeps going. She goes downstairs to the mess hall. In the corner, the canaries' cage is covered with a blanket. The canaries are silent. Viola lifts the blanket. The birds are resting, huddled together. Some stand on one leg, heads tucked under their wings. She puts the blanket back down.

THE COLD IS PIERCING. There is no escape. Like hunger, it is not something you can get away from. Cold days turn into colder evenings and freezing mornings, and then it starts again. There is nowhere to go, nowhere to hide. Even in the kitchen, with the soup pots going, it is still cold, especially for the children and the elderly. No one can get warm.

Josef's concern for his son grows deeper. Once more he turns to the captain. "I am worried about my little boy. He needs a doctor. Perhaps he needs to be in a hospital."

Captain Cassini nods. "You are a doctor, aren't you?"

Josef sighs. "I am a dentist."

Captain Cassini shrugs. "I will try to get you some medicine."

Meanwhile, Anna boils pots of water on the stove in the mess hall. When the steam is rising, she has Rudy bend over the pot. She covers his head with her shawl and tells him to breathe. Rudy breathes in the warm steam, but still, at night, he coughs.

Josef waits for several days for Captain Cassini to provide medicine, but Captain Cassini never brings it up again. Josef rifles through the drawers in the dental office until he finds some penicillin, which he pockets. He gives Rudy a pill every day for a week, but it doesn't seem to help.

ONE NIGHT, VIOLA CAN'T BEAR Rudy's coughing any longer. She slips off her pallet and heads to the doorway. She makes sure no soldiers are patrolling. Then she goes down to the mess hall, to the aviary. Why should the canaries have a blanket when her brother has none? She tugs the blanket off their cage and takes it back to their room. It is soft and warm and she wants to wrap herself in it, but she doesn't. Without waking her father, she tucks the blanket around Rudy. He nestles into it and, to her surprise, sleeps. Downstairs, the canaries sing faintly. Viola doesn't sleep. She sits up, watching her brother. His shallow breathing grows deeper. He is not trembling with cold. At last, he can rest.

All night she watches. Then, at dawn, she removes the blanket. Rudy protests in his sleep but doesn't wake. Viola takes it back to the drafty mess hall. It's freezing cold as she walks in. None of the residents are awake, not even the soldiers. She tiptoes up to the cage. As she approaches, she sees the delicate birds that serenaded them all day, frozen, their tiny legs sticking up in the air. Their eyes are still open. Viola reaches into the cage, stroking their feathers, the tiny talons. Then she covers them. What have I done? Viola asks herself as she sneaks back up to their cell.

Later that morning, she overhears two of the soldiers speaking. They say it was so cold last night. It's no wonder the canaries froze. Later, when Captain Cassini comes in, he stares at his dead birds. He touches one of their bellies. Then he walks away.

115

THE RESIDENTS HAVE LOST TRACK of the dates, but now they know that it is March 10, 1943. A soldier has left a newspaper in the mess hall. Josef picks up the paper, and reads the front page. Not since he read the news of the racial laws in November 1938 has a story so captivated him. On March 5, a group of workers at the Mirafiori Fiat Plant in Turin put down their tools and walked off the job. They're protesting their wages, working hours, and the failure of the Mussolini regime to help them. It isn't many workers at first, but soon their numbers begin to grow. In other plants throughout Italy, workers begin leaving their jobs. Everyone is poor and hungry. And the fascist regime has done nothing. Many return to their villages, where food is easier to find. Josef understands perfectly what this means.

Mussolini is losing his grip, and will soon fall from power.

Josef finds Anna in the corridor. She is heading down to the miserable room where she sews all day. He puts his hands on her shoulders. "Anna," he says, "it won't be long now."

He hugs his wife. He forgets the dream that troubled him just days ago.

116

WARMTH RETURNS. IT CREEPS UP on them. Viola sees it before she feels it. When they first arrived, the fields were turning brown and dry. There was little left growing, only the stubble on the ground. Now as she walks, she sees buds on the trees. Grass bursts from the ground. At night, the wind is less fierce. They are no longer freezing. The birds sing again. The need for blankets is gone. Everyone breathes a sigh of relief.

Even if she is not seeing Tommaso, Viola walks the fields. She finds a grove of trees she did not recognize in winter, but now, in the warmth, they start to bear fruit. One day in June, she plucks one. She has never tasted such sweetness. Figs. Dark, rich, creamy figs. She eats the ripe ones, peeling back the flesh, sucking on the fruit. She fights off the bees and wasps, vying with her for the sweet nectar. When she is full as a bear in a berry patch, she lies down and sleeps.

117

ONE MORNING, JOSEF ARRIVES AT the dental office and finds Tommaso waiting for him. He has another toothache. "I think I have an abscess," he tells Josef. Josef frowns and then motions for him to enter the cubicle where he works. Clearly there is no abscess. Once he is in the chair, Tommaso whispers to Josef, "The Allied forces have landed in Sicily. The invasion has begun."

Josef can barely hide his excitement. "The war will end soon?"

"Yes," Tommaso says, "I think so. Soon you will be free to return home." Tommaso hesitates.

"But that is not all?"

Tommaso nods. "We fear that the Germans might push deeper into Italy."

"What does this mean?" They are both whispering as Josef pretends to probe Tommaso's teeth.

"If all goes well, the south could be liberated soon."

Josef holds his pick. "And if it does not go well?"

"Then Germany could take over."

"And we would all be deported."

"I think it is unlikely."

Josef does not pause from examining Tommaso's healthy gums. He is thinking things through. Mussolini was arrested in July, and he has heard that Badoglio has come to power. He has promised to restore full rights to the Jews, though this has yet to happen. And besides, it is only what Josef has been able to gather from the sporadic news that reaches them. He has come up with his plan. Now Josef leans in and whispers, "Can you find a trustworthy household near Naples where my family will be safe for a week or two?"

Tommaso nods. "Yes, I think I can. I will ask my grandmother."

Josef puts down his instrument. "I don't see an infection," he tells Tommaso, and this time Tommaso does not tell him to pull his tooth. He rises from the chair, thanks the doctor, and walks away.

BUT THAT NIGHT, AS TOMMASO sits in front of Sofia, his head in his hands, she lectures him. She holds a soup spoon in her hand and slaps it for emphasis in her palm. "You cannot return to your job. Ever. You must remove your uniform. If you are captured, you will be forced to fight with the Germans, or worse. They will take you prisoner and send you north. I will never see you again." Everyone knows that no one comes back from the north.

He listens as she repeats the same words over and over again. "You must remove your uniform. I will burn it myself. You may never go back to the Red House. If you do, you will be arrested."

"But what about Viola and her family? What is going to happen to them?" He looks at her with pleading eyes. Sofia Bassano remembers what it was like to be young. She longs to tell him that this will pass, that there will be others, but she doesn't dare.

"I will ask the priest. I have heard of a family in Benevento that might take them in. But you must promise me." She clasped her grandson's hands. "You must promise that you will never go back there again."

The next day, instead of returning to work, Tommaso slips into the dental office. "My grandmother will find someone to help you." Then he slips out again as stealthily as he entered.

THAT EVENING, THE RESIDENTS GATHER and Josef shares what he has learned. "The Allied forces have landed in Sicily," he tells them. "The liberation has begun. If the Allied forces win, then we will be freed."

"And if they lose?"

There is quiet among the men. "We will be sent north," Angelo says. "It is inevitable."

Now there is more mumbling. "How do you know?" someone says, but Josef replies, "It's true. We could all be deported to the north."

Angelo nods, taking this in. Then he steps back as the others listen to what Josef has to say. While they are trying to determine the best course of action, Angelo slips away.

118

WHEN EVERYONE IS ASLEEP, ANGELO goes to the chapel. Turning on the light, he stands looking up at the ceiling, the panel, the walls. He is amazed at the work he has done. He has been thinking about the news, mulling it over. He has been trying to make sense of what will happen next. Soon, they will leave this place. It has been their prison but also their safe haven. No one can know what lies ahead. Only what your gut tells you. Angelo gazes over his creation. At times, it has felt as if he has been guided by the hand of God.

Standing in the center of the room, he turns until the saints walk, the angels fly. Jesus writhes on his cross even as Mary, in another panel, cradles him as a baby. Then Angelo stops spinning. He is dizzy and almost stumbles, but he catches himself before he falls. The chapel is not quite finished. But there is so little left to do. He closes his eyes, and the angels come in faster succession. They fly through his mind. He knows what he will do.

He picks up his brush and dips it into the paint. He must fill every space he can with goodness. The demons are soaring as well, struggling out of the fires of hell, trying to bring him down. He must paint even Satan, with his horns and red trident, as he sinks farther into hell. Angelo paints with a frenzy that he has never felt before. It is as if he is merely holding the brush as it is being guided by another's hand. He cannot give up. He cannot stop. His eyes burn. In the dim light of his single bulb, he can hardly see. Into the night, he works.

And then he is done. He steps back and surveys what he has made. It is beautiful. Perhaps it will last. Perhaps he will be remembered. Dipping his brush into the pigment once more, he signs his name and the date in a corner of the chapel.

He steps outside. It is a clear morning, not yet light. The sky is still filled with stars. The moon has slipped below the horizon. In another hour, the sun will rise. Angelo stands, feeling the freshness of the air, the wind through the branches of the entwined oak trees. He looks up. There is a branch within his reach. For a long time, he has followed his good angels. His demons have burned in the fires of hell. Now they soar. He cannot contain them.

Why now, when he has arrived at his purest state? When the line from his paintbrush to his soul is complete, why have they come to torment him? At first, they are terrifying. Fiery faces of those long gone. But suddenly, the light changes. He sees the future. He's been traveling through an endless tunnel and now there's a sliver of light. It grows brighter as he makes his way toward it.

119

UPSTAIRS ON HIS PALLET, JOSEF THINKS about pigeons. How he and his father would release them, and the birds would swirl until, with a flick of his wrist, they headed home. He touches Anna's cheek, and she opens her eyes. Gently he leads her to the window.

"I have found a family where you and the children can stay, here in the south. I will go back to Turin and find Michele and your parents, and make certain that everything is all right. I will write when it is safe for you to join me."

Anna trembles. There are so many stars tonight. The sky makes her uneasy, but how can she explain? Josef pulls her to him. "Anna," he whispers. "We are going home."

120

SOMETHING WAKES VIOLA AT DAWN. A sound she has never heard before comes to her in a dream. She's sure it's not real. She's sweating. The air is thick with the smell of ripening figs. But it is not the heat that wakes her. Or the sweetness in the air. It's a sound. A creaking, a branch, perhaps, blowing in the wind.

Viola slides out of bed, careful not to disturb her mother, and peers down through the bars, but she sees nothing. Slipping into her shoes, she wraps a sweater around her and makes her way down the stairs. The exterior door is ajar, and she slips through.

Outside, the world seems as she left it, yet something has shifted. On the oak tree, a dark shadow looms. As she steps closer, she sees what she thinks must be a doll or a scarecrow. But as she approaches, she sees that it is not a doll. It is not a scarecrow. Perhaps an angel—the kind that she and Angelo painted and carved into the wall. Viola stands beneath the shape that blows in the wind. It is an angel.

Then she cries out and falls to her knees.

121

VIOLA WALKS THE FIELDS. It's a beautiful afternoon, and she's sobbing. She's run away from the arms of her father, who tried to console her, and her mother, who called out to her. First she ran, and now she walks. All she wants is to talk to Tommaso, to tell him about Angelo. About what she saw in the early-morning light.

Why did she have to be the one to find him? And why did Angelo do this? Why now, when they are about to be free?

It was her father who heard her screams. Her father who rushed down and made her turn away. He was the one who pronounced Angelo dead. The others stood nearby, shocked, not understanding. They, too, asked why now, when their freedom was so near?

All afternoon, Viola walks the fields, but Tommaso doesn't come. She goes to their shed and sits on the cot, but the room has not been aired, and it smells musty and stale. There are no fresh-cut flowers, no oranges or figs waiting for her in a ceramic bowl. Mouse droppings on the bed. Tommaso has not been here in a while. She sees her mother watching her from the upper window of their cell. She turns away, ignoring her. Where was she when Viola needed guidance?

Viola asks around, but no one has seen Tommaso. One by one, the other soldiers begin to disappear as well. Every day, Viola walks to the shed and waits for Tommaso. He does not come to comfort her or bring her food. He does not leave her little gifts. At every sound of a car or a motorcycle, she rushes to the long drive, hoping it's him, but still he does not come. She has no way to reach him. No way to get a message to him. She worries that he has been injured, or even killed. He wouldn't just leave her like this, would he?

Meanwhile, she mourns Angelo. Why would he do it? She cannot get it out of her mind. How could the man who saw so many angels leave her? But then Tommaso did, didn't he? And she understands that all men are destined to leave.

A FEW DAYS LATER, THE RESIDENTS are assembled in the mess hall. The captain is there, along with the few remaining soldiers. "You are going home," he tells them. "You are not being deported. We have kept you safe during this difficult time. And you will be safe where you are going. Your transport is being arranged. Please gather your things."

There is mumbling among them, then elation. The war must be almost over. They are free to leave, to return to the lives they left behind, as if this interval never happened. They scramble to collect their possessions, and the next morning, they board the yellow school buses that brought them here. Most head back the way they have come. Some opt to remain in the south, though it is safe to return home, they are told. They believe the Allies have won. The Jews will not be deported from Italy. Anna and the children are to go to Benevento until Josef can send for them.

On the train, Viola stares out the window. She cannot believe that Tommaso never came to say good-bye. That he just left her. As did Angelo. She does not want her father to go north without them, but they have tried to convince her that it is best.

In Naples, they separate. Anna and the children get off the train. "It won't be long," Josef reassures them as he clasps them to him on the platform. Rudy clutches his father around the neck. Josef has to pry him away. Viola sobs into his chest. Anna tugs the children.

She stands back stoically, that curl of her lip quivering. Josef kisses it one more time.

Then he jumps back on the train. He waves until his train rounds a bend, and they don't see him again.

122

JOSEF SETTLES INTO HIS SEAT. The train is hot and stuffy, as it was when they first traveled to the Red House, and Josef's heart is heavy. He knows leaving Anna and the children behind is right, but as the train leaves Naples behind, he is filled with doubt. He wants to jump off this train, but it's too late.

They will be safe in Benevento, Josef tells himself. And once he knows that all will be well, he will send for them. For now, he closes his eyes and rests. He has not rested in a long time.

123

AS TOMMASO FINISHES HIS STORY, I stand, gazing up at the angels and clouds and saints my mother, a Jew, helped an artist who lost his way paint on these walls. I am now fairly certain that my mother lost her way, as well. But there are still pieces missing for me—things I don't quite understand.

Tommaso stands beside me, staring at the walls. "And you never saw her again?"

He shakes his head. "I did. Once." He can't look me in the eye. "I'm not proud of what I did, and I have suffered for it, but she suffered more." Again he hesitates. "It was not the same."

I can't bring myself to look at him, either. I ask the question I am afraid to ask. I speak in barely a whisper. "What happened to them there?"

Tommaso sighs. "I don't know that I can answer that exactly, but I know who can." We leave the chapel and he locks it with the padlock. He motions to me, and I follow him out of the labyrinth, back into the sun, where he pauses. Reaching into his pocket, he hands me a crumpled slip of paper.

I unfold it. On the slip of paper is a name I don't recognize— Rodolfo Umberto—and an address in Naples. "Naples?" I ask.

I've never been to Naples, despite the fact that my mother met my father there. She never had any interest in returning. She'd flick her wrists and say, "Naples. Who cares? It's a filthy, disgusting city," and that was that.

"Who is this person?"

Tommaso shrugs. "Just go to this address. Show up in the afternoon. No need to call ahead. He won't answer. Just go." He's tired, I can tell. He starts walking toward the car. He's ready to drive back to town. "The rest of what you need to know is there."

124

I LEAVE THE CAR IN BARI and take the train to Naples. I'm rattled by all that Tommaso has told me. I'm too distracted to drive; I don't trust myself on the autostrada. The train has tattered leather seats—some that face forward, some backward. As I settle into my seat in an almost empty car, it occurs to me that my family took this train north when they left the Red House. It seems as if they just disappeared, evaporated. If they were from Turin, why did my mother always claim she came from Naples? Why did she meet my father there? I am left with so many ricocheting questions. I have the pieces but cannot seem to make sense of the puzzle.

The train jerks to a start, but once it's moving, I'm surprised at how comforting the ride is. I lay my head back and let the motion carry me. Vineyards and olive groves zip past. Soon the land becomes hilly, almost mountainous, as we barrel through long tunnels carved out of sheer rock. We careen in and out of darkness.

I close my eyes. When I open them again, we are pulling into Benevento. The place where the green walnuts fall and the witches fly. The place she claimed to have come from.

WE SLIP INTO ANOTHER TUNNEL and then out again. Suddenly, there is light. Huge pewter clouds skid across the sky. They cross the mountains, carrying sheets of rain, bursts of lightning and thunder that seem to subside as quickly as they came. I am tempted to stay on this train, heading north, straight to Rome. But I touch the crumpled slip of paper in my pocket. My journey, it seems, is not done.

I change trains at Caserta for Naples. Soon we round a bend, and Vesuvius appears, skulking over the city, gray and ominous. And then as we pull past it, glistening, almost burning my eyes, is the blinding sun on the Bay of Naples. The water sparkles like a million stars. A vision of what heaven must be.

THE

FOURTH STORY

———

125

DOWN A NARROW ALLEYWAY named Purgatorio, there is a church with many skulls. Years ago, believers adopted these skulls. They visited them, cleaned them, brought them flowers. They talked to them, sharing their troubles. In this way, the believers eased the journey of the souls to the other world, hoping they would be less lonely in their passing. I stop at the church to see the skulls. A tour guide leads us down the cellar stairs and speaks in rapid-fire Italian I can barely follow. Skulls surround us. Some have dried flowers poking through orifices. Each has a story of its own, I'm sure.

I leave Purgatorio behind, though I remain in a strange limbo of my own. I have an address and a name. Clues that lead me further along this quest into the underworld. I am on some mysterious scavenger hunt. Perhaps I am looking for a guide. Perhaps the answer lies in the slip of paper Tommaso gave me. As if in some spy saga, I have memorized it in case I lose it, or my wallet is stolen in this uncertain city.

I check into a small hotel near Piazza Bellini, where I'm offered a glass of Prosecco. My room is bright and airy. It has a small balcony, where I stand, sipping, as I gaze across the piazza and the rooftops of Naples. Below, jazz is playing. A lilting saxophone. All around me this city is pulsing. Nothing here is familiar. Yet this is where my parents met, courted, fell in love. Just one more place she never went back to.

IN NAPLES, I LOSE THE ability to sleep. It's not that I cannot sleep, exactly; I cannot seem to remember how, what is required of me. I'm not sure when I finally drift off. I read somewhere that pregnant women often lose the ability to sleep before the baby comes. It means they are about to give birth. So perhaps I have come here in some way to give birth, but to what? A monster from the deep?

I recall her eyes. Brown and doelike as mine. She was more like a mirror than a mother. As if, without gazing at her, I could barely exist at all.

IN THE MORNING, I'M UP EARLY, though I don't want to be. I know what awaits me today, but it will have to wait until the afternoon, per Tommaso's instructions. I have time to kill, so I head over to the archaeology museum near the hotel. The museum is almost empty as I amble through its cavernous rooms, filled with Greek and Roman mosaics, tiny clay figurines from Sardinia, Iron and Bronze Age tools. Giant sculptures of gladiators and gods.

I wander upstairs to the Pompeii exhibit and enter the room of everyday objects. Before me are vitrines filled with oil lamps, door knockers in the shape of lions' heads, utensils, household gods, ceramics and porcelain. Cases filled with cooking utensils, work implements, jewelry, hair clips, chisels. A dog's leash. It gives me such a palpable sense of people going about their business, tending to their lives as we tend to ours, before everything came to a sudden, crushing end.

I come to a vitrine of medical instruments, including a vaginal speculum that hasn't changed in the last two thousand years. I pause before the dental instruments—probes and pincers. Exactly what my grandfather would have used, the objects he took with him first to his exile at the Red House and then, I assume, wherever he went next.

All these objects found in the House of the Golden Cupids, the House of the Colored Marbles, the House of the Tragic Poet.

Houses where people lived, where children played, where the first signs warning BEWARE OF DOG were ever posted. I find I can barely breathe. It's as if I am suffocating, the way these two thousand people did nearly two thousand years ago. The thought that life can be snuffed out in an instant. That everything can change in a heartbeat. And then, somehow, life goes on. One city was built upon the ruins, and soon the whole tragedy that happened here was forgotten, until a chance discovery seventeen hundred years later.

On 9/11, I was staging a town house that was for sale in the West Village. The owner, a widower, said he couldn't live there since his wife passed away. He was moving to be near his son, in Portland. I was trying to decide between a creamy leather couch or a plush gray one. The two couches gave different feels. Did I want this living room to have a serious look or a more lived-in, family feel?

I was mulling this as the first plane hit. I was leaning toward the lived-in look when the towers came down. I didn't know anything until Patrick texted me. "I love you. Come home." I had to walk across the Williamsburg Bridge with hundreds of others. Three thousand souls vanished that day. Those left behind were desperate for remains, for proof that their loved ones were there, that they died that day.

It's better to know than to be left in limbo, isn't it? I've understood this since I was twelve years old. Not long after 9/11, I ran into an acquaintance whose father had been missing since that day. "Except he wasn't supposed to have been in the World Trade Center. There was no reason for him to have been there." His family was left to wonder. Did he choose that moment to run away?

It is the unknowing that kills us, I think. Actually, I know.

Shaken, I leave the museum. Those everyday objects left behind. Bread crusts, car keys, cigarettes. I stop at a trattoria, where I eat a salad, which I pick at, and gulp down a glass of wine. In my pocket, I finger the slip of paper. What if I just tear it up, toss it away?

What if I get back on the train and head home? I can't help but think about my grandfather and his pigeons. He loved how they found their way home. But there are times when life takes on a momentum of its own, as if you are a boulder, rolling down a hill. You can't stop until you hit the bottom.

126

I WEND MY WAY THROUGH a crowded Port'Alba, the street of the used booksellers, through the old archway. I step into the blinding sun of the Piazza Dante, and for a moment the glare is so bright, I cannot see. Naples is all sun-drenched glory. I begin my descent to the sea. I make my way along Via Toledo, where immigrants sell ripped-off handbags, promising real Prada or Louis Vuitton, scarves, jewelry that glitters in the sun and promises to be one hundred percent gold or silver. A beggar with three small dogs at his feet holds out a cup. Sailors saunter by, their dress whites almost too bright in the afternoon sun.

The street is redolent of grilling meat and tomato sauces, the sharp odor of trash and human sweat, the urine-streaked lampposts, where late-night drunks relieve themselves. Meanwhile, all along this strip, there's pizza and gelato and coffee, always coffee, a crush of people going up and down, eating, shopping, stopping, moving in no discernible order at all. I cut through the maze of streets that make up the Quartieri Spagnoli, making my way through the throngs until I reach the enormous Piazza Plebiscito.

I'm in the Chiaia district now, where the breezes are fresher, the pungent smells gone. All I smell is the brine as the tide pulls away from the shore. I continue down Via Santa Lucia until I come to the sea. I follow the promenade, where the street is lined with restaurants and cafés. I keep walking until I reach a stairway that descends onto a black lava sand beach. Its darkness is haunting, yet I long to jump into the water and take a dip in the bay. In the surf, children splash their parents, mothers laugh, friends shove one another into the water.

I think I may have walked too far, so I turn back and stop at one of the cafés that line the water. I order an espresso and show the server the address where I'm headed. He points to the street just behind the café and shrugs. "It's there."

"So close," I reply, and he smiles as I drop a couple of euros on the bar.

I take a side street to the road that's just a block from the sea. I get turned around, but then I find it. It's an old palazzo, with enormous double doors below huge windows. I hear opera blaring from up above. The beautiful, mournful voice of a woman calling for her lost love. I stand outside, listening to the aria, gathering my courage. What is this person going to think of a stranger ringing his bell? Will he answer at all? Or slam the door in my face?

The giant wooden doors are twice my size, and I cannot help but feel as if this is just another portal. Another way for me to slip deeper into this sinkhole. At last, I ring. There is no answer. I wait. Then ring again, holding the bell longer this time. I can hear the buzzer above the soaring music that blares above me.

Finally, I hear locks opening, a bolt being shoved aside, and an old man peers from behind the huge door. He has leathery skin from too much sun. He resembles an ancient Greek god, risen from the sea. He stares at me, squinting, as if he cannot stand the afternoon sun. He is a small, dark man with thick white hair. With his dark eyes and olive skin, the roundness of his face and fullness of his lips, he looks like her. If she had aged, that is. Because he is an old man and she remains frozen in time. I suppose, as Tommaso made clear, I look just like her.

Suddenly, I understand where this journey has been taking me. I stand, staring back at him. "Rodolfo Umberto?" I ask timidly. He looks at me askance, as if he's trying to place me. "I am Viola's daughter." He steps back, shocked, and suddenly I know who he is. "Uncle Rudy," I stammer, "I'm your niece."

Then he says what I am thinking. "I feel as if I am looking at a ghost."

I nod. "So do I."

"How did you find me?" he asks, sad, it seems, at being found.

"Tommaso in Castellobello. He knew where you lived."

"Ah." Rudy sighs. "Of course. Tommaso." He shakes his head, as if coming out of a fog. He motions for me to come inside. "Watch your step," he tells me. "Come in." And I follow him into the large cobbled courtyard, which seems to double as a parking garage. Without a word, he begins to climb the old marble stairs. After three flights, he turns, walks down a long vestibule, and opens the door. I walk into a dark entryway. Opera blasts through the rooms.

"*Tosca*," Rudy says with a heavy sigh. "Heartbreaking."

He guides me into a spacious living room with all the curtains drawn. Here he turns down the music. "Sit," he says to me. "I will make us some coffee. An espresso?" he asks. He is robust and sturdy, which surprises me.

"Yes. One sugar."

"*Va bene*," he says, and disappears down the hall.

While he is gone, I take it all in. This enormous apartment by the sea. My uncle, whom I learned existed only a few days ago, making me an espresso. None of it seems real. Naples is where my parents met. So it would make sense that my search would bring me here. But why did Rudy and my mother end up in Naples? Why didn't they go home? And why didn't I know about him until now? Why did my mother always pretend she was an orphan? That she had no one, when clearly she did. The man making coffee down the hall is living proof.

"So." Rudy returns, setting down a tray. He hands me a small cup with a double espresso and two lumps of brown sugar in the saucer and a small pot of warm milk on the side. There is also a tiny spoon and a plate of cookies. "So you speak Italian?"

I answer in Italian. "Well enough. It is coming back to me."

"You were born here, weren't you?"

"In Brindisi," I tell him, and he nods.

"Yes, I think I knew that."

He coughs, then takes a lozenge, pointing to his throat. "It's nothing," he says. "Just a cough I've always had." He sips his coffee. "Anyway, I never went looking for her, you know. After she left me," Rudy says. "I didn't see the point."

"She left you?"

"Ah, so you don't know very much, then, do you?"

I shake my head but can't help but feel as if I am being scolded. "Tommaso didn't say . . ."

"She left me at a convent that was also an orphanage. I believe she sent money for my care." He coughs again. "I have never been well. Ever since I can remember, I have had problems with my lungs." He points to the oxygen machine in the corner. "I couldn't really expect her to care for me."

As we sip our coffee, he asks me very quietly, "How is she? Is she . . . alive?"

I realize, looking at him, that until this moment I had held on to a hope that perhaps I'd actually find her here. That, somehow, all these years ago she'd come home. And now I know she didn't. I shake my head. "I honestly don't know." Rudy stares at me, his head cocked. "She left me, too. When I was a girl." I sigh. "I was twelve."

Rudy nods. "I'm sorry, but I'm not entirely surprised."

There's a clap of thunder. He gets up and starts closing his open windows. He disappears down a dark corridor just as the rains come. I hear the shutters closing as drops strike the panes and the skylight above. Once the many windows are all closed, he comes back to me. His shirt is speckled. He picks up the conversation exactly where we left off. "As children, we were forced to leave so much behind. I suppose it became a habit. Still, for years I could not forgive her."

"And have you forgiven her now?"

He sighs. "I've made my peace with it."

And suddenly I blurt out everything. Coming home to the empty house, the crusts of bread left on the plate, her vanishing into thin air. My years without her. My life cracked in two. "I don't know," I tell him. "I don't know what became of her."

He nods again. It seems as if we have reached an understanding. "Well, then, we have that in common, don't we?" I think of my mother and everything she had to leave. Her grandparents, her cat, her home, her school, her friends. And those who left her, Tommaso, Angelo, her father. Until, finally, she began leaving. First Rudy and then me.

He listens, taking it all in. And then he says, "I will tell you what I know. Perhaps it will help you understand."

127

IN NAPLES, THERE'S NO CLEAN WATER. People drink from open sewers. There is no food. Everyone is covered in lice. Typhus is rampant. It's September 1943 and the Germans still control Naples. They shoot people at random. They use a baby as a football. They drag young girls into alleyways and ruin them. If a German soldier is killed, they round up ten random Neapolitans and shoot them.

Meanwhile, Anna waits for a letter, some word from Josef. Day after day, she hopes that the family in Benevento will do as they promised—forward any letters to her. But no mail comes. And no bank wire. Anna writes to him every chance she gets, telling him about where they are living, hoping for a reply. Viola could feel her mother first seething, and now, something worse. Anna has creases around the sides of her mouth as she sews. More streaks of gray have appeared in her hair. She drifts. At times, Viola catches her talking to someone who is not there.

The family they lived with in Benevento soon grew weary of their guests. They asked for more money, which Anna didn't have, and then told them to leave. It was too dangerous, they said. And Anna, like Rudy, was coughing. In Naples, Anna found a basement room below a tailor shop. A windowless hovel with two cots, a small table, and two chairs. She convinced the tailor to give her work in exchange for rent. In their dank basement, she sews hems and buttons, and makes shrouds for those who die in the myriad ways one can in Naples—from typhus, from hunger, or the random cruelty of the Germans. There's hardly any money left over for food. And even if they had money, there's little to eat. Even the fish in the aquarium have been eaten. It is rumored that a baby manatee was served in a stew.

But the sewing is only in exchange for rent; Anna has no money for food, so she must forage. She rifles through trash, but there is nothing being wasted or thrown out in Naples. Everything is eaten. She climbs higher into Vomero to forage in the fields for greens, but she finds little. One day, on her way down the hill, she sees a line of German soldiers in front of a doorway. Inside, a young girl lies on a mattress, her legs spread. A sign her father has written reads THE LAST VIRGIN IN NAPLES. He is charging admission.

Anna continues down the hill. Is she too old to sell her own body? She's seen women who look older on the streets. Would a soldier want her? Or Viola? Is Viola too young? For a moment, in her hunger, she contemplates the unthinkable. Selling her own daughter? Shaking her head, she banishes such thoughts. "I'd rather starve," she says out loud, though no one is listening.

128

THEY HAVEN'T BEEN LIVING IN the basement long when Anna becomes feverish. Perhaps it is just dankness, or an allergy to the mold. Or the heat. It is sweltering in Naples. Still she sews. Somehow, the tailor doesn't notice that she is ill. There's a pile of shirts and dresses stacked in their room. As she works, sweat pours from her forehead. When she takes to her bed, Viola dabs cold water on her brow. When she grows delirious, Viola runs to the tailor for help.

For days, Anna stays in bed. The tailor's wife brings down soup, but it is not enough to stave off their hunger. And she has her own family to feed. One morning, Anna wakes, feeling stronger. Though she is afraid, she must find food. She pulls Viola to her. "You stay here," she tells her. "Watch your brother while I'm gone."

"Let me go with you," Viola protests.

Anna shakes her head. Gently she strokes her daughter's cheek. "No, you must stay here." How could she have contemplated, even for an instant, selling this precious child? She kisses her daughter on the forehead. "Take care of your brother. That is how you can help me."

Anna heads out with the bucket she uses for foraging. She climbs the hills, past the rubble and bombed-out buildings, to barren meadows. Several other women are already here. Anna walks to the back of the meadow, where she finds dandelion greens, mushrooms, and a neglected potato that someone must have dropped. She cradles it like a gemstone.

Looking down over Naples, she sees the sun shimmering on the bay. She holds the potato in her hand. It is small and hard, covered with earth. Anna ponders how distant this existence is from her old life. It is unrecognizable to her. Then she gathers what she has found and hurries back to her children. As she descends the hill, she passes an alleyway, where something catches her eye. A German soldier lies near a trash heap. Anna approaches cautiously. He has been shot through the head. Anna knows about the reprisals for killing a German soldier, but he was already dead when she found him. She is frightened of being caught up in a roundup.

Soon her children will need warm clothes. They cannot pass another winter like the one they just survived. She reaches down and touches his coat. It is made of good wool. It seems almost new. Looking around, she sees no one. She stoops and removes the coat from the dead soldier. Carefully, she folds it and stuffs it into her sack. Then she continues down the hill.

As she descends, a truck with a swastika on the side races past her. In the back there are a dozen people who look down at her forlornly. Anna knows that they are Jews, being taken to the station. She skulks down a side street, clutching her sack.

WHEN SHE RETURNS, THE CHILDREN are waiting. They marvel at the potato. Viola holds it as carefully as if it were an egg and could easily break. Then Anna shows them the coat. She doesn't show them the bullet hole. "I will make jackets for you. So this winter, if we are still here, you will be warm." She does not tell them what she saw in the truck. Instead, she says matter-of-factly, "Our name is no longer Malkin."

Viola and Rudy look at her, perplexed. "Why?" Viola asks.

"It doesn't matter why," their mother replies. "From now on you will call yourselves Umberto. Rodolfo and Viola Umberto."

"But that is the name of our street," Viola protests.

"Exactly." Anna smiles.

Rudy chimes in. "I don't want to be named after a street."

"This way, you will never forget where you live." Then she boils the small potato and cuts it in two.

129

IN THE MORNING, ANNA DOESN'T venture out. She is too frightened. What she saw in that truck terrified her. What if something happens to her? What will the children do? How will they survive? So she stays in. She had a handful of flour that she mixed with water and cabbage, but now that, too, is gone. The room is dank, and Rudy's cough has worsened. Instead of foraging for food, she proceeds to cut the cloth from the soldier's jacket. If she is careful, she can make two jackets from this. First she stitches up the bullet holes. "Come here," she says to Rudy. She takes his measurements and then Viola's. She has never made jackets for them before.

As she cuts the jackets for her children, the Nazis begin rounding up Italian men. They are shipping them north, as laborers. The women of Naples have endured every privation. They have starved, suffered typhus, bombardments, watched their men go off to war, but this is too much for them. "You will not take our men," the women cry. A group of street urchins, joining their protests, hurl rocks at the back of a Nazi soldier on patrol. The soldiers turn to shoot as the boys scamper away. Suddenly the *scugnizzi,* the street urchins, begin hurling rocks at all the passing soldiers. They shout obscenities and disappear down the alleyways they know well. Then, to everyone's surprise, the people rise up. They toss their washtubs and mattresses, pots and pans, even their tomato sauce down on the German patrols. Young girls distract the Germans while the boys rush their tanks, dropping inside them grenades stolen from dead soldiers. The Nazis shoot randomly at the balconies and windows, but still the tables, chairs, and heirloom dressers rain down on them.

The uprising goes on for four days, until the Germans realize that they have been defeated, not by the Allied forces but by rogue battalions of women and children, wielding rocks and tomato sauce. On the fifth day, Anna wakes and hears something she hasn't heard in a long time. Nothing. An eerie silence prevails. For the first time since they arrived, she doesn't hear the planes overhead. The world has grown still. She ventures out of their apartment. No Allied bombers flying over. No sounds of gunfire or Nazi jeeps driving by. Nothing but silence.

Back inside, Anna sits at the edge of the cot where her children sleep. She doesn't know what to do. Why hasn't Josef gotten word to them? Their money is low, and it's been weeks. But, at last, this quiet. The Germans must be in retreat. Soon Naples will be free. Anna cannot help but feel something she has suppressed for so long. A ray of hope. Even if Josef does not get word to them, they will find a way to travel north. She will return to Turin, join her husband and her parents. They will be a family again.

She observes Viola in her steady slumber, her dark hair fallen across her face, sleeping so peacefully, and Rudy with his raspy throat, his struggling breaths. Once again, she must find food. She waits until Viola stirs, then tells her, "The bombardments have stopped." She clasps Viola in her arms and strokes her hair tenderly. "I'm going to look for food." For weeks, all they have eaten is boiled grasses, a crust of bread, tepid tea. That lone potato. Even when Anna has some money, she cannot buy ingredients when there's nothing to be bought. "I'll be back soon. You stay here. Watch your brother."

She kisses Viola on the forehead. Then she heads out. As she walks, she smells the sea breezes, the brine. There is a lightness to her step. It is a bright, sunny day, and the Nazis have abandoned Naples. They are heading north to Rome. In their wake, they flood the fields. They create stagnant breeding grounds, hoping that the mosquitoes will finish the job that they began. The Allied forces must be near. The streets are eerily quiet. There is a lull. A calm over the city that she has not felt since she arrived.

Today, Anna decides not to go into the hills to gather weeds. She will go down to the port. She has not wanted to risk it before, because of the Germans' presence there, but today she feels safe. Perhaps if she is lucky, she will find limpets and even snails.

130

FROM THE DOORWAY, VIOLA AWAITS her mother's return. She, too, is struck by the silence, interrupted only by Rudy's breathing. Suddenly, she hears an explosion. She rushes out to the street as others flood from their houses. A plume of smoke rises from the direction of the port. But Viola heard no planes, none of the telltale sounds of a bombardment. Vesuvius must have erupted, but no smoke rises from the sleeping giant. Only a fluffy white cloud skims its crater. Viola will listen for planes in the days and years that follow, but for now, one thing is clear. The explosion didn't come from the sky. It came from the sea.

"Those bastards," a neighbor says, spitting at the ground. "They blew up the port."

For the rest of the day, the children huddle. They are hungry, but Viola is afraid to step outside. She holds her brother, rubbing his arms to keep him warm. When he whimpers, she reassures him. "She will be back soon. I promise."

Viola thinks about how many times her father and Tommaso said "I promise." And they could not keep their promises. Is this what it means to become an adult? You lie to children to placate them?

131

AS TANKS PARADE DOWN VIA TOLEDO, the Neapolitans rush to greet them. They blow kisses and toss grain. One excited man runs up to the conquering heroes with a bouquet of flowers, and is accidentally run over by a tank. The Germans are gone and the Americans have arrived. The people of Naples switch conquerors easily.

Viola has climbed into the hills to search for their mother. Now she heads down to the sea. She doesn't know about the parade until she comes upon it. The tanks roll by. The Americans wave from their armored vehicles. They are handsome, smiling. They have white teeth. Some leap down to hug women and children. Others throw chewing gum and chocolates into the crowd. Viola waves back, then continues on her way.

When she reaches the sea, she stops. The port has been reduced to rubble. Huge boulders have cascaded onto the promenade. Rescue crews pull bodies from the piles of toppled buildings. Viola stands, stunned. She begins clawing at the rocks with her own hands. She digs and scrapes until a rescue worker gently puts his hands on her shoulders.

"Please," he says to her, "you must go to the morgue."

But Viola just watches as bodies are removed, then wrapped in sheets. She cannot seem to move. She understands that her mother is not coming home. Viola staggers back through the crowds. People are celebrating, shouting. She has no idea why. She trembles as she makes her way back up the hill.

BY MORNING, RUDY IS CRYING again. But Viola moves list-lessly. She can barely drag herself out of bed. "Listen to me, Rudy," she says, "I need to go out. I need to find something to eat. You must stay here."

"No, please," he begs. "I don't want to be alone again. What if you don't come back?" She considers taking him with her but thinks the better of it. His breathing is so labored, she doubts that he would be able to climb into the hills. He will slow her down. She can go and return before dark if she hurries. She has watched her mother go that way and return with whatever she managed to forage. Viola has no idea how they will survive.

She is thirteen years old and still a virgin. But she has seen girls younger than she is selling themselves on the streets. She has seen fathers and brothers offering up their daughters and sisters for pal-try sums. The streets of Naples—the alleyways and doorways—are filled with women selling themselves. Ordinary women. House-wives, mothers who must feed their children. The husbands who cannot provide for their families look the other way.

As Viola walks, she thinks about Rudy, alone, waiting for her. What if she doesn't return? How would he fend for himself? He's barely eleven years old. But she will be back for him; meanwhile, her hunger and her rage propel her. She is furious with her father for leaving them. And she is furious with Angelo and Tommaso for leaving her. She wishes she had understood the depth of Angelo's despair. His fear of being deported. But Tommaso? How can she explain that? How could he just leave her without a word? She loved him. She would have stayed with him. What a coward he was. And suddenly, as she walks, she knows that she will never open her heart again. She will be ruthless about it. Even cruel.

A woman drags past her, carrying a bucket filled with dandelion greens and grass. Before, Viola would have wondered what the woman would do with this, but now she knows. She will boil the weeds for her family's soup. That night, starving, she goes back to the room she shares with Rudy. All night her stomach rumbles. In the morning, she wakes early and heads out again, with no idea where she is going. She wanders the twisting back alleys of the Spanish Quarter.

A man steps out of the shadows. He wears a uniform, a soldier from somewhere. Maybe English. Maybe American. Not German. The man is not very tall, but bulky, with an angular jaw and a small mouth. He's not more than thirty. When he smiles, he shows his bright white teeth.

She nods at him, and they do not speak, but he takes her by the arm. As they walk, he mentions a price, and she nods. He leads her to a pensione that rents rooms by the hour. Viola pays close attention to where the pensione is located and to the cost of the room.

THE ROOM IS DARK AND MISERABLE, with little light coming in. There are stains on the bedspread. The man goes to the window and pulls down the blind, darkening it even more. It is hot and stuffy, with a moldy smell. There is nothing special or out of the ordinary about him as he begins to undress. Unsure of what is expected of her, Viola undresses, as well. She is indifferent to the man as he watches her, as he grows hard gazing upon her. She folds her clothes, placing them in a neat pile, then walks over to the bed.

As she stands at the side of the bed, the man studies her naked body. He runs his rough, warm hands over her skin. She tries not to think. She floats, flying over the earth, over fields and hillsides and cities. As she moves through space, she moves through time.

Her father carries his satchel of instruments off to his practice. Her mother with a mouthful of pins, gently turning a woman like a dancer in a music box. She's running in the playground with her friends. Then with Tommaso in the shed. His gentle touch, his deep kiss. The man runs his hands over her breasts, her thighs, touching parts of her that no man has ever touched. She closes her eyes. She tries to return to the shed that smelled of oranges and a scratchy wool blanket to lie on. The man pushes into her, and the pain is sharp. He grunts. It is a sound that will always disgust her.

When it is over, she rinses in the bowl on the washstand. She ignores the blood. The man, who is getting dressed, doesn't seem to notice either. He hands her some bills, which she counts as if she's been counting money her whole life. She looks up at him. "It's less than we agreed." These are the only words she will say to him. He smiles smugly as he hands her two more bills and leaves. Next time, Viola tells herself, she will charge more.

She finds Rudy in his bed, trembling, face turned to the wall. She clasps her brother in her arms.

"I'm sorry. I'm sorry I left you," Viola rocks her brother in her arms.

"Promise," he says to her, "promise you'll never leave me again."

Viola hugs him more tightly. "I promise," she says, though she's not sure if she can keep her word. She knows that they are alone now in the world. The next day she stays in, but soon they are hungry again. She must find food, and now she knows how to do so. She waits until Rudy is asleep. Then she heads out.

IT IS A WARM, RAINY NIGHT as Viola makes her way up the hill to Vomero. The cobblestones are slick and shiny beneath the streetlights. In the rubble, cats fight, children sleep. She has some luck tonight. Two English soldiers who are content to wait their turn. They are polite, do their business, and they're gone. As she's leaving the pensione, where now she rents a room by the hour, she hears laughter. It's a high-pitched giggle that sounds vaguely familiar.

Viola turns to see a gaunt, ashen-faced girl with thick strawberry blond curls. Her face appears old, but looking again, Viola can see that she is only hungry. The girl looks up at Viola as well, and catches her by the arm.

"Let's get out of here," Leila says.

"How?" Viola gasps. "How did you end up in this place?"

"How?" Leila laughs that maniacal laugh of hers. She has dark circles under her eyes. Her skin is sallow, as if she is ill. She coughs from deep within her lungs. "Like you, I suppose." Leila tells her story. The father, who decided to go north, alone, leaving Leila and her mother behind. The father never returned. The mother died of typhus. "So, I earn my living the way the rest of Naples does."

"Not everyone." Viola sighs.

"No," Leila agrees. "Just the women." They duck into a café, where Leila orders two coffees. The coffees arrive tepid and small, but at least they can sit inside. Leila insists on paying. "So," Leila continues, "how long have you been on the streets?"

Viola blushes at this. She doesn't want to think of herself as being on the streets, though she is, of course, isn't she? "Not long. Just a week or so. I have my brother . . ."

"Oh." Leila nods. "Of course. I have only myself to worry about." As they are finishing their coffee, the café is closing and the bartender shoos them out. "Hey," Leila says, "maybe we could work together. Share clients? Also, have you shaved your pubic hair? You have to get a pubic wig."

Viola gulps. "A pubic wig?"

"Yes, a merkin." Leila laughs that coarse laugh, then raises her skirt for Viola to see. Where her pubic hair should be, she wears a blond wig. "No one wants pubic hair. It's bad for business, and a breeding ground for lice. So get rid of yours. American servicemen, they like blond hair."

It occurs to Viola that Leila has gone mad. She continues: "I'm told that if you really want to get off the streets, you have to find yourself a soldier to marry you. Preferably an American. That's the real prize."

"An American?"

"If you meet one, don't sleep with him. Just string him along. You'll see." She laughs again. "He'll marry you."

Viola needs to get back to Rudy, but she gives Leila a hug. Then she scribbles her address on a piece of paper. "We're staying here," Viola tells her. "Come anytime."

Smiling, Leila tucks the slip of paper into her blouse. "I will," she says. "I'll see you tomorrow." The women embrace again before going their separate ways.

132

VIOLA RETURNS HOME WITH PROVISIONS. Rice, bread, cheese. She even managed to get some carrots and an onion on the black market. Rudy is sound asleep. She covers him gently. In the morning, she shows him what she was able to procure. Rudy eats one of the carrots. "No more," Viola says. "I'm going to make us lunch." As the water is boiling on the small burner, there's a knock at the door. Viola assumes that Leila has come to see her, as she said she would. Perhaps they will team up. What difference would it make, really?

She flings the door open, and then covers her mouth, afraid she will cry out.

"How did you find me?" Viola says coldly, stepping back.

"I asked the people in Benevento where you were staying," he says. "Your mother left an address. In case your father wrote or came to find you."

"I was expecting someone else," she says, gazing out into the street. So, he tracked her down. "What do you want?"

"May I come in?"

Viola shrugs. "As you wish," she says, sounding like an old woman.

Tommaso steps into the shabby room with its gray stained walls, the tiny window that gets no light. A dark, dreary, musty place. She points for him to sit on the one chair in the room. She perches at the edge of the bed.

"I owe you an explanation," he tells her.

She shrugs. "There is no need."

"But I must." He gazes at her with those blue eyes only matched by the sparkling sea. She ladles Rudy a bowl of the rice and vegetables. "Go sit outside and eat," she tells her brother. "I will open the door when you can come inside again." Rudy scurries onto the stoop with his bowl.

She closes the door and settles back. "We were told that if the Allied soldiers saw us in uniform, we'd be shot, and if the Germans caught us, we'd be conscripted. My grandmother told me I had to take off my uniform and never go back to the Red House. She was right. I know other soldiers who weren't as lucky. I did what I had to. And we found you the family in Benevento." He rambles on, and Viola listens in silence.

When he is done, she looks at him. "Is that all?" He nods. "Well, thank you for coming."

She gets up to show him to the door. Tommaso rises as well, but instead of heading to the door, he grabs her. He pulls her head back and kisses her deeply. At first, she feels his urgency, even a sense of violence, but after a moment, the gentleness she knew in his arms comes back, and his touch is kinder. His kiss is less ferocious, and once more she feels his love.

"You know what I do for a living now, right? You understand how I survive?"

He perches at the edge of her bed as she unbuttons his shirt. She tugs his undershirt over his head. She undresses slowly. She is not in a hurry. She takes out the hair clasp he stole from his grandmother and puts it on the table near the bed. Tommaso looks at the hair clasp as Viola shakes out her thick dark hair. She knows that once this is done, she will never see him again. He kisses her, touches her, and then he is inside of her, and he is weeping. When he is done, he strokes her head. "I'm so sorry," he says. "I am truly sorry."

Viola gets up from the cot. She hands him the hair clasp. "Do you want it?"

He stares at it blankly. "No," he says. "My grandmother died last week."

Though Viola never met Sofia, she'd heard about her. "I'm very sorry."

She begins to dress. "You could have married me. You could have asked me to stay with you. Instead, you left me and my family to fend for ourselves, and now they're all gone."

She opens the door. Tommaso tries to say something, but she puts her finger to his lips, touching the philtrum—where an angel places its finger on a newborn to take away knowledge. "Shush," she says. Tommaso steps out and she motions for Rudy to come inside. Then she shuts the door.

133

I DIDN'T KNOW IT WOULD BE the last time I'd see him. I didn't know it as I drove up to his apartment complex on a warm summer afternoon, locked my car, and walked toward the red-and-gray cinder-block building on a generic tree-lined street. We'd been seeing each other on and off for a few years. I'm sure he saw other women, and I had started dating a boy at Pratt. But I kept coming around. He'd call me, or I'd phone him when I was in New Jersey, visiting my dad.

Over the years, he'd grown heavier, and his hair had thinned. His blue eyes dulled. But none of this mattered to me. I was drawn to him in an inexplicable way. I couldn't stay away. As I punched in his code and buzzed myself in, I was aware, suddenly, of the building itself. The tattered carpet, the smell of soup. His apartment was on the third floor, and I always took the stairs. Normally I raced up, but on this day I walked slowly.

It was an early-summer day, and Charlie was on his sofa. He'd finished a double shift, and was drinking a beer and watching a game. He was in shorts and a T-shirt, and it seemed odd to me that a grown man would sit around like a college student. I flopped down on the sofa beside him, and he handed me a beer.

I sat there, turning it in my hands. While he watched the game, I gazed around the apartment. The tacky tables and chairs, the generic posters on the wall—the Rolling Stones, Joe Montana. The Formica counters, the mismatched plates. I took it all in as if, even then, I knew that one day I'd be staging apartments to make sure they looked nothing like this one. And suddenly it occurred to me that fucking my mother's detective was never going to bring her home. That I had been in some strange trance.

For a long time, I had been going to see him or begging him to meet me. And he did. We fucked in cars, in his kitchen, and once even in my bedroom. We fucked in a million different ways, but the void, the darkness, the black emptiness of the sea still stretched before me. Sitting there on his sofa, as he watched a game in his shorts, it was as if I'd awakened.

I left his building. I never went back again.

134

A FEW DAYS LATER, WHEN VIOLA goes upstairs to pay the rent, she is surprised at the brisk business happening in the tailor's shop. It seems he has diversified. Hanging on the wall is a display of tiny wigs that his wife has begun making in the back room. They are made from horsehair, old carpets, and even human hair. They come in all colors. Some are bright red. Some have feathers like a bird. After she pays the rent, the tailor's wife gives her a blond one. "On the house," she says, laughing. The woman points to her crotch.

Then Viola goes to the pharmacy, where she purchases a razor. When she gets home, she shaves.

THAT EVENING, VIOLA GOES OUT and picks up two American servicemen. One is Black and he likes the blond hair between her legs. He licks her there and she is surprised at how much pleasure it brings her. She returns home, her legs sticky, but she has managed with her earnings to purchase a sack of rice and a fish head on the black market. Rudy is elated. He stands beside her as she puts the rice in a saucepan, which she heats up on their small gas stove. Then she drops in the fish head and covers the pot. That night, they have a feast.

But in the morning, Rudy has another one of his fevers, and this time it seems serious. His skin is yellow, and he trembles. No matter how many blankets she heaps on him, he shivers. His eyes grow more and more glassy.

When at last Rudy is asleep, she heads out. She picks up an English sailor. He reeks of drink and smoke. Before she has undressed, he forces himself into her. He jabs her with his finger, then thrusts himself inside of her from behind. Afterward, she is raw and sore. She can barely walk. She decides that is enough for one night. It's not late as she strolls back up the hill where they live. The sky is purple, and the thin crest of the moon seems to be mocking her.

She misses her father in moments like this. She thinks of their early-evening walks along Via Roma. How they'd amble until they reached the Caffè Mulassano, where they'd munch on little triangular sandwiches—*tramezzini*. Her father favored those made with smoked salmon and watercress. Viola loved the egg and tomato. They would order a plate, then another while Viola enjoyed a cold chocolate drink and her father sipped ever so slowly on an espresso, holding the handle of the cup daintily in his hand.

Afterward, they'd continue on their walk—sometimes to the river. They'd pause for a gelato, which they always shared, having stuffed themselves on sandwiches. She liked the pistachio and lemon ice. Her father preferred chocolate, but he deferred to her. She ate most of it anyway. They'd make their way home. When they walked in, her mother would invariably say, "I was about to call the *carabinieri* to go find you."

With Anna, it's different. She only recalls her mother during these last weeks in Naples. Sick and feverish, her fingers worn to the bone. The gay, robust woman who hugged her children every time she could has slipped away. And with her, Viola's childhood is lost, as well.

AS SHE MOVES THROUGH THE winding street of the Spanish Quarter, making her way home, she hears a cry that has become all too familiar. "Poggioreale. Poggioreale!" A black cart sits at the top of the street, drawn by two horses. Poggioreale is the name of the cemetery. The carts that once comprised the Municipal Cleaning Service no longer pick up trash. Instead, they gather dead bodies—some of which have been sitting for five or even ten days, waiting for the carts to come around. There is not always room on the carts for all the dead, so the families race out of their homes, carrying the dead in ersatz coffins or wrapped in linen. Wood is too scarce for coffins.

As she is walking, a man races down the alley behind her. "*Aspetta,*" he shouts. "*Aspetta.*" He carries in his hands a small bundle wrapped in red cloth. Weeping, he tosses the body of his child onto the heap of other bodies.

135

WHEN SHE GETS HOME, RUDY is more feverish, his breathing labored. She sits at the edge of their cot, watching him. How can she care for him? What can she possibly do to make him well and safe? She waits until first light. Then she gently wakes him. "Get up," she says.

"No," he shouts, pulling back the tattered sheet that covers him.

"We have to go somewhere," she tells him. "I have to get you somewhere where they can help you." Still he won't budge. "There will be food. You'll like it."

At the word *food,* Rudy agrees. He pulls on his threadbare shirt and trousers, and together they walk out into the October morning. It's still warm in Naples. Not even a hint of winter in the air, but Viola knows it won't be long before they'll be cold again, and how can she care for her brother, let alone herself?

She takes Rudy by the hand and they walk slowly up the hill. "Where are we going?"

"It's a surprise," she says.

The church bells ring. The city, still reduced to rubble, is starting to come out of its darkness. Bricks and stones are being piled along the side of the roads. There is a sound of hammering, saws. "We're going to where the church bells are," she assures her brother, tugging his arm. At last, they stand in front of the convent. Huge imposing doors. Viola rings a bell and moments later the door opens. Viola steps away. A nun appears, looking around her. Then she spots the little boy on the doorstep. Without a word, she takes Rudy by the hand and ushers him inside.

As soon as the door closes, Viola turns down a narrow alleyway. A shudder runs through her. She feels something in her bones. It's a chill, as if she has walked into the shadows. At times like this, she tries to remember the faces of her parents, her grandparents, her brother Michele, and now even Rudy. Their voices have drifted away. Now she can neither see them nor hear them. And she knows that they are gone.

136

RUDY HOLDS HIS ESPRESSO CUP in his hands, as if he can't bring himself to put it down. Yet his hands tremble slightly. Outside, the storm is letting up. He glances at his windows. A ray of sunlight filters in. With his rheumy eyes, he looks at me. "That was it," he says. "I never saw her again."

"You never saw her?"

Rudy shakes his head. "No, I never did. In all fairness, she might have come back to look for me, but I wasn't there. I was moved to a monastery in the hills after a few weeks, and later a family took me in. But no, I never saw her again." He sighs deeply. "I did hear about her. After the war, she managed to leave the streets and worked for the tailor for a while. Then she got a job doing what Angelo had taught her to do. She helped restore the walls of churches. She knew her angels and demons." He shakes his head, chuckling to himself.

"And you heard this how?"

He cocks his head and gives me a little smirk, as if he must state the obvious. "Tommaso knew where I was. He came to check on me from time to time. He kept tabs on her in his own way, as well. He even worked in a restaurant in Naples for a while. He always hoped she'd change her mind." He shakes his head again. "But she never did."

"I thought . . ." I hesitate but then say it. "I thought she might have come here. After she left us." I have been holding vaguely on to the hope that she returned to Naples, but now I am fairly certain she didn't. I have a feeling she didn't go anywhere. Not back to Italy or even down to Florida. A shiver runs through me. Perhaps the Pine Barrens was as far as she got.

"If she did come back, I wouldn't know." He shakes his head. "In the end, it was probably for the best. A kind family took me in."

He pauses. "They did their best, but that didn't end well, either. I was never really right after everything that transpired. I think she dropped off money for me when she could."

I sigh. "Yes, she probably would do that. However flawed, she had a kind heart."

"Truthfully, I assumed she was long dead." He points to me. "Until now."

I feel as if our time is drawing to an end, but I'm not ready to leave. "But what about you?" I ask. "What has your life been like, for all these years?"

He seems taken aback by this question. He puts his coffee cup down and arranges his hands in his lap as if he's folding an origami crane. "It has been what you see. A life of routine. There was no other way for me to survive. I had the same job for forty years as an accountant in a small corporate firm. Very dull, but the orderliness of it suited me. As to my personal life, well, I've had the occasional relationship, but nothing stuck. I've made my peace with it. I enjoy my friends, my apartment. And I swim in the sea every day. It's a small but satisfying existence." He pauses. "It is not that easy to be, well, such as I am in Naples."

I know better than to ask what he means by this last, cryptic statement. But I understand that he does not wish me to know anything more about him than what he has already shared.

"Ah," he says, clapping his hands together. "The rain has stopped." He rises, and I understand that our time together is done. "I am tired," he says. "It's time for my nap."

I look at him, smiling.

"As I said, I'm a very regimented man," he tells me.

As I get up to leave, Uncle Rudy writes something on the back of an old envelope. Another clue on my scavenger hunt. This one is an address in Turin. "You should probably go there, Laura," he tells me. I am touched that he calls me by my name. "As long as you are here, you may as well."

As he heads down the hallway, I follow. He pauses at the bookshelf and takes down a thick, tattered volume, its spine torn, the pages yellow. "I want you to have this." It appears to be an old library book. "He never returned it." Rudy chuckles. "This may be the only crime my father ever actually committed." He opens the book to its last page and reads, "All of human wisdom is contained in these two words—'Wait and hope.'" He shuts the book, and dust rises from its pages. He hands it to me. "Now you know the end." He chuckles. "I've been waiting too long to return this book. You should have it," he says.

I tuck the volume under my arm as he walks me downstairs. "I am happy to know you," he says. "I am glad to know that you exist." Then he shuts the door.

137

I CAN'T RECALL FEELING AS CLOSE to her as I do now. I feel her presence walking these streets, searching for the man who will take her away, who will become my father. I no longer see the narrow warrens of streets, their crush of people. I see my mother, wandering the rubble, foraging for food, doing what she must for money. I wonder how she lived for those ten years after the war, before she met my father.

She was beautiful when my father met her. He always told me this. And I remember her from when I was small. So she could not have lived on the street all those years. It made sense that she worked for the tailor. She knew how to sew. And, of course, Angelo had taught her how to paint churches. So many had to be rebuilt and repaired after the war. More angels and demons and clouds? And then at night, she'd go to the bars.

It is odd to feel her presence, like a bird that hovers overhead. Now, it seems, I know everything I can know. My grandparents went to the Red House in 1942, when my grandfather was forty-two years old. My mother and Uncle Rudy did what they could to survive. Then she left her brother behind. She did what she had to do to survive. She never looked back.

There was no snake to account for her hunger, except for the one in her heart.

But the cold she always felt, the cold was real.

She met my father, had me and Janine, and, it seemed, lived a happy, fulfilling life. Until her demons caught up with her. And then she was gone for good. She reached the age she could not see beyond—forty-two. A year, her father's age, her own, and now mine.

We are all mysteries—even to ourselves.

138

LEAVING MY UNCLE RUDY, I follow the street that takes me to the sea. At the water's edge, there is a small staircase littered with beer bottles, filthy rags, cigarette butts. I walk past them to the thin strip of black volcanic sand. Ahead of me, a line of boulders creates a seawall. In the small swimming area, the water is relatively calm. Kicking off my sandals, I roll up my pants and wade in.

The water is warm as a bath, the volcanic sand black as night. Mothers swim with their children. Boys toss balls around. One splashes me accidentally and apologizes, then splashes me again. I know what they say about Naples. That it's riddled with crime and corruption. But here, it seems at peace.

I step in farther and a wave comes from a passing speedboat. I dive into the baptismal waters. The warmth of the water is almost disconcerting. I lie on my back, my clothes soaking wet, thick clouds passing overhead. Another storm threatens. I stay in the sea until I feel cleansed. As I leave, the skies open. I'm drenched from above and below. Everywhere, everything is water. Others race beneath nearby awnings, but I walk in the downpour along Via Partenope—the road that follows the bay.

Ahead of me, Vesuvius looms, a cloud crowning its peak. Neapolitans live in the shadow of its destruction, always there, like a promise. I pause at the Castel dell'Ovo. It was here that a mermaid named Partenope tried to lure Ulysses into her arms. She sang her sweetest songs, but Ulysses had his men tie him to the mast, and despite her singing, she could not lure him away. Instead, she tumbled into the sea, became tangled in her own hair, and drowned. The story goes that on the rock that became the castle, Partenope left one egg from her own body and that the poet Virgil hid it in a secret place—never to be found. If that egg is ever lost or broken, Naples will fall into the sea.

It is dusk as I reach my hotel. Already, the ladies of the night are on the streets. I pass one—a young woman in a black bodysuit, pink fishnet hose, stiletto boots. She's in a phone booth, talking to a john, I imagine. But as I walk past, I hear her say, "I've got to get to work now. I love you, Mama." She blows a kiss and hangs up.

I head back up Via Toledo and try to imagine what it must be like to live in a place where there are resident mermaids, where people adopt skulls that they tend and talk to, where a rainbow arcs over the volcano that can destroy this city in a heartbeat, and an egg can rule your fate.

139

THE TRAIN IS PACKED WITH families returning from their seaside vacations, students heading to Rome and beyond for their studies, sun-drenched tourists. There's the usual shouting and jostling for overhead bins. I have a seat in a corner, riding backward. It's one of the things I've never liked about European trains. I never know which direction the seat will face when I buy my ticket. Still, I settle in.

As we head north, I stare outside. Behind me, Naples and the sea recede. Then the train plunges into a long, dark tunnel. This is the train they would have taken had they ever returned home. When we come back into the light, I take *The Count of Monte Cristo* out of my bag and lay it open on my lap. I begin to read. "On the 24th of February, 1815, the lookout at Notre-Dame de la Garde signalled the three-master, the *Pharaon,* from Smyrna, Trieste, and Naples. . . ."

I read a chapter or two, and then I drift off. I keep wanting the swashbuckling adventure to enchant me, but instead it makes me drowsy. Perhaps I would have enjoyed it more when I was a girl. It wasn't in the house when I was a child. I wonder if my mother intended it that way. It seems long and tedious, but it is the book that entertained my mother and Rudy when they were interned at the Red House.

I hug the book to me, even in my sleep. My grandfather held this book. He read it aloud to his children. Rudy kept it all these years. He never let it go until now.

140

THE NORTH IS NOTHING LIKE the south. And Turin isn't anything like Naples. If Naples is a wild, pulsing city, Turin is an organized and intellectual one. It lacks the crush of humanity you feel in Naples, and that weird feeling that death is everywhere, but it has beautiful wide boulevards and wonderful little cafés and gelaterias everywhere. It is order compared to chaos. Though I have my destination on another slip of paper—this time from Rudy—I decide it will wait. This is the city where my mother was born, where my grandparents lived. After breakfast, I decide to walk around.

I head down the pedestrian mall at Via Lagrange until I reach the duomo, where the Shroud of Turin is housed. I decide to skip the tourist site and cut over to the Piazza Castello, where I pause under a portico at the Caffè Mulassano. This is where my grand-father used to bring my mother on their Saturday outings. This is where she ate *tramezzini* with their crusts cut off. Now I think of that sandwich my mother left behind when she disappeared. She ate everything but the crusts.

I take a table outside and order an iced coffee. At the table next to me sits a large woman with a lot of makeup and four-inch stilet-tos. Her husband, who is also rotund, sits across from her, watch-ing as she dips into the pile of small sandwiches they have ordered. One after another she pops them into her mouth, wipes her lips, then applies more makeup. I try to imagine this couple in their youth—the wife trim and wild, the husband endlessly amused by her. It is as if I can glimpse into the past and see them as they once were. And then it occurs to me that my grandparents came to this very café. Perhaps they even courted here.

I pay my bill, check the slip of paper in my bag, and head down to the Corso Re Umberto. This is the street where my family lived. I come to the address that Rudy gave me. It is on an elegant residential street. All of the apartments have wrought-iron balconies, French doors. There are trees and shade. I can picture my mother coming home to this building from school. And now that I look again at the street address, I realize that, of course, Umberto was not her last name. Her name was Malkin—a Jewish name. Umberto was the name my grandmother gave her children so, like the pigeons, they'd always find their way home.

I gaze up at the window where she must have stood, looking down at the school she would never return to again, at the friends she would never play with again. The school is gone, replaced by a modern apartment building. There, on the fifth floor, is the apartment where my great-grandparents lived, and two floors down, the apartment where my grandparents lived with my mother, Rudy, and Michele.

I am surprised at how close the train station is to the Corso Re Umberto. This sends a chill through me, because now I can see for myself, as if guided by an internal map, the trajectory that my great-grandparents and my uncle Michele took when they were deported from the Stazione di Turino Porta Nuova, the same one I had just arrived at, in the fall of 1943, just weeks before my grandfather returned. He was wrong about many things, but he was right about this: It was not safe to return. Perhaps he hoped against hope. Perhaps he thought, even as the cattle cars carried them north, that this was just another leg of the journey and not its end.

I imagine my grandfather coming up this street, still wearing the wool suit he wore when he'd left. His keys jingle in his pocket. He unlocks the heavy front door and lets himself in. He does not bother glancing at the mailboxes. He heads straight for the lift. It is broken, as usual, so he takes the stairs. He climbs three flights to his apartment and uses his key. The door doesn't open. He tries again. There must be something wrong with his key. He climbs another two flights, to his in-laws' apartment. When he knocks, there is no reply. He has their keys, so he tries them, as well. But they don't work, either. It occurs to him that the locks have been changed.

Confused, Josef climbs down the stairs. Perhaps the locks were changed for some reason. He goes down to the old porter and jangles his keys. "I can't get into my apartment," he tells the man. He has always been on good terms with the porter, but the man barely looks at him.

"We had to change all the locks. There have been many robberies," the porter replies.

"And my in-laws?"

The porter shrugs. "I believe they have gone to the sea."

"Ah." Josef breathes a sigh of relief.

He tells Josef to wait at a nearby café, and that he will fetch him when he finds the right keys. Again, Josef does not bother to check the mailboxes. If he did, he would see that other people's names are now on the box. His in-laws, his own family, all have been erased. Josef heads to the café, stopping to buy a newspaper. He sits at a table, tapping his fingers, barely glancing at the news of Hitler's advance into Northern Italy. What has yet to be reported is that in Merano, a tranquil mountain village in the occupied north, twenty-five Jews, including six children and an old woman, are torn from their beds and arrested by the Germans. In another village sixteen people, three of them children, are executed. A grandfather begs for the children's lives. They are shot and dumped into Lago Maggiore. Their belongings are sold off in the town square.

But Josef knows none of this as he waits for what seems like a long time. He is about to leave, when the police arrive. He is not entirely surprised when they arrest him. But he did not know that the porter would receive five thousand lire for turning in a Jew. He smiles wryly when he learns this.

There is no trial. No legal proceedings. All of his identity cards are taken from him. This he does not protest, but when they try to take his dental instruments, he grows furious. Josef is sent to Bolzano prison because, as Mussolini has said, we will not deport our Jews, but we will not send them to vacation spots, either. Here he languishes for weeks, in a cell with nine other men. They have little to eat, and only the clothes on their backs to wear.

Eventually, he will be transferred by train from the Porta Nuova station to the Milano Centrale station. Here, along with hundreds of other deportees, he proceeds to track 21 on the lower level, a track used to transport merchandise. Here he is packed into a railroad car with nothing but straw on the floor and a bucket in a corner, which soon overflows. It takes several days to reach their destination.

Years later, I will find my grandfather's name on a ledger. He arrived at Auschwitz in December 1943. He died there in the spring of 1944.

STANDING IN FRONT OF THE building where they lived, I find it difficult to leave. I will probably never be back here again. But I know where I must go. I follow the Corso Vittorio Emanuele II until I come to the small Piazzetta Primo Levi. At each end of the piazza, soldiers in full uniform stand guard. In the piazza, there is only one building, and the soldiers are guarding it. It is the old synagogue, built in the Moorish style. It was completely destroyed in 1942, then rebuilt after the war. Once a year, on Yom Kippur, my grandparents worshipped here. My mother probably came, too. Now two young soldiers are stationed out front. They are smoking and joking, even as they hold their machine guns. Security, it seems, is lax. With a nod, they wave me toward a gate, where I ring the bell. A man opens the gate, asks to see my identification, then steps back and invites me inside.

There is a staircase that leads to the sanctuary. I descend to a lower level, where services are being conducted. The room is made of pale wood, shaped in a circle around what I have previously called a pulpit but now I know is a bema. A man waves his hand, and I am motioned up to the women's section, directly behind the bema. A woman hands me a prayer book. I open it, but it is written in Hebrew and Italian, neither of which I can read. Beside me, a woman dressed in black reads the Hebrew and rocks back and forth on her heels. Another younger woman pats her chest, where her heart is.

I feel the loss of those I never knew. I mourn people I didn't even know existed until now. I am surrounded by ghosts. I do not understand the words that are being chanted. I do not know what the rituals are, but as I listen to the songs, I envision my ancestors here—perhaps in these very pews. I see a family of acrobats in a pyramid, and I am standing, perilously alone, at the top. Then I rise along with the others, in this room that circles back on itself, and I do something I have never done before.

I pray.

141

IT'S MARCH 1972. AN ORDINARY DAY, except it isn't. It's mud season, early spring. The ground is loamy. There's that fresh smell of trees budding, and plants pushing up from the soil. My mother, Viola, sits at the kitchen counter, eating her sandwich. It's almost thirty years since she dropped her brother, Rudy, off at the convent in Naples. Nearly three decades that she has not been able to forgive herself.

She doesn't finish her sandwich. She leaves the crusts. She goes upstairs. She ties her hair up in a bun with an elastic and puts on an old cap. She had not planned to do this today. She walks out the door. No one sees her go. If the neighbors are home, they aren't watching. She walks to the end of our street and turns right. She keeps walking until she gets to the bigger road that feeds into the Garden State Parkway. She flags down a car. It's a battered two-door Ford with Florida plates. "I'm so sorry," she says, "but my car broke down and I need to meet my husband."

"Oh, I can take you back to your car, if you like."

She has to think on the spot. "No, thank you. It's better if you take me to him. It's just a few miles down the road."

"Well, that's where I'm headed. Going home." Home, he tells her, is Tampa.

The man is older, slightly overweight. His paunch touches the steering wheel. He looks at this well-dressed woman. She doesn't seem dangerous. Her story is believable. It's not out of his way. "Hop in," he says. "I could use some company."

As they drive, my mother chatters, as she always does. "That darn car of mine. I just need a new one. It's better if Jim—that's my husband. It's better if he just drives me to pick it up. That way, at least one of us can get home to the kids."

The kids. Is it the first time she thinks about us? Does she register what she's doing, or where she's going? I don't know. I just know that whatever the reason, she lets this man drive her away from her life. "I was just visiting my daughter up here for a couple weeks. Since the wife died, I'm still trying to make it up here once a year, like we always did."

"Oh, I'm sorry," Violet says.

"Oh, it's been a while. I've gotten used to it, I suppose. If you can ever get used to such a thing."

Ten, fifteen miles until she sees where she wants to get off. "There's a turnoff into the Pine Barrens a few miles up the road.

If you just pull in, I can walk. My husband's a ranger. He'll drive me home."

The man glances at her. "Are you sure? Why don't I drive you in? Just in case he's not there."

"No, no, I talked to him not long ago. He's there."

The man makes a clicking sound with his teeth. He's not sure whether to believe her or not. It's not his concern, really. He's done his good deed. They will never cross paths again.

He drops her off, as she asks him to. He watches as she disappears down the trail. He wonders, briefly, if anything she said was true. Then he drives the rest of his way home to Tampa Bay.

Violet walks. She knows where she's going. She takes her time, heading deep into the Pine Barrens. But she can walk to her destination in the hours of daylight that remain. There's a chill in the air. Violet hates to be cold as much she hates to be hungry. As she walks, she ponders the eternal present in which she has lived all these years. Her parents lost, Tommaso gone. And Rudy, the only person she had in the end, left behind. Leila was wrong. She could not leave it behind. All of it, even as her life travels backward, has stayed with her.

She comes to the ghost town. She is the most at home here, among these ruins. They are so like the Red House, the last place where her life resembled what she had once known. For a few moments, she rests. She is so tired, she could just drift off to sleep and then return home. Instead, she forces herself to rise. The lake is not far.

She reaches it half an hour later, and sits at the water's edge. No one is here. It's the middle of the week, too early in the season. A lovely breeze blows. She takes a deep breath. The world springing back to life. She wants to lie back and smell the earth. Instead, once more, she forces herself to get up. She gathers stones. She puts them into the pockets of her jacket. The pockets have zippers. She zips them shut.

Then she steps into the water, where she meets the devil. The one she's been looking for all along.

142

I KNOW WHY CHARLIE HENDRICKS called me. Perhaps, after all this time, the lake has spewed up its secrets. Perhaps a passing hiker found a bone. Something a predator scavenged from the shallows. Who knows how long ago they found her? Perhaps her remains have been sitting in a vault for years, waiting to be identified.

Remains. That's what we call them. What a strange notion. In truth, nothing but what we remember remains.

143

PATRICK IS SITTING ON OUR STOOP, nursing a beer. I don't expect him to greet me, but he does. As my taxi pulls up, he stands to help me with my bag. I search his face for clues, but he doesn't look angry as I get out of the taxi. He just looks sad. He kisses me on the cheek and on the top of my head, the way a parent would. He goes into the house to grab me a glass of wine. While he is inside, I think how it is good to be home. Oddly comforting to see the cars going up and down our street, hear a distant siren, children playing at a nearby playground. "I was having an affair," I tell him, "but I'm not now. This wasn't about another person."

I tell him everything. It pours out of me—Castellobello, the Red House, Tommaso, Rudy, the apartment building in Turin, all of it—and soon I am sobbing. Patrick strokes my head. We sit like that for a long time. Finally, he says, "Do you want me to move out?"

It's so hard to explain that this isn't about us. It's as if I've lived my life as an absentee landlord—as if it were happening while I was somewhere else. I've been a good actor, learning my lines, following stage directions. But now, it seems, I've forgotten my cue.

I shake my head. "I honestly don't know what I want. Can we sleep on it?"

"Of course. Take your time." He stands up, dusting off his jeans. "I'll make us some dinner." I take a long hot shower and come down to a tofu stir-fry over rice. It's simple and delicious.

"Thank you," I tell him.

He shrugs. "Dinner was the easy part."

We are like old friends, roommates. And yet there is comfort here. This is my home. "Are you going to leave me?" I ask him.

He understands. My fear of being left. Then he almost smiles. "I don't want to, but it depends. . . ."

Suddenly, I can barely keep my head up. "Can we talk tomorrow?" He nods as he starts taking the dishes to the sink. "Thank you for being here." Again, that faint nod.

I SLEEP FOR A FEW HOURS. A long nap, really. It's jet lag, of course. I'm up in the middle of the night. I go into the garage that Patrick designed as my studio long ago. It's a place I haven't used in a while. I come upon my snails. Snails—what Anna was looking for when she died at the port. My snails are in a large bowl, a terrarium, and they look alive. Patrick has given them water while I was away. He's thoughtful that way. I take them out one at a time and hold them by their shells. I look to see if their feet move, if they reach for something to hold on to. This is what snails must do, after all, hold on. As one stretches out on my hand, I know what I'm going to do.

The next morning, I get up early and make a paste of flour and water. I mash the mixture, softening it with a fork. On each snail I put a dab of paste. I begin to arrange them on the wall of my studio. First an N, then an o. I spell out these words: *Non sarò qui per sempre.* I shape the letters carefully with my snails. Now they will sleep. In three years they will awaken, eat the paste I have provided, and when they are nourished, they will walk away.

I work feverishly, creating this installation, which I will photograph and document over the next three years. It will be the work I am remembered for—if I am remembered for anything.

After I am done, I go back into the house, find Patrick in his woodworking studio. He has taught me about wood. How a damaged tree creates a wood wound. It will heal, but it leaves a scar. Once inside, I wash my hands. I shower.

Then I take a deep breath and go to the phone. He answers right away. "Detective Hendricks," the voice says.

"It's Laura," I reply, tears welling up. Then he starts to speak, and I listen as he tells me what I already know.

ACKNOWLEDGMENTS

In 2016, we were doing a house exchange with a family, the Marangis, who lived in Puglia. This was our second visit to the area, and one of the daughters in the family, Cinzia, wanted to take us to visit the town of Alberobello. I knew enough about the area to know that Alberobello was a tourist town, famous for its strange conical-shaped houses. I was reluctant to go, but Cinzia insisted and off we went. As I'd feared, the town was packed with tourists and shops that sold trinkets and T-shirts. After a little while of trying to navigate the crowded streets, I saw a bench in a churchyard and told Cinzia that I was going to take a rest.

It was pleasant, sitting alone in the shade, watching kids eating ice creams and dogs running around. I wasn't sitting in that churchyard long when I noticed in front of me a scrawny-looking olive tree with a plaque around its trunk. Curious, I got up to see what was written on the plaque, and, to my surprise, the words were in Italian and Hebrew. I can read a little Hebrew and was able to make out a few words. But I could read the Italian. The plaque declared: "This olive tree from the hills of Jerusalem to the people of Alberobello for the hospitality your citizens offered during the racist persecution." The tree was planted in 2002.

I was stunned. What could this strange, isolated town have to do with the persecution of the Jews? I am basically a secular Jew, but Jewish history, and especially the Holocaust, have a deep interest and meaning for me. When I met up with Cinzia and asked her what she thought, she had no idea. I went to the tourist information office and they also had no idea. But I could not walk away from this tree, its plaque, and whatever its story might be.

This book is the result of years of research, travel, just plain digging to find out. It would not exist without the help and friendship of the Marangi family. Not only Cinzia and her sister, Analisa, but also her wonderful parents, Maria and Nino, who as I say in my dedication have become family to me. They, along with their spouses, children, and grandchildren, have welcomed us now over many years.

I also want to thank my neighbor, Robert Bergen, who first made me aware of this unique history in Puglia, and Andrea Glover, who was his teacher in the class on the Jews of Italy. For help with Naples, I want to thank John Domini, who shared copious information as well as his own work and who helped me get contacts in Naples. I want to thank Angelo Cannavacciuolo and Suzy Carbone in Naples for their assistance. Also, my first readers—Marc Kaufman, Caroline Leavitt, and Barbara Grossman—for their insights and their friendship.

I am deeply grateful to my agent, Ellen Levine, and her staff, who have helped shepherd this book every step of the way, and to my excellent editor, Carolyn Williams, for her thoughtful edits and insights, as well as the whole team at Doubleday, who have been terrific, including designer Emily Mahon and production editor Kathleen Cook.

And finally, I am beyond grateful to my loving family. My daughter, Kate, with her eagle-eyed read, son-in-law, Chris Heim, and our two grandchildren, Sonny and Charlie, who are the lights of my life and the promise for the future.

And of course, Larry O'Connor, because if not for him, none of this would be. He is my husband, my partner, my first reader, and, perhaps most important, my friend. I am beyond grateful that so many years ago our stars aligned.

Mary Morris is the author of numerous works of fiction, including the novels *Gateway to the Moon, The Jazz Palace, A Mother's Love,* and *House Arrest,* and of nonfiction, including the travel classic *Nothing to Declare: Memoirs of a Woman Traveling Alone.* Morris is a recipient of the Rome Prize in literature and the 2016 Anisfield-Wolf Book Award for fiction. She lives in Brooklyn, New York.